Sikandar C

NEELUM SARAN GOUR

PENGUIN BOOKS

PENGUIN BOOKS
Published by the Penguin Group
Penguin Books India Pvt Ltd, 11 Community Centre, Panchsheel Park, New Delhi
110 017, India
Penguin Group (USA) Inc., 375 Hudson Street, New York, New York 10014, USA
Penguin Group (Canada), 90 Eglinton Avenue East, Suite 700, Toronto, Ontario,
M4P 2Y3, Canada (a division of Pearson Penguin Canada Inc.)
Penguin Books Ltd, 80 Strand, London WC2R 0RL, England
Penguin Ireland, 25 St Stephen's Green, Dublin 2, Ireland (a division of Penguin
Books Ltd)
Penguin Group (Australia), 250 Camberwell Road, Camberwell, Victoria 3124,
Australia (a division of Pearson Australia Group Pty Ltd)
Penguin Group (NZ), cnr Airborne and Rosedale Roads, Albany, Auckland 1310,
New Zealand (a division of Pearson New Zealand Ltd)
Penguin Group (South Africa) (Pty) Ltd, 24 Sturdee Avenue, Rosebank, Johannesburg
2196, South Africa

Penguin Books Ltd, Registered Offices: 80 Strand, London WC2R 0RL, England

First published by Penguin Books India 2005

Copyright © Neelum Saran Gour 2005

All rights reserved

10 9 8 7 6 5 4 3 2

This is a work of fiction. Names, characters, places and incidents are either the
product of the author's imagination or are used fictitiously, and any resemblance to
any actual person, living or dead, events or locales is entirely coincidental.

Typeset in Sabon by S.R. Enterprises, New Delhi
Printed at Chaman Offset Printers, New Delhi

To Vera, Labonya and Kaka

Acknowledgements

I thank Dr Lalji Singh, Director of the Centre for Cellular and Molecular Biology, Hyderabad, for sorting out my queries about DNA fingerprinting, and R.K. Singh of Allahabad University for putting me through to him. The *Times of India* of 1 January 2000 carried a news item about the fax from Egypt which I have used in my story. The translated nursery rhymes were the work of T.F. Bignold, ICS (1863–88), and I have taken them from *British Life in India* by R.V. Vernede (OUP). Professor Mathur explicates lines from 'The Darkling Thrush', a poem written by Thomas Hardy on the last day of the nineteenth century, and Munna writes a parody of Wordsworth's 'Three Years She Grew'. Halim's tales belong to several popular Partition anecdotes which were put together in an article in the *Northern Indian Patrika*. I also thank the now-anonymous student of mine whose essay 'My Struggle with the English Language' forms the basis of Munna's essay of the same name. Finally, the poem on John Moyse by Sir Francis Hastings Doyle is on display in Canterbury Museum from where it has been borrowed.

This is the story of eleven people and a bomb blast. Eleven has by now become a mythic number in the history of blasts but the events in this book occurred a bit earlier than 9/11, and without further preamble let me acquaint you with three out of those eleven. Let the date be the thirty-first of December 1999 and the time roughly eleven-thirty p.m. when the countdown to the new millennium had begun. The world's premier cities had been blasting away all evening, strewing the December sky with spectacular displays. Rockets shot across, went pop over the Statue of Liberty. Fizzing fountains sprang into the stars, arched and spouted cataracts of flame over Tokyo. Spitfire wheels sprang phosphorus spokes over Sydney, unreeling miles of dizzy ribbons of light, and magic dragon banners fluttered in the heavens above Hong Kong, gold-fanged letters licking out the words: Welcome 2000!

But all this was happening on the TV screen.

This other bhutbhutbhutbhut—a multiple-bang serial cracker of Mau-aima make that sent Vakil Sahib's wife scurrying on her sluffing slippers to the balustrade to look—hadn't emerged from the TV screen at all.

The busteewalas—reeling drunk, chanting and stomping, flushed with arrack and song—were having a field day. To the howling frenzy of blaring loudspeakers and pounding tin cans they had just added the riotous joy of a fireworks display.

The sight that met her eyes made her gasp: *Hai Ma*! Her hand flew up to her throat. *Hé Ram*! What ill luck! Who was he?

She groped for her spectacles. Couldn't find them. Then a further suspicion assailed her. Looks more like a baraat than a funeral. Those madcaps capering around like Lord Shiva's gibbering imps, those trot-trotting kettledrums. But that dead body there ... surely ... ah, the spectacles. Surely not! Oh Shiva! Oh Devi Ma! How inauspicious! There on the funereal bamboo ladder, laid out in the rigid repose of death was a figure like her ... her very own husband, Vakil Sahib Mahendra Chandraji!

For a micro-second the unspeakable horror of it stabbed her to the heart, before Vakil Sahib Mahendra Chandra's zestful baritone droned up behind her: This is the great millennium exchange marketing scheme, Nirmalaji. Pack up your old century. Bring it along. Pay up the forty-odd years you've lived so far and we'll give you, at an attractive discount, a brand new-model century. Better picture quality, superior sound, more channels, greater historic excitement, more sex-violence-drama, you name it. Even a chance to win a lottery. Fabulous prizes! Marvellous exchange offer, but, of course, no money back. Can't return the used years of your life, eh heh?

But Vakilin wasn't listening. She was appalled, incensed, mutely pointing. He joined her on their third-floor balcony.

Satyanash! he swore. If that isn't me lying there!

She whirled round, aghast, and shushed him up.

But if that isn't my old kutchery coat-pant! he spluttered.

It is, she snapped. In his anarchic state of mind, Vakil Sahib imagined he was looking back at his life across the great divide. Faced with the soul-shaking spectacle of his own dissolution, he grew pardonably slow of wit. His hand went up to his head in a hushed gesture of awed respect. But the question in his brain still demanded an answer.

Who in Bhagwan's name is that ... that person there dressed in my clothes?

Before his wife could offer a solution to the mystery, activity intensified in the yard below. The crowd of mourners hoisted the corpse on their shoulders and proceeded to frolic around the court, jiggling the cortège playfully about. Ahead of the crazed procession, prancing and galloping like a hideous goblin gone berserk, was the rascal, Nankoo. Palm-leaf bugles split the air, the kettledrums beat a flourish and a cry arose: *Ram nam satya hai, khaye piye mast hai*!

It was the latter reference to his own epicurean disposition that momentarily confirmed Vakil Sahib's certainty that he had indeed quit the land of the living and had returned as a mournful phantom to oversee the despatch of his perishable remains.

The bizarre process of despatch was one unsanctioned by any scripture.

Seven times round and round the court amid songs and shouts. Then the cot was set down, the pyre lit to the accompaniment of halloos and claps and cheers. A crescendo of mega blasts rent the air, each louder and more ear-shattering than the last, and all emerging from the epicentre of his sorry effigy on the pyre, now turned into a glorious blazing bonfire, kerosene doused and rejoicing in cheery oblations of arrack.

Ish! How inauspicious! murmured his wife, thunder on her brow. Starting a New Year like this! It's that badmash's idea of a joke.

But Vakil Sahib's sense of humour had risen from the dead and convulsed him. Boys will be boys, he chuckled.

Boy! That one is thirty if a day! No matter his beardless baby face and idiot gawp!

But the coat-pant?

Oh, that! she remembered. He begged them of me. Said, Bahuji, so, so cold this winter. My old pant is torn, here and here, look. I said, All right, I'll see. The kutchery coat-pant— the old set—was all worn out, so ... but never, never, Hé Bhagwan, did I dream what the wretch wanted them for!

Let the saala come! I'll take the stick to him. I'll take the hide off his saala arse!

Vakil Sahib's mock rage was belied by his delighted smile. He had just spotted a hilarious joke to crack when his card-and-chatterbucking gang came. He risked cracking it now. Cautiously. To try the effect on her.

All this buck-buck about awarding the first millennium baby! If you ask me, Nirmalaji, I'm in the run for the trophy for the first millennium corpse ... only nobody's announced a prize, so how do I stake my claim?

One look at his spouse's face discouraged any further exercise of wistful fantasy. No sense of humour, this woman. He was sure it would go down better with the card group. No, why not, honestly, why not? A fabulous idea had just started in his head. It would need softening and humouring her up a bit. The Millennium Corpse! Called for a grand thirteen-day obsequies feast. Thirteenth night, ho! The entire chatterbucking horde en masse. A millennium party with a difference. A rip-roaring, belly-tickling guffaw of a party. The host as ghost! He saw himself, solemnly ushering in his guests at the head of the stairs, the offending Nankoo beside him.

This salt-betraying dolt, he'd tell his guests, lit my funeral pyre on the thirty-first of December, before I had had a chance to bid farewell to my choicest mates. I am obliged to celebrate my obsequies feast myself, my yaars. The first time in history—not in one millennium but in all the world's past—a man stands before you, milords, hosting his own funeral feast. Won't you shave your heads for me? Ha! he thought, that last bit was a jewel. They would try every ruse to scuttle out and he would magnanimously settle for one token mourner: the rascal Nankoo. This son of my soul, he would announce, who lit my funeral pyre, yes, dressed me up in my kutchery coat-pant, filled my belly with crackers, laid me out and danced me round the bustee, howling *Ram naam satya hai*! Yes, even he, after twenty years of feudal kinship, this blower-up of his old-time master, shall shave his head as ritual decrees. Where is Ram Saran, the barber?

And out of an alcove would step Ram Saran, complete with scissors and razor and neck cloth, and seize the offender! If there was one thing that vagabond was vain about, it was his opulent locks, combed now in a Bachchan, now in a Salman and now in a Shah Rukh. Vakil Sahib's fantasy enlarged, filling him with immense satisfaction, even as merriment grew in the yard beneath. Let the lout come, he chuckled, let him, aha, I'll teach the haramzada!

Aloud he told his lady: Thirteen days from now—the thirteenth night of the New Year, Nirmalaji—make ready for a largish dinner feast. No table-chair feast. A real old-fashioned wattle-mat and banana-leaf banquet. There. Diners sitting in twin rows on the floor down the length of the baradari. Serving men in spotless dhotis, ladling out your choicest dishes. Puris in wicker baskets, vegetables in steel buckets, water in earthen tumblers and papad and laddoos in leaf-bowls.

What's this place, a temple yard? she spoke with an ill grace.

This is to be my thirteenth-day shraddh feast, Nirmalaji. To celebrate my winning the Corpse of the Millennium trophy.

This millennium-shillenium! she exploded. Going to be the death of me, it is!

Shabash! The runner-up trophy is yours then.

Her husband's perversity did nothing to improve Vakilin's already peevish mood. Six times had she picked up the telephone receiver, to be addressed by a clanging female voice: Namaskar. The telephone department wishes you a Happy New Year. *Nava Varsha ke uplaksha par door sanchar vibhag ki hardik shubh kamnayein.* Until, seething, she had flung down the receiver and sat, glowering at the instrument in mute rage.

***

In an old kothi off the east bank of the river and just across Sikandar Chowk Park, Professor K.B. Mathur had been haranguing his landlady, the long-suffering and all-approving Sakina Bibi, known to the inhabitants of the crumbling tenement simply as Bibi.

First of all, Bibi, it isn't a kambakht millennium. It's just nineteen hundred and ninety-nine years! It's like saying that nineteen rupees and ninety-nine paise is the same as twenty rupees. These computers have made us forget simple counting. Secondly, he went on, I'm sick and tired of this statesman of the millennium, actor of the millennium, cricketer of the millennium, criminal of the millennium, clown of the millennium litany. How do you know I'm not the greatest Indian of the millennium?

Sakina Bibi rested her poignant old eyes on him, eyes that said, yes, in her opinion he surely was that and much more.

Thirdly ... He turned irritably on the divan and, with a vengeful grimace, switched off his portable black-and-white TV. Thirdly, he continued, I detest this endless song-dance-mime-wisecrack-vaudeville going on inside that fool box.

When hijackers have got those poor blighters held up in Kandahar! Such rotten taste!

Like his own, Bibi's concern for the hijacked passengers of the Indian Airlines plane IC 814 had mounted to fever pitch. It had even exceeded her anxiety about the cricket score on India–Pakistan match days. Every hour, during the last few days, she had keenly followed the negotiations and reported them to the professor.

Allah be thanked, the relief plane reached Kandahar at five-thirty p.m. today, Professor Sahib.

He turned sharply. What are they saying now?

They are saying: We will release women and children and the sick only in exchange for Maulana Azhar.

But at Dubai they promised to release all seventy of the women and children. How many did you say they let free there?

Twenty-six. And ... and the body of that badnaseeb young man.

Stabbed for lifting his head. Returning home from Kathmandu. From a honeymoon!

She shuddered, thinking of his young corpse rolling down a chute in all the asymmetry of misshapen matter.

And his young wife?

She shook her head. Ah, poor *jigar-figar* young woman. Married on the third, widowed on the twenty-fourth. Allah give her *rahat-e-rooh*.

They still refuse?

She nodded, and padded back to her room in her loose slippers.

Some time later:

Now they're asking for two hundred million dollars and thirty-six militants. That and the body of that one—Sajjad Afghani.

All this in Allah's name, Bibi?

It is not written that the innocent be tormented. But they say, those zalims, don't teach us Islam.

The plane had begun smelling of vomit. Toilets overflowing. Food packets from the UN. Sitting there, heads down. Ah, their poor aching backs, necks, legs. The danger of paralysis. All the world watching. Allah, the food will not go down the throat. And what one must swallow, to keep body and soul together, that nigora sits like lead in the pit of the stomach. No taste in the mouth, no sleep in the eyes. What is to happen, when shall it end? Allah, Most Merciful, Most Benevolent, hear our entreaty. Restore those misguided ones to their senses, restore those helpless ones to their families, grant that young couple submission to Thy will, peace to that dead young man, comfort to that destroyed young woman. And so on and so forth, five times a day, on the prayer mat, facing holy Mecca.

Until the suspense reached such an intolerable pitch that even the pretence of sleep was abandoned. Landlady and tenant sat, each in their room separated by a narrow corridor, one glued to her TV set, the other switching on his own and snapping it shut and alternately shaking his fist and uttering imprecations at its bland, rectangular face.

Morning came, no one knew how. A killing cold. No sun in the sky. The terraces clammy wet. Dense, impenetrable fog. She took him his five a.m. cup of tea, sat down for her usual chat, warming her stumpy old toes at the coals burning in the rusted iron brazier.

He surveyed the darkness outside, blew upon his tea.

The last day of a century, Bibi, he said meaningly.

She understood. A day that called for significant utterance. A day for a clutch of couplets. That is, if one still found poetry in one's heart.

But what despair there would be, Professor Sahib.

He agreed. There was a shayar, he told her, who had felt the same way, not ten, twenty, fifty years ago but full one hundred years back. An English shayar who wrote of the selfsame despair—on the thirty-first of December, 1899. Wait, he used to teach that poem to his undergraduate students long years back. His memory wasn't what it used to be but ... how did it go? *I stood at the coppice gate* ... No. I *leant* upon the coppice gate ... Coppice gate? You know, Bibi, that sort of gate between country fields in the paintings in my old *Encyclopaedia of Art*? Good, you know the kind. Next line: *When frost was spectre grey.* Spectre grey? See that fog outside. Five-thirty in the morning. Sightless charcoal ...

Surmai? she suggested, catching on.

That's it. And the next two lines: *And winter's dregs made desolate the weakening eye of day.* Dregs? What remains at the bottom of the glass when the glass has been drained. Winter as a draught.

She nodded.

The weakening eye ... ah, we old ones know that so well, Bibi. The light of day like the weakening eye of age ...

Subhanallah, but he was good, this English shayar!

Now mark the next lines, Bibi: *The tangled bine-stems scored the sky like strings of broken lyres* ...

He pondered. How to explain that bit now? He tried. She understood. When a taanpura or a sarangi string snaps, Professor Sahib, there is a twang, a sting and it curls back and then trails ... so ...

She showed how, traced the movement with her now mottled, chilblained fingers. After all, she had been a nautch-lady, this venerable danseuse turned patroness.

And then on to the next thought: *The land's sharp features seemed to be the century's corpse outleant, His crypt the cloudy canopy, the wind his death-lament* ... The shayar compares the earth to a corpse laid out. Lifeless. Pulse stilled. And the sky the dark pall. The wind grieving in maatam.

Izhar-e-afsos? she suggested, struck.

Excellent! he beamed. Or *afsurdgi*. You get the idea?

So it went, line by line. English–Urdu, Urdu–English. And it came to the thrush.

Notice, Bibi, this wasn't a young bird flushed with the hot blood of youth and springtime and melody. No. This was winter. Surmai fog. The century's funeral. The wind howling. This was an aged thrush, *frail, gaunt, and small*.

Mundaris? she offered.

Exactly. *Mundaris. In blast-beruffled plume*. The storms of life had scattered its scanty feathers. This bird had nothing, nothing to sing about, Bibi. But it sang, all by itself, up in its bare, leafless tree. And it sang joyously: *had chosen thus to fling his soul upon the growing gloom*. It was ... it was rapturous as it sang, Bibi, it was ...

Shigufta-khatir, she deduced.

Of course! *Shigufta-khatir*! Blossoming in joy! The gloom could do nothing to suppress its pleasure. There was absolutely nothing, visible or sensible, Bibi, to occasion such rejoicing. But still the old bird sang. And the shayar gave the bird credit for some larger knowledge that he himself had missed—something that spelt hope for his desolate civilization. Consider the final lines, Bibi: *That I could think there trembled through his happy good-night air, some blessed hope whereof he knew and I was unaware*.

Wah! she breathed. How true, Professor Sahib, it is the beasts of the earth and the birds of the air that better know the tides of life.

He waved her words off. *Then*, he objected shortly. Maybe *then*—a hundred years ago. The world's changed beyond recognition since. That shayar knew nothing of the world wars, nuclear energy, chemical and biological warfare, so many things. He could still trust the instinct of a bird above his own. But where are we, Bibi, where? Nothing but display and profits and braggart ambition. I should like to ask this cyber-cipher world what hope it has to offer. Alas, are all our lyres broken? Can no bird sing us to sanity?

She knew he was having one of his poetic seizures. The paroxysm used to come on with cyclic regularity once every seven or eight days. His metaphors would inflate, classicize. His eyes might smoulder and spill. His voice spark and choke upon an overpowering epiphany. She was used to it.

Time to fetch the milk and double-roti and give that one in the barabar chamber his tea, Professor Sahib. Poetry will not warm the gullet or set the bowels a-moving of a morning, you know. She heaved her massive bulk on to her slow, lumbering feet. But first I must save the newspaper from the dew. Soaked it was, all soggy, yesterday.

He heard her huff and puff up the stairs. She left the damp newspaper on his rickety old table and went back, muttering, to switching on the water-pump and filling her cranky collection of plastic buckets, iron tubs, brass and copper urns, earthen matkas, even kitchen bowls and jugs and her indispensable spouted hand-pot. The water was cold, made her lumpy chilblains flame with pain. But Allah's karam it was that the taps still ran from five in the morning till seven, else the house would be like the barren desert 'neath the foot of Sinai and Hazrat Moosa might have to be summoned to strike water out of a rock!

Waking up her other lodger was a demanding job. Some mornings, she swore, she felt like splashing his head with ice-cold water. If he hadn't been a grown man—twenty-five at least, if one took a measure of his face—she would have done it too. Instead, she stood patiently by his bedside, teacup and saucer in hand, entreating: Suleman Bhai, it is six-thirty. Be so good as to rise before your tea turns cold as the dews of Jalwa-Sharif.

Looking down on his sleep-bleared face with its tousled beard, she was touched by its unguarded simplicity. Poor, unemployed boy. Working so hard. Must have worked at that book of his till late in the night. When he did not stir, she sighed, left the cup on his bedside chowki, covering it with the saucer. It would have to be warmed again when Professor Sahib's second cup of tea was made at seven.

She heard Professor Sahib calling for a pair of scissors. When she took it up to him, along with his tea, he held the *Times of India* across to her. She took the page he indicated, took another look at him. Some frenzy was on him, an ill-suppressed excitement. Another poetic seizure, who knows, she reflected, as she read the column he tapped with his finger:

Militant's Father Condemns Terrorist Act to Free Son

By a Staff Reporter

New Delhi, 31 December. In a fax message to this office, the father of a militant, who appears to be among the thirty-six whose release the IA plane hijackers are demanding, on Wednesday said he did 'not wish his release to be secured through such terrorist means'.

The fax has apparently been sent from Egypt. The fax number, from where the signed fax originated, didn't respond despite being contacted on several occasions. The authenticity of the fax message, therefore, could not be confirmed beyond all doubt.

Saeed Ahmed Sheikh, father of Ahmed Omar Saeed Sheikh, who is in an Indian jail and is facing trial for his involvement in the 1994 kidnapping of four foreign tourists, sympathised with the family of Ripen Katyal and said: 'As a grief-stricken father myself, I convey my heartfelt condolences to the family of Ripen Katyal. I join them in their appeal to the hijackers to free his widow, Rachna Katyal immediately, irrespective of all demands.'

Apparently, the Sheikh's son had kidnapped the four tourists— who were later released, unharmed—in an attempt to seek the release of Maulana Masood Azhar. Azhar's release from jail is the main demand of the hijackers of IC814.

Assailing the hijackers, the Sheikh said: 'I wish to place on record my strong condemnation of the hijacking and all demands made by the hijackers. Though I have not seen my son for five years, I do not wish his release to be secured through such terrorist means. I am certain that my son Omar would also be of the same view if he had any means of communication to the outside world.' The statement condemned the acts of the hijackers and all similar actions of terrorist groups directed against innocent civilians, mothers and children.

Her English was shaky, although she had passed the Middle School exam privately and had known the difference between infinitives and gerunds despite the bells on her ankles. She spelt through the paragraphs with some labour, not rendered any easier by her constantly slipping spectacles and his muffled humming of that annoying Sehgal song—*Aye dil-e-bekaraar kyun*—of which he knew but one line that he ground out in irritating repetition: Oh heart, why still unconsoled, oh heart, why still unconsoled, oh heart, why still unconsoled, oh heart why still ...

She helped him cut out the snippet in silence, patiently tolerating the tuneless grind. Then she ventured to remark, almost coyly, every nuanced grace and courtly coquetry in her nautch-girl ancestry intact: May the temerity be forgiven, Professor Sahib, but the bird, it is singing. Hearken you. It is singing, Professor Sahib.

He turned to stare as her meaning got across to him, his lank, uncombed hair thinly starting up round the sparse balding pate, looking oddly like a moth-eaten, scanty-feathered, wind-ruffled bird.

You're right, Bibi. If this world can still hold a father who can say, don't release my son at this cost, it can also hold an old bird's song. How did it go?

Shigufta-khatir, she prompted softly.

***

In the small hours of the morning of the first of January, Masterji Hargopal Misra was woken by a curious creaking. Then a soft clang. He recognized that as the dull tinker of the three-linked chain on his old groaning door.

It had rained all night. Not thick strands of monsoon rain but a ragged drumming in the antechamber of one's sleep—a steady accompaniment to the more pressing urgencies of Masterji's garbled dream. Now, at that stealthy grate and stir, he sat bolt upright in bed.

A burglar! He groped for the electric switch. Snapped it on. Nothing. A power failure. He fumbled beneath his pillow for his torch.

Something crept in. Small and slinking. The beam of the torch made it shrink in recoil, tail between its legs, lozenge eyes radium-glowing. Masterji's heart relaxed with love. Kurkuri, the little black bitch!

Come, child. Oh-foh, how wet her fur feels! Bristling up in a thousand soaked needle-tufts. Come, Kurkuri, now there. That dratted cat's got your milk again. And where've you been prowling this icy night? One of these nights you'll get my room burgled and my throat slit, then who's going to look after you, my vagabond girl?

The dog sniffed at her empty bowl, looked up, sorry. The look was not lost on Masterji, who caught the reproach, rose, abashed, and stumbled to the far wall where his sherwani hung upon a clothes peg. He groped in the long, capacious pocket, brought out a packet of Parle G biscuits and gave six to the dog. There, that's for missing meals, Kurkuri.

Then, just as he was about to lie down again, the old panic gripped him. I leave the door open for this little thing but I sleep so sound, who knows who can slip in, slip out? He went down on all fours, close, close to the dog's reeking black fur, felt under his bed and dragged out the violin-case. Ah, still safe, thank Ishwar! He took out the violin and tested its glossy weight against his chin. Willowy in form as a lissom woman, mellow-rich in tone as a much-suffered one, ah, this treasure! He laid it on the bed, focussed the torch into its interiors and spelt over the words in perplexity and excitement: *Antonio Stradivarius Cremonenfis, Faciebat Anno 17*.

What was it? German? But Cremona, he was told, was in Italy. Did Anno mean year? Or century?

He couldn't get over that snippet his colleague Janardan Prasad had shown him. Ever since he had seen that newspaper cutting, Masterji Hargopal had obsessed about burglars and slit throats. But what to do? The door had to stay open for Kurkuri—the nights were so cold. Once she was in, no burglar could harm a hair on his head.

Sleep, Kurkuri, sleep. He put the violin back in its case, the case under the bed, and climbed into bed himself. But he had lost his sleep for tonight. The dog snuffled and scratched, dug its hams with its clashing teeth, hunted ticks while Masterji blessed the comfort of her presence. He had brought her in one dismal winter evening, she and her little twin, Jamun. Two tiny, starving pups, half frozen. Twenty-four hours they had lain, snuggling against the rigid body of their dead mother, the majestic black stray everyone called Juhi. Masterji passed the dung heap—the one where the buffaloes stamped and chomped their fodder—several times on his moped, looking anxiously at the dead mother with her tongue lolled askew and her staring, stoned eyes, and the little ones, still seeking warmth from that stiff body and sustenance from the shrivelled teats. Until evening came and the doms still hadn't come to remove the body, which had begun to stink, the pups still clinging to it.

One thought troubled Masterji. Those doms usually dragged a dog's carcass away, holding on to a string tied to a hind leg, the head bumping over the ground as it scraped after the scavenger. How would the little pups feel? Also, when night fell—this miserable fog and the newspapers reporting a minimum temperature of three degrees Celsius— where would the little mites go? At eight o'clock he went and fetched the pups, folded in his sherwani. He begged two teaspoonfuls of brandy from a neighbour, heated milk, lighted a sigri, and spread sacking on his floor. They grew up there. By night in his room, by day on his doorstep in the lane, until they learnt to forage for scraps in garbage heaps and developed enough traffic sense to avoid getting killed. Jamun died. Masterji still remembered his solemn gold-glinting eyes, his tiger-prowl tread, his devoted vigils upon his doorstep, and his heart winced at the memory. But Kurkuri grew up. She had already littered twice. (Masterji found himself experiencing great moral responsibility for Kurkuri's children and was now supporting them with food, sackcloth, homeopathic doses, agonizing over their deaths, arranging their funerals and unavailingly trying to fix homes for the more prepossessing ones.)

When Kurkuri vanished once, last month, Masterji stopped his music tuitions for four days. The dog van had come and gone, he was informed, and Kurkuri had been taken away. Masterji appealed to the municipal health officer, the chief veterinary doctor (whose kids he taught singing), the driver and attendants of the dog van itself.

Is it true you destroy these poor strays? Place a staff slantwise across their necks and then stand on it till the neck breaks?

No, no, the attendants swore. We take them far out of town and into the wilds and leave them there.

But my Kurkuri wasn't rabid. How'll she survive? Masterji was sick with worry until Mayank came to his rescue.

In my last life that boy was my son, Masterji often reflected. Good boy. Deferential. Gifted. One to whom a musical father might feel fulfilled in handing down the legacy of his art and knowledge. Masterji Hargopal's prize pupil, he was called, and Masterji puffed with pride. When he performed before the examiners at the Fourth Year Practical Exam, ah, such a hush there was, such an intake of breath when he finished playing Raga Jaijaiwanti, such clapping. And when the examiner asked him: Who is your guru? Mayank answered, Pandit Hargopal Misra. Maihar gharana. And everyone turned to look at him and even that Janardan forgot to jeer and scoff as he was always doing.

When Kurkuri was lost, Mayank was quick to grasp his teacher's grief. He turned up one morning, all muffled up against the cold. I've arranged a car, Masterji. Let's drive down to Chak village and look for Kurkuri. I've found out from the dog van men where they left her.

In the old Fiat they drove down. Twenty-five miles out of the city and into the mango plantation belt. They spotted dozens of dogs. Some crushed to a flattened, bloody pulp on the highway, some dozing outside hutments, some prowling around the G.T. Road eateries. But no sign of Kurkuri. After a day's fruitless search they drove back, Masterji's heart stupefied with disappointment. My little girl is lost or run over, who knows. I'll never see her now. But two days later Mayank was back, late at night. He led, at the end of a nylon cord, a much bedraggled, hungry-looking Kurkuri. Here she is, Masterji. Couldn't rest till I found her. Give her something to eat. Mayank was a boy of few words.

Where did you find her? was all Masterji could trust himself to utter.

Under the bridge. She was trying to cross the river flats, answered Mayank.

That was Mayank. Gem of a boy. Fine feelings, no vanity, no cynicism, such simplicity. And he was, believe it or not, a rich businessman's son. An electronics equipment dealer! But nothing of the nouveau riche about the boy. He would go far, he would. Pity he couldn't take the Fifth Year exams. Preparing for his IIT entrance tests. So much coaching. Can't spare any time for riyaz, you understand how it is, Masterji? Of course Masterji did. Oh all right, there's always next year. But you'll keep taking lessons once a week? Certainly. That I will, Masterji.

And by now it was already five-thirty a.m. Time to get up. To be washed and ready for the six a.m. riyaz. The joss stick lit before the small sandalwood Saraswati in the niche. Then that other ritual.

He took the precious violin out of its case. Sat on the mat and drew out the now-familiar strains:

> Ga re sa dha dha
> Pa sa sa ga re
> Ga re sa sa dha dha
> Pa sa ni re sa.

He couldn't read staff notation and Evans knew only that. He had played that tune ever so slowly, phrase by phrase, and Masterji had quickly jotted down the sargam for it. Now, after months, he could play that tune as well as Evans had.

Though Evans had stood, statuesque despite his stoop, the violin propped against his collarbone, and he himself now sat, Indian fashion, on the floor, the melody slipped out just right. Liquid, quivering, a pure, pale gold seam, its charged shimmer vibrating in resonant appeal. Then it drew back gravely, its arches enlarging in slow, tremulous eddies. Until it came to rest in a kind of solemn transport. His fingers unspooled the melody he had come to love and he cursed himself for the nth time for having failed to ask Evans the name of the song.

Once he had played it at the Academy and when Janardan asked what it was, he could only answer vaguely: A sort of hymn. To Isamasih.

And Janardan's lip had curled in his habitual sneer and the old light of battle had sparked in his eye. And why play hymns to Isamasih, Hargopalji?

With Janardan, Masterji always had to struggle to stay composed, seldom with success.

I promised that old Christian who sold me his antique German violin.

Curiosity triumphed over Janardan's scorn. What promise?

That I'd only play hymns to Isamasih on his violin. He taught me some. This one too. Evans, his name was. Migrated to Australia. Old fellow. Getting on in years.

Janardan's ears had caught the operative words. 'German' and 'antique'. How much did you pay for it? he asked.

Very little. Just a thousand rupees. It was the promise that was important ...

Ah, a point of honour. And you've faithfully kept it, Hargopalji. Don't say the Mission is supplying you your daily dole of rice now. Aren't your tuitions fetching enough? Then, slyly provocative: Aren't you a Hindu any more, Hargopalji?

Masterji's voice had begun turning shrill. My Hinduism has lots of room, Janardan. It can hold a few hymns to Isamasih too!

But a German antique ... Janardan's mind turned to practical matters. Suppose you show it to me, Hargopalji?

Now, sitting on the mat, Masterji thought of Evans demonstrating another hymn. *The Lord is my shepherd*. How is your God a shepherd, Evans Sahib? he had asked. Evans explained. The single lost sheep, the Lord going in search, restless until it was found. Masterji understood perfectly. The way he had gone in search of Kurkuri. Our Lord Krishna, he had started telling Evans, he, he too is a cowherd ... But Evans hadn't shown interest.

But this other hymn, the one he now practised daily, this tune without words, had sunk into his memory. Several times he tried finding out the words. He had asked Isaac Theodore Singh, the cashier at the Academy. Hummed it out for him. But Isaac shook his head. Sorry, Hargopalji. We sing all our hymns in Hindi. He sang a few for Masterji's benefit. He sang *Daya ka sagar aaya jagat mein, tere-mere is jahan mein*. But Masterji said, no, this wasn't it. Then he sang *Kiya intezar jiska, woh Yeshu nazar aaya*. But Masterji said, not this one either. Then Isaac sang *Vandanam, deva, vandanam, chinmayanand rupah vandanam*. And Masterji exclaimed: What's this? This is a hymn very like one composed by our Sankara. Isaac looked stung. It was composed by our pastor, the Reverend Dhiranand Biswas. Rubbish, said Masterji, getting heated. Ever heard of Sankara, Isaac? The one who rides a bull? ventured Isaac (and powders his nose with ashes, he thought to himself). Uf! spat Masterji. Bhagwan Shankar and Adi Sankara are not to be confused, Isaacji. (Thinking to himself: What can one expect of these converted half-castes?) He grew agitated, discursive. *Sachchidanand rupah* is Sanskrit, Isaacji. Meaning one whose being is made of Sat, Chitta and Ananda—existence, knowledge, bliss. Brahman, the Formless. Brahma? queried Isaac. Masterji tried again. Adi Sankara was a philosopher, Isaacji. He defined Brahman as the Formless. That's your *Sachchidanand rupah*.

Then Masterji stopped, for he half suspected that laying property rights on the Formless was silly. But Isaac asked curiously: Brahmin? And Masterji found himself floundering inextricably in a maze of incommunicables. Brahmin is one who understands Brahman, the Formless, he answered, resolute like Yudhishthira to the yaksha in the Mahabharata. Then what's Brahma? persisted Isaac. Masterji sighed and gave up.

So that melody remained wordless. A noumenal sweetness in Masterji's mornings. And he didn't know if he would ever track down the fugitive words that might at last give its sweetness a name and a sense.

The mornings followed a precise routine. After the hymn some chants to Lord Shiva and the Maihar Devi. My guru, the legendary Alauddin Khan, he often told new pupils, dedicated all his music to the Maihar goddess and so must I. As he did his riyaz, practising painstakingly, it was often like labouring up the steps to the Maihar Devi's temple. After the first twenty-five notes or so, as his voice began climbing up the antara, his old breathlessness stole in, a wheezy gasp between each phrase. Higher and higher, up the rocky staircase of the scale, the terrain growing ever more rough-hewn, note by persevering note, beyond the reaches of voice or string or breath or flue. But this is my tapasya, he thought. He went through *Rum-jhum, rum-jhum payal baje, Kaise ja-oon main piya milan ko*. He did *Dagar chalat mosé karat raar kanha*.

After that there were dance steps to practise. At sixty, one must keep the body supple. For Masterji was a jack-of-all. Guitar, violin, sitar, vocal, harmonium, even a bit of dance. Fifty rupees an hour wasn't bad but he had to stay in practice, and to the furnace with all the snipers and scoffers who jibed: What more are you planning to teach, Hargopalji? Why not adopt a bandmaster's profession. Very profitable in the marriage season. And with cent per cent versatility such as yours—not just a bandmaster, you can be the entire baraat band all by yourself. Including the dancer boys!

That wasn't Janardan this time. But Janardan's crony, Srikant Swaroop, the official violin man at the Academy. To hell with him!

After the practice hour, Masterji locked up, mounted his old TVS Champ, and clanked off to the doodhwala's stall, where he quaffed a litre of unboiled milk straight out of the frothing bucket. The milk descended in two taut, churring streamlets, a white sizzle squeezed out of the buffalo's engorged udders, and the doodhwala tipped the bucket over and poured out a Patiala glassful for Masterji. Then off to the halwai for a pao of sweets. A high-powered bachelor breakfast. Then he picked up his daily dog ration—three packets of Parle G biscuits for the strays he came across on his beat. Adjusted his helmet like a knight's headpiece, visor and all, and remounted his moped— a large, lanky, unsteady form on a steady little two-wheeler.

two

Vakil Sahib Mahendra Chandra, Professor Mathur and Masterji Hargopal Misra. Much high-powered technology was set in action before the hieroglyphic of their essence was decoded and their mislaid names subsumed. I was angry on their behalf. I felt one with them, one of history's ciphers, unchronicled potential history-fodder. Still I was technically alive and I could ask: Where does this history happen? For those granted merciful, if temporary, exemption from its sting, it happens in the headlines of newspapers, in the TV screen, in internet outcries, on bookshelves, in magazines, classrooms and conference rooms. Or in the reverberation of human voices recalling.

For me, that day in late March, it began with the ringing of my mobile phone and Deb's voice: Siddhantha, there's this blast in Sikandar Chowk Park. I want you to rush down and cover it. Immediately.

My protest: But my train's at five-twenty. I'm off to Mathura to cover the Lathmaar Holi, have you forgotten? Where the women ritually beat up their menfolk with lathis and this year a man's died ...

His irate reaction: Drop that for now. Forget your train reservations. We're terribly short of hands today. Just rush.

No arguing with that. I did that story. It wasn't exactly a scoop. A scrap of news so trivial that the desensitized eye quickly glosses over it in its insignificant corner of the local page, a mere quarter column.

> 22 *March*. A powerful bomb blast occurred at Sikandar Chowk Park in the heart of Sikandar Bagh market in which 57 people were killed and 115 seriously injured. A horde of security personnel and journalists converged on the scene after hearing news of the blast which occurred at 16.25 hours. Eyewitnesses said they saw black smoke go up like a whirlwind immediately after the ear-splitting explosion. The impact damaged the boundary wall of the park besides damaging dozens of shops, vehicles and a number of adjoining buildings. The site presented a gory spectacle with mutilated bodies, mangled metal and broken branches strewn all around.

The frequency of blasts all over the world has generated a now-clichéd vocabulary of reportage and I made use of it:

> Authorities announced an ad hoc ex gratia of Rs 15000 to the next of kin of the dead and Rs 500 for the seriously injured. The defence ministry has impressed on the state police forces the need for extra vigilance to ensure that anti-national elements do not indulge in further disruptive acts. The Swatantra Bharat Party has called for a twelve-hour bandh tomorrow, 23 March.

You can so easily spin off the phrases of a typical blast report. And next morning's sequel story:

> Death toll rising. 300 to 500 pounds of plastic explosives. Police cordoned off the area. The grim work of cleaning up the site underway.

And finally the next to next day:

> Forensic experts have found evidence of RDX. Director of State Forensic Laboratory, Dr Mohan Mehrotra, told PTI

their report was based on samples collected immediately after the blasts. The explosive was kept in the dicky of the car and the CNG gas cylinder added to the high explosive impact. Remains of the CNG gas cylinder were found at the site. The tissues of some of the mutilated bodies where identification was impossible have been sent to the Centre for Cellular and Molecular Biology, Hyderabad, for identification by the DNA fingerprinting technique, Mehrotra said. Police are working on different leads. While refusing to pinpoint responsibility for the blast on any particular group, the police are investigating the antecedents of one Suleman Jameel, who is reported missing since 22 March. A police raid has brought to light a roll of film containing a photograph of Suleman Jameel and also the script of a novel alleged to have been used as a channel for secret instructions from the headquarters of Jameel's militant group in London. An enquiry committee has been set up to look into the details of the evidence. Meanwhile, the police interrogated Sakina Ali, at whose Sikandar Bagh house Jameel reportedly lodged during the whole of the last year, a senior police official told PTI. The police, according to the report, are still not satisfied with Ali's replies during the interrogation. Later, rampaging mobs stormed Ali's house in search of Jameel, and a young girl, a relative of Ali's, is reported to have been criminally assaulted. The police resorted to firing to control the mob. No casualties are reported.

You have, of course, gathered that I am a journalist. Twenty years into it. I became a journalist by chance and not by choice. You could say the job found me, not I the job. I used to tutor fellows rich enough to pay me and patient enough to endure my verbal excesses, and the rest of the time I used to sit doodling and dribbling vinegary prose and verse, my speciality being parodies in a sour-wicked-pseudo-wisdom mode typically my own. This was in the early eighties. But those days you didn't need a Mass Comm. degree to land a newspaper job in a small town. I met my editor, Ravindra Deb, at (but of course) the Coffee House at the loafers' hour. I'd just recited a poem before a tableful of raucous revellers. Something that went, I remember, like this:

> Now I have finally travelled
> Sadly beyond all experience.
> Your eyes have gone silent.
> In your most stale gesture are things
>   which oppose me
> Or which I dare not touch because
> There's so much fear.

A sixties' campus intellectual might have guffawed at the travesty but not old Deb. He probably took it for a sad, serious piece of original poesy, for his eyes rested on me in solemn respect.

Your own? he asked.

In its present form, yes, I replied.

Writer? he pursued.

Of sorts, I answered.

A poet or a story-wala? he queried.

Both on occasion.

Then tell me, Siddhantha, how it's possible for you to write prose and poetry both.

I could see I was up for trial, that this was an interview of sorts. I kept a straight face and looked him in the eye. When I write prose I use words as particles. When I write poetry I use words as waves, I intoned soberly. You could tell he was impressed. Five minutes later I was an employed man, a middle-ranking editor at the *Mashal*.

The *Mashal* outfit those days was housed in a single hall down an alley lined with lace and button shops. You get the scene? Shoddy office, stained tables, half a dozen rackety manual typewriters, a chai-boy doing the rounds with a metal carrier of glasses of sugary, scalding tea. Loud voices raised in noisy certitudes and the occasional hawk and spit of paan. I had an absurdly high-sounding designation. Over the last twenty years the *Mashal* establishment modernized itself a lot with tinted glass partitions, mica-ed plywood cabins, computers, whathaveyou, but during these recent riots I saw it burn down to a shell. I remember how Deb and I stepped in after the firemen had left. The ceiling fans still hung, their blades twisted and drooping like the limp black petals of dying flowers, and a mesh of snarled wires all over the ground. I guess I was partially responsible for the wreckage.

That's again how history goes on happening all around you and sometimes within you, whether in palpable external events or in small, equivocal, time-branded thoughts. It's like a drop of rain here, another there, then a shock of unexpected spray under a gust of wind and you might say to yourself: Soon I'll need my umbrella. Then suddenly there's the spouting downpour, the thrashing drench-broil and the uproar and urgency of clamouring for shelter. The puddles come glushing round your squelching feet and you hurry along, still managing to step round the staining gutter swill. You scarcely notice the water level rising until the flood-broth comes ramming at your shins. Then in a second it's detonating all around you, its high decibel booms imploding in your nerves. It has you capsized, fleeing, blinded. I frequently get the sinking feeling that I'm one of the passengers on that hijacked plane that smashed into the WTC, my illusory identity on a disintegration countdown. Do you hear that sick buzz, behind all the other noises? That's history, its engines never switched off. And try as I might, I cannot chart its movement because, so close up, I can only be sucked into the vibrating grains of the dizzying image racing beyond snare. By the time it has receded and settled into contained focus I won't be around. But at the moment all I can do is clutch at a single news item, a micro-monad of the essential tale, to my mind at least, a minor, practically trite bomb blast in a certain park in the middle of a certain crowded market of an obscure small town.

There were of course survivors who could later tell me: This is how it started ... I'm not very sure of this but I'm relatively surer of that. The threads tie themselves in knots and loops, then straighten as a narrative picks up. But I grew interested in the victims who hadn't had the time to sort it out, or if they had it was in the super-slow instant of ceding consent to death. And there were the eleven of them who were completely pulped, whose names went missing in the first casualty lists. Until scraps of the forlorn matter of which they had been built were put through the high-powered automated sequencers for STR-based DNA fingerprinting. And out of the random mashed mess there sprang personalities, lives, stories of pain and love and betrayed trust and fantasies and forgiveness and fresh resolves. Scientific research has established that the DNA of living beings holds unbelievable quantities of information, past, present, yes, even the future in its intricate network of molecules, that the DNA stores all the records implanted in it and under certain chemical influences cataracts of electro-chemical reaction are activated and the sanctum of so-called knowledge is reached. Then photons of light send out signals of energy, approximately a hundred units of energy per square centimetre per second. And the DNA of the dead might well be a reservoir of all history, their own and that which they shared with the whole of sentience, of which I must be a participating receptor. It is a sort of romantic faith in this source of shared knowing that has motivated me. This is a book about eleven people and a country. Eleven human characters and a twelfth para-human one, you might say. For three years I've carried these eleven people in my head, researching their lives, intuiting what I could not prove, my imagination overleaping the fault lines in the accounts of others as I struggled to experience their realities by proxy. As for the twelfth character, It (one can only use the transcendental neuter) forms the amniotic plasma surrounding, decreeing and sustaining each cellular entity, the living and the dead.

I've already told you something about Vakil Sahib Mahendra Chandra, Professor Mathur and Pandit Hargopal Misra, three of history's ciphers. Let me now go on to another one of those eleven, one who went into the automated sequencer as a sample tissue and came out as a sparkling secretary.

***

My name's Shirin, though Chagrin might be better, she had told the new recruit breezily. With that characteristic devil-may-care-ish shrug that tossed her hair out of its loose bun and made it snake right down her shoulder blades.

In the office they heard her out with respect. Convent-educated English steno. No wonder she used strange, complicated words no one understood. They didn't know what 'chagrin' meant but no doubt it meant something bright and gutsy. English steno who never, but never, made a typing error. Who often strode into the boss's chamber, declaring brusquely: Excuse me, sir, but this word here—'malfeasance'—is incorrectly used in this context, if I may say so. May I replace it with something more suitable?

The funny thing was that the superiors didn't resent it. She reduced them to a state of abject humility, no one understood how. Her English maybe. And something else. Her air of a woman who, having stood a great deal of nonsense in her life, will now stand no more. Bosses, officers and staff, all, all knew the hell she was going through and the way she dared and defied it every working day.

How fresh you manage to look in spite of ... said her women colleagues.

Oh, one's got to muddle through, she answered with untypical demureness, pausing just a split second before letting loose one of her blasts of outrageous humour. Now the docs say he's got to have a brain scan. As for me, I guess what I need is an arse scan, I'm that buggered up by now.

She enjoyed their speechless disconcert.

I said to him: Jus, in four months I've taken you to see cardiologists, gastroenterologists, neurologists, whathaveyou. I guess I'll even have to take you to a gynaecologist one of these days.

They sniggered timidly. She didn't tell them how frightened she had been in the cardiologist's chamber while Juswant's heart appeared on the monitor screen. 2-D Colour Doppler Echo. The pistons of his pumping machine working. Bellows filling and emptying. Like a fat, fleshy fist. Clenching and unclenching. An alcoholic's fist, clenching and unclenching. Ready to hit out.

But honestly, she thought, how do I do it, look fresh, I mean? Dress well. Apply make-up. Breeze around. As she dressed for office, he watched her from the bed, hawk-eyed. As though he envied her. Or mocked her in his heart. Forty-two-year-old has-been nayika applying kohl to her eyes. Why did she do it so carefully? So extra diligently. She didn't care a hang for impressions, for any man under the sun, nor any woman either. Then why?

She had found her answer at the bus terminus, waiting for the nine-twenty number 23. A little, naked beggar kid, nose running, snot-starched, hair dirt-matted, had painted a big, black moustache on his face. As bold as Rana Pratap Singh, if you please! Lush in coal dust and scimitar-curved round his sallow cheeks. Ah, that's make-up for you! she had exclaimed to herself. Now I know why I do it. One's got to be fighting fit. Not a scrap to cover his little brown bottom but the whiskers, wow, what swaggering bravado! That's me, she told herself. And told Juswant all about it that evening as she rubbed Moov into his swollen ankles.

Arse scan now, I told them. I've taken him to cardiologists, neurologists, gastroenterologists. Now I'm thinking of taking him to a gynaecologist. No. I didn't tell them we've been going to Sahai. I know you're touchy about telling anyone you're seeing a psychiatrist. So I never give them so much as a hint ...

That was said to nudge him alive. But he didn't react. He always lay or stood or walked about like a spectre. Completely impersonal. A zombie. A robotic non-person. He wasn't wearing a mask. He just wasn't all there. Sometimes for a flash he became his old self. Just a flicker, before his face locked up again. So absent. I don't know if I've really lost him, she wondered. It frightened her. Will he ever come back? She wanted to shout, as one shouts into a telephone receiver to be heard above the disturbance in the line or the all-muffling barrier of unconquerable silence: I'm waiting just outside this door you're locked behind, Jus. Just outside. Waiting to receive you when you return to yourself.

But would he ever?

It put her in a jibing mood. Partly to provoke him out of this waking stupor, more to vent her own fretfulnes.

So when you were lying in the CCU of Wellington General Hospital, all you could think of was your Provident Fund and how to help me get it! That's all I meant? Didn't you want to see me? Didn't you want to talk to me, feel me beside you? I was nothing beyond being the official nominee in the papers? Writing me off as a duty completed? Deep down she guessed that face to face with death there were perhaps different priorities.

He just looked blank and she realized that none of it had registered. It was scary. It irked her. Left her angry, her nerves jangling.

What further fuelled her restlessness was the sight of her precious Camay submerged like a pat of slow-melting butter in the soap dish. An island in a semeny slop. There was the scum of Camay on the tiled bathroom floor and a pinkish curd smeared on the steel mesh over the drain. A mess he left the bathroom in! What was he using all that Camay for? He couldn't even eat his meals without assistance, much less bathe, and he certainly didn't look recently washed.

If I slip and break my back, a nice soup we'll be in! she jittered aloud. Imagine me laid up and you in this state. But then, she jibed, you walk enough for two.

When the cirrhosis was diagnosed and total abstinence forced upon him, his nerves had revealed the mess they were in. Not only did he turn completely sleepless, he couldn't even sit still. Some frenetic nervous clamour made him pace the floors, hour upon hour. Until the veins stood out on his feet and his calves and ankles bulged with tumid blood. Pale, his face drawn with pain, he walked and walked. Dragging his feet, breathing heavily, walking, walking, fleeing, fleeing. It was like some mythic curse. An epic hero cursed with walking the earth. Endlessly.

If there isn't a myth, there ought to be one, she often thought, watching him, appalled.

Outwardly, she made a jest of it. Hullo, hullo there, Jus! Trekking across the globe? Where have you reached now? Hungary?

When he was tired he stood, ramrod-stiff, face wooden, and his right hand raised chest-high against his torso in an empty, aimless freeze. She pulled his leg. You look like the Emperor Jehangir twiddling a rose. Or George the Fifth holding the reins. He did not laugh. His eyes were glazed, staring straight ahead.

Now time for your Zolam—you've walked enough, she baby-chatted him. You and I must've walked twenty kilometres between us today. I walked half the way home. No auto, rickshaw, tempo, bus, nothing.

Suddenly his old voice! A single phrase of achieved coherence in the confused babel of rioting nervous chaos: Wish I could drive you back.

She started. So normal he had sounded. Human. Even friendly, as he hadn't been in years. It caught her off her guard, threw her off-balance, wrung her heart and nettled her intolerably.

Oh indeed! Indeed and indeed again, Jus. Drive me home you would, would you? I remember that time you drove us back from a party. A wedding it was ... whose? Oh yes— Govind's. As usual you vanished the moment we reached. Sitting in a car with your useless mates, boozing. I've stood through countless weddings, all alone, smiling stiffly, anxiously searching the crowd ...

She had a horror in her that she couldn't handle. Grown weak with remembering, she executed with her tongue atrocities she couldn't perpetrate otherwise.

On our way back, dear Juswant, you, dead drunk, driving the old Standard Herald. You deliberately chose the streets with the heaviest traffic. To terrify me, no?

Those reckless, grinding brakes. Screeching tyres. Jolting and shooting across lanes. Jerking and swerving zigzag across the highway. That teeth-jamming, heart-hammering halt. She had wept, begged: Stop, stop please! Please God, Let's get home alive! I don't want to get all smashed and pulped up in this car. Look out, Jus—that truck! A piercing twinge in her temples, her ears shrieking a siren, her palms sweating. He rammed down the brakes. A sickening, nerve-drilling screech. She flung open the door, leapt out. His brutal smut stinging her ear. She had walked home at midnight. Miles and miles. Breathless, fuming, gritting her teeth.

Remember that night, Jus? she nagged like a contentious harpy. Remember?

Then a thought crept in, unbidden. Now it's he who does the walking. Oh God, if I could only help him stop. But he walks because he must. He took all her lashes meekly, hung his head. His eyes were slack. His lips beaked, gap-toothed. He seemed an old man with a lopsided, slightly crazed look, and suddenly her own feverish eyes thawed.

Wish I could drive you home. No mistaking it. Those were the words. No, she thought, I could have left him a hundred times but I didn't. I may have been a coward but I don't think that's it. I think beneath all my rage, he has been my addiction, as booze was his. And do I then love him? Where in me does this embattled love reside? At forty-two I don't know. It's there—like the covert pain in my limbs. That's silent all day, gathered in a microcellular mist just beneath the level of sensation. But when I'm sitting or lying perfectly still, little runnels of pain erupt. My love is like that. Buried somewhere. Insensate. Threatening to turn active. Best to keep the beast submerged. It hasn't been up to any good.

three

Understand me: This became for me an impassioned personal project. Let me acknowledge my sources: Vakil Sahib's wife; Professor Mathur's (and Suleman Jameel's) landlady, Sakina Bibi, now shifted out of her original quarters after little Rubina's dastardly rape; Rubina's wooden silence which told me ever so much more than her voice possibly could. I owe many fruitful details to Master Hargopal's neighbours, his ex-student, Mayank, and Sukhiya, the kabari-turned-drunk; Halim, the tabla repairer and Raghavram, the crazed mendicant–philosopher on the ghats. I specially thank Juswant Ahuja, Shirin's husband for his laboured, halting accounts. (God knows how tough it must have been for him with his bipolar problem.) Let me also thank Neelesh Trivedi and Parul Chopra for their active cooperation and for helping me across certain opaque patches. My other sources include persons as diverse as the Hindustani classical maestro, Raghunath Rai, the mafia overlord, Kailash Brahmachari, and Mrs Masako Kawaguchi of Yokohama. I acknowledge them all here for sharing what they knew, for suggesting possible answers to what they did not know and for activating in my mind this live narrative in which fact, likelihood and imagination seamlessly blend to form what I can only call, by default, history.

So, like a man with a dousing rod I pursued the ley lines of their lives, the texts, the subtexts and the counter-texts. I am grateful to Suruchi Chauhan's son, Vineet, now in college in Delhi, for putting me right on several delicate points, surely embarrassing and sensitive issues to an adolescent boy. To Vikram Aditya's maid I owe considerable hyphenating details that made the total picture come alive. Finally, I'd like to thank Vani Kabir's cousin, Mrs Vrinda Nigam, for furnishing me with certain papers and Vani's appointment diary which came right up to that fateful day, the twenty-second of March. Through inferences, implications, through the pursuit of strong chances and frequently through pure hunches I got to know those eleven people. Some solid details I managed to secure. But I like to think that I obsessed so deeply about each one that their basic stories offered themselves to my reception. Not factually accurate, mind you, but rather existentially probable. I do not for a moment claim that this is their undeniable history, only that it might well have been their essential story, give or take a few runaway variations of incident or experience. So I can say: This is how they were and how they went about their lives and how they came to be there at that time. I went about postulating, anticipating, where necessary inventing, and that's how I wrote out their approximate stories. But I have always, to the best of my power, fine-tuned it to the last knowable milli-pulse of truth.

Approximate stories, get me? How shall I qualify this dubious achievement? All my life I barely managed to avert failure by a hair's breadth rather than triumphantly ride success. And in this telling of approximate stories I may have just missed tumbling into the pit of the impossible rather than authentically pinning down the unquestionable. If history has only taught us how to make the old mistakes in new ways, all this literature stuff has trapped me into recounting the old tractable sub-truths and flexible personal meanings in new ways.

Something took all those people to Sikandar Chowk Park at four in the afternoon on the twenty-second of March. Exhausted words like chance or destiny need to be upgraded in resonance to mean a bit more than they do. What brought Suruchi Chauhan and Vikram Aditya Singh together? Neither chance nor destiny but a pedestrian semi-official problem. It hasn't been difficult finding out about Suruchi Chauhan. Scores of people knew her. I can close my eyes and see her at her imposing desk. Through the frosted windowpanes the long sleeves of muslin light blowing in, engaging steel and brass and chrome and wood in a different dilution. The wall clock strikes, gold globules of sound bouncing down to the thick carpet, the walls tingling with the vibration, the air wincing. A dozen tiny signals portending something to come.

***

That late February morning Suruchi Chauhan, PCS, Secretary of the Allahabad Development Authority, sat in her official cabin on the eleventh floor of Indira Bhavan. Brooding on the same subject. A matter that had turned into a compulsive preoccupation for several months now, a desperate test of personality. Her clash with Ganesh Agarwal and Co., Building Contractors and Property Brokers, with whom she had engaged in a long and bitter ego clash. Whose latest tenders she had turned down and whose earlier contracts she had summarily cancelled. At the Sriharipuram Township Colony, fifteen kilometres down the Benaras route, the landfills had proved insecure. A general sinkage reported in just three years. Agarwal's brokerage company had purchased and sold half the houses at exorbitant rates and now there were a handful of Consumer Forum cases pending.

She had received abuse, threats on the phone in the dead of night. Anonymous letters charging corruption had been sent against her to the local self-government and PWD ministries. An enquiry had been initiated. Betel-chewing, gun-toting mafias had barged into her office once and assaulted her peon, Chhote Lal. Even her PA, Ramesh Chaturvedi, had been roughed up. It happened during the lunch hour and the 'miscreants', as the local paper reported them to be, decamped before two-thirty. Ramesh had frantically telephoned her at her residence in Ashok Nagar, asking her not to return. But she did. Nothing happened. Except a long, affable phone call from a pint-sized local neta in which, among other small talk, allusion was made to a corporator's death in a recent suburban shoot-out. Ah, times are bad, bad, madam, one cannot be too careful, etc. She had laughed. But the next day a fire had broken out in the records section and valuable files pertaining to the Sriharipuram case were destroyed.

That was more than a year back and the vice chairman of the Allahabad Development Authority, Rajaram Yadav, had revoked her earlier cancellation of contracts. No one knew the extent and nature of Agarwal's influence over Yadav but Suruchi Chauhan had keenly felt the loss of face. It had, in all likelihood, even cost her her long overdue promotion this year. She had sent a petition and copies of her CV to the ministry and to the home secretary.

Meanwhile, the Holi title had grown from the customarily malicious to the brazenly salacious. The last one had been: Jackfruit on tree, oil on the lip. No doubt a penetrating observation on her certainty of promotion and her thwarted expectations.

Since no answer had come so far from the ministry, the thing to do was send a reminder. Before moving a writ in the High Court. She had already discussed the matter with a couple of lawyers.

When her eyes suddenly fell on the odd-looking figure before her, she started, displeased.

Chaturvedi, I thought I'd made it quite clear that I had no appointments in the forenoon, she snapped pointedly at Ramesh, who fussed and pussyfooted in his usual inarticulate flurry, indicating in awkward sign language his helplessness in the present circumstances.

She clicked in impatience and turned her attention on the visitor. A thought flitted across her mind: I believe one's supposed to call them 'physically challenged persons' not 'disabled' now.

He seemed about four feet tall. On closer inspection, she realized, he really wasn't small-built but was a tall man almost bent double, his chest shrunk into a misshapen concave curve and a large deformity hillocking on his back. Not a growth, just a strange backward looping of the spine. She couldn't see his legs behind the large desk but he rested his weight upon a sturdy cane from the way he stood tilted slightly to the right.

It was the face that was arresting. Not young, not conventionally good-looking but full eyes of a fierce frankness and a strong jaw. Grey hair, thick and wavy, above a faintly lined forehead. Pity, she thought, such a good face on such a stunted body. Probably putting in a request for accommodation in response to that recently advertised vacancy in the Establishment Department—against the handicapped (no, 'physically challenged') persons' reserved quota.

Suddenly she realized that there had been a power failure for more than an hour. How had he managed eleven flights of stairs? Involuntarily she rose from her chair, motioned him to sit, sat down again and waited while he carefully propped his cane against the desk, adjusted his body alongside, held on to the edge of the table and lowered himself slowly into the chair. All done with great economy and precision of movement. A practised manoeuvre.

The lift wasn't working? she asked.

He sensed the guilty concern in her voice, a shabby mode he knew and no longer resented.

No problem, madam. I'd come mentally prepared to climb mountains.

There was a distinguished urbanity in his voice. An aristocratic polish almost. No, no request for employment this. Something else.

It's been like the trek to Amarnath, he smiled.

Mr Amarnath? She had grown confused, hadn't quite caught his words.

No. I said that gaining an audience with the secretary of the ADA is like the trek to Amarnath. This is my fourth pilgrimage here.

There was a pleasant tang of acid in his speech.

She looked suitably shocked. Really? You went back four times?

Thrice. This is the fourth. Achieved by paying a handsome—what's it called in your offices?—a 'convenience allowance' to quite a few peons and babus. *Suvidha shulk*, is that the term?

She had recovered her poise. Grew professional. Solicitous. So sorry for the trouble. I've tried very hard to uproot some of these practices here, but you know, the system ...

Darkness beneath the lamp, madam, he remarked, idiomatic.

What can I do for you?

I've brought a letter of introduction, madam. From someone you knew.

She was instantly on her guard. Another one!

He placed an envelope on the table.

She didn't want to reach out and pick it up. Hostile. On the defensive. Her lips set tightly, waiting for his next move.

He rose with some difficulty and shifted the envelope closer. Then he looked intently at her, took in her cold eyes and constrained smile, her pigment-spattered face, her plump arms in gold bangles, placed, resolute and unmoving, on the desk. There was a long, awkward pause.

She put all her resistance into her next words. What's this? Pressure from above?

But he was unfazed. He had obviously come well briefed and rehearsed for the act.

Something like that, madam, but not quite the way you imagine.

The pause grew disconcerting. She chose the simplest way out of the stalemate.

Now that you've come up eleven flights of stairs in your condition ...

That sent the signal across loud and clear: I don't usually relent but you're subnormal, hence this concession. She was half ashamed to hint at his disability, but you never knew what to expect in her kind of job. Avoiding his eye, she reached across, picked up the envelope and was surprised to find it unsealed.

Now what would Chaturvedi think? There was a suspicious crackle as she drew out what appeared to be bank drafts. She hoped Chaturvedi would stay out. Her worst suspicions were getting confirmed. Business and sympathy had no truck with one another and had best be kept apart.

The papers lay before her. She put on her glasses and studied them curiously. No, not bank drafts. These appeared to be signed cheques. More than a dozen. Faded and yellow with age. The ink paled, the central fold brittle. The amounts ranged from two hundred to a thousand rupees. The Imperial Trading Bank, Colonelgunj, Allahabad. The year: 1939. And the signature, in a bold and affected hand: Gajendra Singh Rathor.

And it was here that she was rendered utterly witless. She didn't know how to react, realized she was clean out of her depth. She looked up at him, speechless.

What's all this? I don't understand ...

He was mindful of her confusion. Sympathetic.

Of course you know who that was?

My grandfather, she said.

He raised himself slowly, leaned across, supporting himself precariously, and gathered up the cheques.

Don't get me wrong, he said. These are ... kind of ... letters of introduction. From your own grandfather. That's all and nothing irregular. My name is V.A. Singh. Vikram Aditya Singh. And I must first apologize for resorting to this measure and the shock I've caused you. But do understand, a fellow in my position, without any social patrons or godfathers, must utilize whatever resources he's got to gain the bureaucratic ear, don't you see?

He smiled with great reassurance but she didn't trust him. He guessed as much.

You are naturally intrigued by these uncashed cheques. I'll put you out of your trouble, madam. These cheques were sent by your grandfather, Gajendra Singh Rathor, to a person in my family. Sixty ... no, sixty-one years ago. But it is, as they say, a long story.

By now she had somewhat recovered her composure. In that case, Mr Singh, I'll order tea. Do chai, she instructed when Chhote Lal appeared. And rang the bell for Chaturvedi and sent him off on a useless errand that would occupy him for the better part of an hour.

four

There wasn't much data on Swati Maurya except a handful of snippets in a regional-language daily in the archives of the Public Library, and a floating rumour, in the area in which she lived, of a withdrawn FIR. There had been some unpleasantness some time back but not the poor girl's fault at all, was the general opinion. But there were, as my investigations revealed, as many as three different claimants for the ad hoc ex gratia of fifteen thousand rupees and ironically the amount was awarded to the party rumoured as having been named in the withdrawn FIR. But for my purposes there was that plum find, a real live witness to the blast, Neelesh Trivedi. When I asked Neelesh to describe Swati Maurya to me he grew confused. Her face had, you know, changed beyond all recognition after all that ... was all he could say offhand. It was the giddy Mrs Goswamy, whose small son, Kartik, had also died in the blast, who, in the midst of many weepy outcries, brought Swati Maurya alive in my mind's eye. She looked, well, like anyone else, she was this-high, thin, tired-looking, no, definitely unbeautiful, but very, very determined about everything she undertook. Neelesh's non-accounts, turned inside-out, gave me Swati Maurya's mind like a roll of negative film which when developed gives you dozens of positive images. They had met about a year ago by appointment, not with one another, but with a third, common party, Mrs

Goswamy. And after the deal had been clinched they had come away, looking for public transport and spoken to one another, for the first time, at the gate of Sikandar Chowk Park of all places.

A giant pipal guarded the entrance to the park. The white morning had calcified on its jingling leaves but by ten-thirty a late sun had come squinting down through the mesh. Swati Maurya, waiting at the gate, experienced an overwhelming feeling of relief. It hadn't been such an ordeal after all. She hadn't been at all sure of this fellow here, this Neelesh Whatzisname. Nor of this weird kid beside her. But the Neelesh guy had, after committing three choice blunders, got the hang of it and performed tolerably well. And the kid had, thank god, had the presence of mind to say 'Kartik Goswamy' when the principal asked him his name.

While she was grooming him for the interview—in the brief two hours she'd had—he had come up with bizarre answers. When she asked him, And what is your name? he had answered with a devilish perversity: AB.

She had put on a 'friendly auntie' voice (remember, teachers are called 'auntie' in some of these primary schools, she reminded herself).

And what does AB stand for? Amitabh Bachchan? Or Atal Bihari?

He had answered, prim and poker-faced: Also Binnu. And sometimes I'm called Et Cet Ra.

A precocious brat with a bitter pout. She had forced a laugh to cover her nervousness.

Really? Also Et Cet Ra, what unusual names!

When Papa writes home from Dubai, he says, Give my love to Vijoo Et Cet Ra. Vijoo's my big brother. I'm Et Cet Ra.

Oh-foh! That's funny, na?

And when Mummee has visitors, she calls us in and says, Meet Vijoo. And Also Binnu.

Once he got started there was no stopping him. Strange that his mother had said he was a silent kid. Problem child and completely closed.

In the course of that brief getting-to-know-each-other session he airily mentioned the time he had experimented with rat poison (after watching *Mahayagya* on TV) and the time he had swallowed a button trying to scare his Mummee. And the time he had run off and changed his mind when he was on the bridge and slunk back and sulked on the back stairs instead. All this while his mother held a long phone conversation with his father in Dubai. By the end of the session, Swati didn't know whether to be terrified or touched at this enigma she had taken on. Eight years old and still not in school. Couldn't clear a single admission test in the classy schools despite donations and all the rest; and his swanking parents wouldn't dream of putting him in anything less than standard.

And now that parents were to be interviewed by school admission committees, the chances of selection were, if anything, bleaker as Mrs Goswamy's vapourings conveyed.

Ek toh I've studied only up till my Inter and that too quickly-quickly before my marriage and then Kartik's papa is away and Kartik—you can see how he is. Now my Vijoo was admitted into Jesus Marry Convent the first time he appeared for interview but this other one ... always I am getting after him to study, study like his brother. I say to him, competition everywhere. Study is must. *Yeh toh very must hai*. But he doesn't. He is like this only.

Swati had taken an instant dislike to the woman. The deal had been clinched at one thousand per head in case of selection and four hundred per head in case of rejection. The terms had been closely haggled and only when Swati had put on her in-that-case-I'm-not-interested act that the final agreement had been reluctantly and rancorously reached.

The Papa had been arranged by Chunni Lal, godknowshow! Chunni Lal sat in the sentry-box at the gate of St. Dominic's School and had proved a mine of inspiration and a resourceful think-tank for scores of people. He had surreptitiously displayed for Swati's benefit a handbill when recently she had gone job-hunting to the Primary Section and was coming away, dejected:

> *Coaching, All Subjects, All Classes. Home*
> *Tutors Available*
> *Reasonable Rates. Guaranteed Sure-Shot*
> *Success.*
> *I.C.S.E., C.B.S.E, U.P. Board.*

And the small print, down in the lower margin: *For Admission Interview, Parents on Hire. Smart, Convented, Ladies-Gents. No Risk. Super Successful Performance Assured.*

There was only one leaflet. Chunni Lal couldn't risk circulating it but he let prospective candidates read it. Then he explained the business with many thumb and finger clicks, many nods and winks. She got the general idea. Twenty per cent for Chunni Lal, the rest for self. Good, paying social service. Better returns than primary school salary for non-BEd candidate. She had put down her name and address in Chunni Lal's secret pocket diary.

Looking back, she was fascinated, aghast, at her own readiness for corruption. If that hadn't been a particularly desperate day, she would never have taken the plunge. But the Monster had come again, sometime during the night, and punctured both the tyres of her Hero Puch and that had put her in a tearing frenzy of rage. It was one thing to refuse maintenance, quite another thing to torment her with malicious damages to property and person. One of these days I'll put an attempt-to-kill-for-dowry charge upon the badmash and then ...

Now that the morning's job was satisfactorily over and Kartik Goswamy's mother expected to drive up any moment to pick up her son after her shopping spree, Swati felt relaxed enough to study her companion, the hired 'Papa' arranged by Chunni Lal. Another desperado like me, she thought.

Tall. Powerfully built. She approved of the broad planes of his chest. But he had a pinched, consumptive face, a parrot-beak nose and adamant, querulous eyes. Eyes of a manic single-mindedness. At the moment they were fixed on her face in impatience and accusation. As though he held her responsible for the Goswamy woman's delay.

A universal malcontent this, she deduced. One of life's permanent dissidents. But she had to confess it, even on that first occasion, he was oddly attractive.

She tried to make cordial conversation. The Goswamy woman, their temporary client? Employer? What to call her? Did she ask to see your school and college certs too? she asked him tentatively.

She couldn't understand why a crooked smile of the purest poison came upon his face.

Yes, he said. Chunni Lal got me some.

I only brought photocopies of mine and she asked for the originals, Swati spoke on, admiring his surly profile as he turned to buy a single fag from a passing vendor. I had to tell her the management of the school I work in takes our original certs away from us so we can't apply elsewhere. Yes, it's true. But she didn't believe me. Stupid woman, didn't she realize our real names are on the certs, so if the principal asked to see them the truth would slip out? But schools don't ask for the certs of parents, thank god.

She stole a furtive look at his now expressionless face, puffing away at his fag.

Maybe they only want kids from educated families so they don't have to work too hard educating them, na?

The vendor returned with the change and he stuffed it into his cheap plastic wallet. And as he did so, a scrap of paper fluttered out and fell close to her feet. She bent to pick it up.

What's this?

My cert, he answered with a short laugh.

But this is a blood report! she exclaimed, puzzled.

That's my cert, he said.

She wondered if it was her cleavage he was looking down at as she bent. She had a nice one, she knew. He probably thinks me a practising slut. For some mysterious reason, it was important to her that he shouldn't.

I had to take leave from my school today. My principal is a real vulture. One day's salary knocked off. But I thought—can't be helped. Anyway, this morning's takings will more than make up ...

He didn't seem interested. A polite show of interest, that's all.

To be honest, she went on, I'd never have taken this on if yesterday and the day before hadn't been so awful. Yesterday after school—we get over at twelve—I went selling soap from door to door. Every thirty packets of detergent sold, seventy bucks for me. But such a hot sun and the basket so heavy! My arm ached all night.

He organized his bored face into a suitably sympathetic expression.

And the day before that I worked as a daily wager—the two o'clock to five o'clock shift in the BSc exams in the university. Such ill-behaved rascals there! If you stop them copying, they threaten you. There was this shameless fellow who took out a screwed-up paper chit with tobacco powder in it, emptied the tobacco on his palm, bolted it down and then smoothed out the chit and began copying out of it. But forty bucks per invigilation is okay by me. At least it takes care of the day's vegetables and milk ...

Was she chattering on too giddily? But no, he actually asked a question.

Isn't your salary enough? How much the school is paying you?

Oh, they make me sign a bill for sixteen hundred but actually give me only six hundred. They are like that only. And all the time I am working. I am working extra even. So when Chunni Lal told me about this thing, I said, I'm going to go and try this out.

But he seemed restless, impatient to get away. Maybe he didn't take leave from wherever he works.

Did you take leave too? she ventured timidly.

He shook his head curtly. Looked at his watch. Late for something. Getting restive. What time did she say she would be back?

Ten-thirty or eleven. Do you have to reach anywhere?

He swung round, irritable. The Benarsidas General Hospital, he answered. Clipped voice. Man of few words.

Someone ill?

Yes.

Is it serious?

Might turn serious. If I don't reach on time.

Someone in the family? Really, she thought, I'm getting too busybodyish, but I rather like his curt way of speaking.

No, he said. Never set eyes on him. Or her.

Who?

This patient in Benarsidas General.

She was taken aback. Then how—

He decided to shut her up by answering her fully. It's an A-Positive blood group. I'm to supply a bottle of blood. Six hundred rupees a bottle. My best renewable resource!

She was stunned into silence. A professional blood donor!

If this bitch would only turn up fast and fork up the cash ... he muttered.

She had always thought of professional blood donors as destitute, uneducated. But look at this one now. Is it a sideline? Is he on dope?

He read the question in her face.

You could call it a summer job, he supplied dryly. Till I get at least one answer from all the wretched companies I've applied in.

Applied for what?

Accountancy. They'll have to pay a decent price for a bottle of strong, pedigreed Brahmin blood. Produced under strictly sanitized conditions in a five-thousand-year-old genealogical laboratory!

What an unexpected outburst of words! So that's why he had made that blunder. When the principal of St. Dominic's asked him his line, he had said accounts. And the principal had looked at the form and remarked, It says here: Business in Dubai. He had recovered instantly and said, Yes, I have a chartered accountancy firm in Dubai. The principal had made no comment.

She essayed a cliché: Better to donate blood than spill it, na? Then she offered: In case you're getting late, I could collect the cash and drop it at your place. Or maybe we could meet somewhere ...

How bold I'm getting, she thought. But, hell, it's now or never, before he's lost in the crowd.

He studied her suspiciously. Weighing her moral credibility.

No, thanks, he said at last. I'll wait.

She subsided, crushed.

But when, after half an hour, the Goswamy woman still hadn't shown up, he said: All right then, you can pick up the cash and give me a ring.

He fished out a piece of paper from the pocket of his jeans. Scribbled. Handed it across.

Any time after four in the afternoon.

She looked at the paper. Neelesh Trivedi. Prakriti Diagnostic Lab, 16 B-Block, Kareli, she read. And a couple of telephone numbers.

He stopped an auto, gave hurried instructions, got in and was whisked away.

Well, Et Cet Ra-ji, she said, her spirits unaccountably soaring. Why's your Mummee so late?

So you see where all this research took me. It became a piece of compulsive reconstruction, an obsession with a sample tissue of history that I put through the automated sequencer of my mind. Sequencer—I like that word. It goes well with my theme and has resonances of quintessential blueprinting and an ordering in time. For me this has involved visits to the city morgue, hospitals, homes, igniting a preoccupation that absorbed me for three intensive years. It has brought me lasting friends like old Sakina Bibi, who now lives in Nakhas Kohna, the old Mughal horse market on the eastern edge of Sikandar Chowk.

When I first approached her I found her a strange combination of obduracy and timidity. A shrinking, elderly Muslim woman who shuddered as she spoke, whose voice had turned flat and had acquired the squelch of tears, and who repeatedly reached for the end of her tinselled head cloth and dabbed her eyes hastily, breathing heavily to herself. She had had enough of interrogations, she implored. First the police, then that mob and then those camera and mike-toting paperwalas and even some TV crew. When the mob had broken in, the Swatantra Bharat fellows, she had barred and bolted the heavy haveli doors. But she heard them ram it down, thud on thud that slammed upon her heart like a doom-crash. And when the doors fell off their tired hinges, what should the mob see? A shapeless old Muslim woman, kneeling alone on the ground, hands joined in speechless supplication.

But the child paid for it, the little Rubina! she lamented. Ah, what kayamat, beta. My whole body shakes still ... still. I lie awake nights, hearing the blood-freezing shrieks and sobs, the deafening roars. I will never be granted Maula's mercy of forgetting; this is my punishment for harbouring that guileful one. I shall never again be what once I was, Siddhantha bete.

Nor will she be the imperious dowager queen of the lane, the one with the chilli-hot tongue. I portray her for you as she was. Then, not now.

***

She sat on her chowki in her first-floor baradari draped with chiks. Peering at a brass dish of golden selha rice through thick, owlish post-cataract glasses. The glasses kept slipping down her pudgy nose and she kept jolting her head backwards to toss them in place, synchronizing her movement with the jerk with which she picked out minute stones in the rice and flung them over the rim of the dish.

She was in an aggrieved frame of mind, her concentration fine-tuned to catch what the cricketer layabouts were chattering on her doorstep facing the cobbled close that had come to be known as Bibi ka Haatha.

Between Bibi and the cricketer louts there existed a sportive state of declared war which ranged from jesting banter to fiendish combat. Her ears seized upon their words with bloodthirsty relish, raring for a bracing dose of mud-slinging.

Nathan Astley, yaar. One day when he was practising, this paanwala got to slip past the guards. Went bilkul up to Astley. Said: Sir-ji, I want to play a game of cricket with you. Astley said: Okay, just as you like. The paanwala beat Astley soundly. Astley said: What you wasting your talent for, selling those munching leaf things? You should be in the Indian team.

Wah!

He gave the paanwala a cheque of several thousand dollars ...

How many thousand?

I've forgotten.

Abbé, you're speaking all gup.

Kasam se, it's true. Astley gave the fellow a cheque. Several thousand dollars.

Lucky bastard.

No, wait till you hear this. The paanwala didn't encash it. Laminated and preserved it. Hanging on a wall, yaar.

Fool.

Why?

Not to encash it. I mean, what a waste, saala!

What would you have done?

I'd have photocopied it. Encashed the real. Hung up the copy. Simple.

So, there's hope for you still, beta ...

Here, Bibi's voice shrilled down from the baradari above like the judgement of a teeth-gnashing God:

Arré, you nikamma slackers! Have you no work, nigoray? What do you imagine my doorstep is—the diwan-khana of a nautch house where your nawabships can while away your idle hours? Be off! Be off this minute! Shouting loudly-loudly at the top of your voices, enough to rouse the dead in their graves before kayamat-day and visit their wrath upon us all! Ulloo ke patthe!

There was a chorus of guffawing protests.

Arré, Bibi, have a heart. We're only resting from our labours, practising to join the Indian team and bring glory to your haatha.

By the way, what's the score, Bibi? Don't pretend you don't know.

Twenty-five for one in six overs, she answered, grim.

Who's batting?

Sourav Ganguly. Now go to jahannum, the lot of you! Cricket should be banned in this country.

An outcry outside.

Oh, come on, Bibi. You're getting to be a crotchety old maid. Why don't you go marry our Lalloo Prasad in Bihar?

Let my enemies go marry him, namakools!

No, seriously. Lalloo said cricket should be banned in India because whenever there's a major match there's the spirit of war. Why don't you go wed him, Bibi? Two of a kind. You'll do better than his wife, Rabri, as an administrator.

For shame! A married man. Nine children.

So what? You Muslims can marry four times, Bibi. He will have to convert, you know. How many husbands have you been married to at a time, Bibi? And dozens of kids are right up you people's street.

There was a cackle.

Only a man may marry four wives at a time, mian. That's a man's privilege. But no woman, my ignorant oafs.

How dare you marry Bibi to anyone else! She's my betrothed, yaar. Even if she isn't a day less than sixty-five.

Yours? She's mine! You less than a pubic-hair louse!

Whose?

Mine, eunuch!

Hair or louse?

Here Bibi screeched forth from behind the dusty chik: Arré you! Can't keep a clean tongue in your mouths?

Ha! Look at her ... she is mad as a galloping cow. Bibi will chomp us with her golden teeth.

If my faith didn't forbid it, beta, I absolutely would.

It took a second to register and when it did a loud laugh went up, Bibi laughing loudest of all.

Ha ha ha, she called you a pig, yaar, didn't you catch on?

Now be off! shouted Bibi. Befouling my yard with gutter-speech! Be off! Before I empty the kitchen slops on you.

There was a burst of laughter, a clatter of running feet. Ten minutes later they were back in position at her doorstep. The chatter a little muted but still audible to her sharp ears.

Classes suspended today?

Don't know. Bunked my practicals. Everyone's watching the match, yaar. But my papa-jaan's after my hide. Says the country stops functioning on cricket match days and the leaders should do something about it and one of these days he will lead a protest march. I told him he's fighting a losing battle. Told him: Papaji, too bad, but there's nothing you can do about it. See what the papers say—in Mumbai a shoeshine man polished shoes for free all day long to celebrate India's victory. Four little girls ran away from their homes in a West Bengal village, boarded a local train and went all the way to Nabalia Para, Behala, to see their idol, Sourav Ganguly. Riots break out when crackers turn to bombs. And in Kargil, as soon as the bombing ended two young labourer blokes started playing cricket with a rough plank of wood and a piece of rubber pine ...

Why, even in heaven the gods must be either watching the score or playing cricket themselves.

Ha, what an idea!

Yeah, just think ... Lord Krishna must be a bowler. Indra too. All that experience with Sudarshan chakra and thunderbolt.

An audible chuckle.

And Balaram must be a batsman. Bhim, Hanuman, Parashuram ... all the mace and hatchet bearers, all, all batsmen ...

Ya-Allah, exclaimed Bibi. These Hindus! So irreverent, even with their gods! But Allah help us from the reverent ones. Dousing men in kerosene, setting them alight because they wouldn't say Jai Sri Ram! Ransacking churches, desecrating altars, dishonouring nuns! Saying all the time they are avenging past wrongs!

Aloud she shrilled: And do you hold nothing sacred in earth or heaven, kambakhts? A cricket team of your gods, forsooth!

Uff, Bibi, don't be such an old stick! Our gods are as sporting as we are. Absolutely flexible. Before the World Cup, do you know, a grand yagya was performed in which fellows from different faiths worshipped a bat and a ball.

She was incensed. This frivolous idolatry!

Very sweetly she called down: No wonder your India lost the World Cup. Didn't even get to the semi-finals.

They were quick to trip her up: *Our* India? Caught you, Bibi. Isn't it *your* India too? Or are you with Pakistan all the time?

And why did Pakistan lose the World Cup, Bibi? Is Allah Mian jealous of the new icons?

Bibi decided to manifest herself in all the authority and imperious amplitude of her person. Till now she had been just a cantankerous, disembodied voice. Don't dare question my loyalties, bewakoofs! she thundered. I sent a hundred rupees to the *Times of India* Kargil Martyrs' Fund.

They crowed, seeing her provoked.

Oh ho ho ho ho! That's no big deal, Bibi. Beggars who lick the leavings of others got together forty thousand rupees for the fund.

Yes, and jailbirds donated blood and all their savings. Eunuchs too.

She ignored them with splendid dignity.

As for the reason why Pakistan lost the World Cup, listen, bewakoofs! Pakistan lost the World Cup because their army did un-Islamic things. Like gouging out the eyes and ears and noses and ... and other parts ... of those poor boys.

She shuddered as she spoke. The fate of young Saurabh Kalia, mutilated heinously, the heart attack of his poor mother, continued to trouble her deeply and had been added to her long list of deserving recipients of Allah's grace in her namaz.

Now will you shut those municipal drain mouths of yours? You are disturbing Professor Sahib.

Okay, okay, but Bibi, be a sport and return those cricket balls you've confiscated. My good, sweet Bibi, there's a dear!

To the furnace with you! She lost her temper. Get out, else I'll make kofta of your balls!

They howled with delight and scattered in mock panic. Run, run, Bibi will make kofta of your balls. And hack off the 'other parts' too for her mutton biryani tonight, haw haw haw!

A nd there was the gentle professor, teaching English and history. Writing monographs, giving radio talks, fretting over falling standards, recalling anecdotes of honour. He lived, trying to understand history and died inadvertently enacting it. His pupils greeted him with, Sir-ji, manny, manny happy New Year of the day!—little realizing what the year would bring for their teacher. Let me share my conjuring of a typical morning at Professor Mathur's with you.

In his spartan room, Professor Mathur struggled with his new pupil, perspiring despite the cold with superhuman efforts to untangle the complications of the English language.

No, no. This is incorrect. Absolutely wrong. There was a rising note of despair in his voice. The plural of 'fox' is not 'foxen'. And this sentence here is all wrong—'The solicitor was soliciting in his office.'

When Munna had first appeared in Ray-Ban goggles, Sachin Tendulkar cap (flap turned to the back), Newport jeans, Reebok shoes and Adidas bag, the effect on Professor Mathur had been intimidating. A metropolitan mongrel type, he had observed. But over the weeks he had had time to revise his opinion. Munna's costume, as Munna had himself admitted, was all footpath 'duplicate'. One had only to scratch the surface to unearth the rustic son of the soil who lurked beneath the get-up. Which made his tryst with the English language that much more grotesque.

His questions were often painfully urgent: Sir, is it wrong to say to girl, May I eavesdrop you?

What's that? Do you know what eavesdrop means?

I know what 'eve tease' means. So 'eavesdrop' must be ... drop girl home ...

Or drop her off a mountain! groaned the professor. What have you been up to, Munna? Eavesdropping or eve teasing?

I making friendship with one girl. Nice girl. Sweet face. Long, open hair ...

Loose hair, prompted the professor.

No, not loose girl. Good girl. I say to her: Hayloh! Myself Munna. What is your good name, please? She say: Gate out! I say: Gentle my lady, may I eavesdrop you? She say: Saala dog. So I shout English abuse at her.

What might that be now? ventured Professor Mathur in trepidation.

I say: Aroint thee, witch! Thou rump-fed ronyon!

The professor choked in his chair. Munna went on, flushed with victory. Zounds! he exclaimed. The hoyden was much affrighted ...

Stop! cried the professor. Where did you pick up these words?

Why? You give me one book—Mack ... Muck ... McDonald? Munna racked his memory.

Macbeth? suggested the professor feebly.

Ah, yes. Muck-beth!

The language of Shakespeare can't very well be used by us in its original form, Munna ...

Munna looked at the professor, surprised. Shakespeare use wrong English?

No. But we can't use his language the way he used it.

Munna looked dejected. I will never get my fundas clear, he said ruefully. How to say my fedupness with this all!

The professor resumed his heroic efforts: A language changes from age to age and place to place. There's a standard norm but, above all, it must not be artificial or forced. Shakespeare was completely natural but we can't use his words that way, you know.

But Munna looked deeply disappointed and personally injured. Even Shakespeare didn't have his fundas clear, he thought.

To eavesdrop means to listen secretly to something which we are not supposed to hear, persisted the professor. In his heart he heaved a deep sigh. Lay on, McDonald, he thought.

seven

I don't have to confess that I've grown attached to all these people, having lived with their lives as long as I have, in fact having banished my own in preference to theirs. Surely I have a claim on their retrieved histories. I re-embodied them in their ex-incarnations, gave them back to themselves, but maybe I've only gifted their crypto-histories to myself, feeling strongly for them as I do.

I have my favourites. Sakina doesn't count because she's alive. But there's the professor and the endearingly silly and kind old music master. And there's Lynette Shepherd, slow, grey and powder-dusted, in her creaky shoes. You'll say more women went through those automated sequencers than men. Call it chance or destiny or some third kind of pseudo-determinism. This individual, Lynette Shepherd, in the wholeness of her age and doubt and hurt, emerged when a sister in Auckland was traced and a specific region of the mitochondrial DNA, the hypervariable region, was sequenced. In her case no one bothered to claim that ad hoc ex gratia. Her only daughter had migrated long ago and fifteen thousand Indian rupees, converted into dollars or pounds was peanuts.

In Lynette Shepherd's life the big railway bungalows had gone, the vast lawns, the flowering gardens, the orchards. Her habit of drinking her mid-morning coffee under the spreading boughs hadn't. Now limited to this single cup (with the only spoonful of sugar she allowed herself in a day) in Sikandar Chowk Park. She carried a small flask of coffee in her broken plastic basket and treated herself to the pleasure of sitting under the trees for half an hour every morning before hobbling off to the vegetable market and picking up her daily packet of Parag milk which the grocer saved for her. Coffee had become frightfully expensive now, what with India exporting all the coffee it grew. Who could have imagined that a fifty-gram packet of Nescafé would cost fifty rupees!

Her favoured bench stood in a pleasant clump of laburnums, half concealed from the main walks. Here she sat, savouring the morning, the sun spraying down fine spurts of light as if from a perfume atomiser. Branches snarled in sun-yarn. Clusters of leaves splayed wide in a soft gold plasma. Stretching it thinner and thinner like balloon skin until by noon there would be a soundless snap and it would all come spilling out.

The park repeatedly reminded her of a cathedral. St. Andrews, where she was married. In the layout of the giant neems and pipals, the sloping guava and mango groves, the jasmine bushes and grape plantations, the terraced flower beds, she could actually pick out nave, chancel, altar. Even a vestry and line upon line of pews where rows of crotons stood like solemn guests when she swept down the aisle on Brian's arm. Overhead, the branches interlocked in a soaring green vault. Poor, dear Brian. Never learnt how to unhook a woman's brassiere, not till the end. He was all fingers and thumbs. He cursed and she laughed. Then a goblin thought gatecrashed into her carefully built peace. Could he manage it when he was with that one? Did it ever reach that stage between them?

Suddenly she was afraid of being alone with herself. Didn't know if the quiet park would lay her misery to rest or only loosen her internal self-commands, bringing it all up, turning it into a sensate suffering.

Each winter she sunned her late husband's letters. Unpacking them from the large cardboard cartons where they were stored, untying the ribbons and spreading them out on a rusty camp cot on the terrace of her tenement flat. But this year she noticed that the ballpoint ink was smudged in illegible patches on the grain of the faded paper. The seepage of purplish stains around the words, like the dried blood of a wounded relationship. From the folds there slipped out frightened silverfish. And she was filled with alarm.

She always avoided reading those letters. If by chance her eyes happened to race hungrily down a para, her heart began to pump painfully, her temples drummed, her throat dried up and she thrust the page away from her.

But the thought of their falling to pieces was not to be endured. Should she photocopy them all? How? An old lady photocopying ancient love letters! Embarrassing. Too naked a display of self. The problem lay heavy in her head—along with that other, more persistent one. The telephoning business. She had tried so hard to dismiss the impulse as a senseless whim but nothing had worked against the inexorable compulsion.

She had the old address—a Calcutta address. But the first time she tried she drew a blank. *This number does not exist. Kindly check the number you have dialled* etc etc.

She had got hold of a Calcutta directory. Gosse ... ? Gosse ... ? Gaus Mohammad, Ghoshal ... Ghosh-Dastidar ... Gosain ... Goswamy ...

Ballygunge, Beadon Street, Behala, Belgachia, Beniatola, Broad Street, Burra Bazaar ... until in Bow Bazaar she came upon Alexander M. Gosse (who, for Pete's sake, was he now?).

The PCO man dialled for her and passed the receiver across.

Hullo ... hullo! May I speak to Mrs Gosse? Marcia Gosse.
Her voice sounded thin, alien.

Ghosh?

No, Gosse.

Hullo! cried the practical joker at the other end. A brilliant
young spark, no doubt playing truant from college. *Mashi*
Ghosh? Which one? Renu Mashi or Pupul Mashi?

Gosse. Marcia Gosse. G-O-S-S-E.

Goose! cried the joker, disbelieving.

No, GOSSE.

Gosh! There was a titter of laughter. Then the disclosure:
Sorry. Wrong number.

The line disconnected. The meter whirred. A long strip of
paper came lolling out like a mocking tongue and the PCO
man tore it out. Seventeen fifty, he said. The queer way he
regarded her disturbed face, she would have to go to a different
PCO next time.

The shady vegetable market with its fresh greens and reds
and whites helped somewhat to calm her working head. She
vented her agitation on the vendor boys.

What cheek! she hissed. *Uske vaste four rupees, mere ko
five*? Her habitual brown memsahib voice. The rice-doll, puri-
tak voice: *Kya bolta tum*?

Bass. Four twenty for you, no more.

Tum ek four-twenty chokra-boy hai!

The vendors protested: No, no, Miss Sahib. *Kasam se*, Auntie-
ji. This special discount just for you, Maidum-ji.

From Missy-baba to Miss Sahib to Auntie-ji to Maidum-ji.
The last the highest tribute of public esteem that she could claim
by reason of her knee-length print dress and snowy hair.

She worked off her smarting hurt in spirited haggling:
*Gobhi kitna? How much yeh? Tum sub gurbur prices bolta,
chaaloo mafik. Tum ek tikrumbaaz boy hai*!

If Vakil Sahib's wife had a name it had been forgotten by the neighbours. Yes, her husband called her Nirmalaji but to everyone else she was plain Vakilin. Vakilin was an exacting woman with a face like a long, dry, brown nut. Hard and grained. And a strident voice delivering inflexible domestic strictures. Like exchanging street-soiled footwear for clean house slippers laid out at the bottom of the staircase. Like the strict observance of the kosherness of chappaties and rice. Like not sitting on her special chair or bed. And the ritual, scripture-decreed starvation on all sacred days.

When I sought her out and requested information about Vakil Mahendra Chandra, I met with sulky resistance.

How can I tell you anything? she reacted sharply. He had so many secrets from me.

And she proceeded to expand on the subject with pained relish. Like that maun vrat of his, for example, she cited. Told me he had taken an oath of silence from eight o'clock in the morning till ten so as to concentrate on God and the good life. Went around like a deaf-mute, oh, I could talk till I was purple in the face but would he deign a word? Then all these years, all these years later, along comes that upstairs Osman Bhai and tells me that the maun vrat was just for me, that out on his bazaar walk, your Vakil Sahib was the soul of laughter and chatter!

It still rankled. What else did I wish to know? she demanded. Did I want to know how Vakil Sahib always cheated in the Navratra fast and went eatery-crawling with that upstairs Osman Bhai? Maybe I had better consult that upstairs Osman who surely knew more about his dead crony than the latter's own seven-times-round-the-fire spouse! But of course it was too late to consult Osman. No one knew where Osman and his family had gone. Some said Canada, some said Singapore. Ah, how his yaar, Vakil Sahib, would have grieved and missed him, two good-for-nothings though they were and a trial to their wives!

I saw that she was working herself up into a state and tried to pin down the interview to a specific question: Vakil Sahib and his servant, Nankoo, were both victims of the Sikandar Chowk Park blast, wasn't that so?

Her underlip trembled and she hastily looked away to hide the glitter of tears. Ah, it had been an inauspicious beginning, this millennium-shillennium, as she had repeatedly told him. It had been unlucky for that Nankoo as well though his brothers seemed to think otherwise when they learnt of the fifteen thousand rupees. A noisy and shameful tamasha it was, four of them trying to split the money, such is this world! She had known that joking about death was a no-good thing but master and servant had courted this peril, jesting about funerals and funeral feasts!

She was weeping openly now. To think that master and servant had a thirteen-day feast on the same day! Had they dreamt of it turning out that way? And what had he called her? A first runner-up for the millennium funeral trophy. Ah, would that she too were dead like the devoted Hindu wife that she was, never mind his little deceptions. Would that Ishwar had called her up!

It was hard getting things out of her without provoking fervid reaction. Yes, yes, Vakil Sahib was a big-big joke teller and a big-big laugher. Such a laugh he had. He was a big-big eater and shouter. Yes, and also a noisy singer.

What did he sing?

Bhajans mainly. Would I like to hear his voice on tape?

I said I would.

A big, broad, sentiment-sodden voice, singing: *In thy mighty universe, nothing is ever lost, O Lord. It is we who flounder in this immense sightless maya and that is why we weep.*

She sat staring glazed-eyed, at the Sony cassette player, seeming to read signals in it she had missed before. Until the curtains parted and in tore a small dog, barking madly, his tail flailing in a feverish wag, the fur on his neck bristling in massive excitement. He pranced around the cassette player, producing short, sharp, joyous barks which competed in volume with that of the heavy baritone issuing out of the instrument. The association was inescapable.

HMV, I said.

She was offended. No HIV, she retorted, stung, and tried to shoo away the dog and failed. I decided to let it go but suggested switching off the cassette player. That's when she understood what I had meant though neither of us said a word. She switched it off and the little dog froze, disoriented. She reverted to her earlier complaints about her late husband and his friend, Upstairs Osman. Only Osman Bhai knew Vakil Sahib's secrets as only Vakil Sahib knew Osman's. No, neither Sarvar knew what Osman Bhai was up to nor did she, Vakilin, know what her Vakil Sahib did. What unholy food they ate together, where they went. Why, twenty-two years ago when Vakil Sahib and his parents had come to view her before fixing up their marriage, Vakil Sahib had been bashful as a bride and kept his eyes fixed on his shoes and never once looked at her for all her georgette and tinsel finery. It had been Osman who, with an expert aesthetic eye, had examined her appearance and later conveyed to Vakil Sahib the general impression. She had taken issue with her brand-new husband over this: I told my amma that evening, if this-one doesn't know his mind, then let that-one marry me, how does it matter? He's like my own cousin-brother, Vakil Sahib protested. Then, did *you* go to view *his* wife? she pursued the point. How could I? She was in purdah. Vakilin had snorted at that one.

So you see how close the two were and suddenly they began talking of migration and Sarvar dropped her cultured airs and said: If ever there's trouble, behen, I'll just drop a glass or a plate from my terrace down to yours. Please, behen, hide my little daughter in your house, that's all I ask. Of course, dear, Vakilin had replied, not just the little Bilquis but all of you. It's your very own house too. This was of course long before that third closely kept secret slipped out in an unguarded moment, that evening when the Pakistani relatives came to dinner.

There may have been a last secret, one which she never knew or suspected. It was left to me, merciless journalist-sleuth of the dead, to unearth that bit. But maybe my sources were wrong. Maybe they were just two men who were very close friends, nothing more. But nothing less, as my reification of a customary day between them shall show.

***

The fifth day of the Goddess had found Vakilin in a foul mood of which the causes were multiple and complex. That rascal Nankoo's disappearance since she sent him to the grocer was one. Her old grouse against her husband for his refusal to vote had simultaneously surfaced. Along with her abhorrence for Sonia Gandhi's short hair. A suspicious mother-in-law/

daughter-in-law hatred, Vakil Sahib often thought, bemused. To hear her rant: Remember the time the Italian mem-ji visited her husband's samadhi, remember? Didn't have the right nuance at all. Nor the proper shade of reverence in the tilt of her neck as befits a Hindu widow, hah! And Atalji lost by a single vote that time! Here you sat, refusing to vote, here you sat, chewing your cud like a lazy temple bull, here you sat!

There was also the little matter of the voice in the telephone. Vakilin was specially angry with the affected voice that would turn up each time: *All lines in this route are busy. Kindly dial after some time*. Or: *Aapka dial kiya hua number ghalat hai.*

Ji nahin, beti, ghalat ho hi nahin sakta! retorted Vakilin, launching into a tirade against the hare-brained chits who lurked in her phone. She almost reproached her husband for their presence. She almost suspected him. Women's voices in their phone! Never had it happened before. All these years. Since that old black 2260 they had had twenty years ago, the one with the whirring dial. But when a man turned forty-five who knew what folly might befall?

Excuse me, please, she spoke firmly into the phone. First you kindly check the number I dialled, then say.

Having told off the entelechy, she replaced the receiver in its cradle with an expression of masterful contempt. Only to spot Osman Bhai slink in, shamefaced.

Osman Bhai couldn't have chosen a worse moment to arrive. He was not at all sure of his hostess's favour. Luckily for him, he stumbled upon the very issue that had originally roused Vakilin's ire.

It's about that servant boy of yours, that Nankoo, Bhabhi Sahib, he stammered. You'll never believe what the namakool lout is up to now. Yes, at this very minute. He stopped to smirk. I thought I'd take Mahendra Chandra Sahib to see for himself.

And probe and prod though she did with utmost vigour, Osman Bhai resolutely wouldn't divulge, beckoning mysteriously to his crony, Vakil Mahendra Chandraji, across the terrace to rise and follow. Which Vakil Sahib did with gladness and haste, relieved to be out of his spouse's firing range.

Vakil Sahib and Osman Bhai were united by, among other more important things, a common fondness for food, Vakil Sahib's for Lucknavi and Osman Bhai's for Hinduana. Vakil Sahib had a weakness for rich meats and sauces, strong, spicy blends, hot unguent textures, heart-haunting fragrances. Osman Bhai had a hankering for sour-tangy vegetables, scented dal and aniseed-stuffed loaves fried in ghee, turmeric and asafoetida aromatic gravies, milk paste desserts. Each satiated the other's taste from time to time—at roadside eateries when their spouses weren't helpful. On Id day, Vakil Sahib not only made a round of all his Muslim friends' houses and formed an invaluable and appreciative member at their tables but returned home with large, steel tiffin boxes full of packed delicacies. Which his wife wouldn't hear of eating (those Shias spit into the food they serve, chhee chhee, for shame!) but that was just what his hedonist heart desired.

Once out of the lane and across the road, Vakil Sahib's spirits soared.

Where is the kambakht? he asked Osman Bhai.

Osman Bhai lifted an arm and pointed in a direction across the park. Near Phool Bagh Mor, he answered. Come.

They entered Sikandar Chowk Park through a wicket gate, taking a short cut to the bazaar area beyond. The light was a fine silver pollen afloat in the air. The shaft of the marble fountain wobbled faintly on the cut-glass surface of its brimming pool. It had rained at dawn. Diamond chips sprinkled on the leaves, small, grainy crystals. The sloping lawns looked iced to a crunch.

Twenty minutes' brisk walking took them across the park. Then, crossing a road, and another, threading their way through bicycles and scooters and snazzy new cars and horse-drawn tongas leaving smoking dung pats, and shrill delivery vans and rickshaws and scurrying along with all the rest, a few wooden leper trolleys trundling wheel-barrow fashion, pushed by competent young assistant beggars.

They took up their stand beneath the canvas awning of a chaat stall.

Look, pointed Osman Bhai.

Vakil Sahib followed his gaze and stood speechless for an entire minute. Then, of one accord, the two burst into a thunder-squall of rumbling, belly-rippling guffaws.

Oh-foh! Vakil Sahib mopped his pinked eyes. What do you think the fool imagines he's doing?

Just what he seems to, replied Osman Bhai.

Stationed high above the milling traffic, confident usurper of the British viceroy's now-empty pedestal, planted erect, arms moving with puppeteering precision, now commanding a summary halt, now beckoning a slow come-hither, now a languid, eurhythmic ballerina-sweep 'pass', Nankoo stood, solemnly directing the traffic. Causing endless bewilderment, jamming down of brakes and screechings of tyres, shoutings and cursings, rearings of tonga horses, swervings of rickshaws and, every now and then, a last-minute averted collision between various parties.

Stop him! Before he causes a major accident, suggested Vakil Sahib.

They have got the hang of it now. After all, they can see he isn't in uniform.

Ah, true.

Do you think he's all right up there?

Looks like a spell of bhang to me. He was a bit queer this morning.

Ah, that's it then.

It's happened before. Not traffic-policeman fantasies but other things. Like acting out women's roles in Ramlila groups and continuing the role the whole of the following day. It wears off ...

Shall we haul him down?

No, wait. Let's watch a bit, Osman Bhai. He will tire himself out presently.

They seated themselves on a couple of wooden benches beneath the chaatwala's canvas awning.

Whether it was the piquant scents emerging from the chaatwala's cauldron and giant sizzling griddle alongside or whether it was the two friends' natural disposition for gluttony, their talk turned to temptation. Osman Bhai recounted the spiritual dangers of greed and Vakil Sahib told the story of the pious dog who sat before Lord Hanuman's temple and who ate no meat on Tuesdays, no, was known to refuse all food except prasad and had consequently achieved distinction as a canine saint of a modest, local renown.

It's true, Osman Bhai. There was a write-up in the papers.

Osman Bhai nodded vigorously. But of course, Vakil Sahib. Such things are known to happen. Now Amin Sahib once went to visit the Lucknow Residency. This was many, many years ago when the city looked different. There used to be a small, elevated gatehouse and a tiny kothri beneath. Now Amin Sahib pushes open the door and sees what?

What?

He sees a swarm of plump pigeons gadding about inside. So Amin Sahib enters the kothri, shuts the door carefully, thinking: Aha! Got them now! Must get the Begum to prepare her Afghani pigeon salan tonight. But lo! Where are the pigeons?

Where?

Vanished, Vakil Sahib. All gone. Not one. And a horrid dread—a chill—clammy darkness. Amin Sahib tugged at the door. Lo! The door was jammed. Wouldn't open.

Tajjub!

Amin Sahib in a cold sweat. Literally. He tugged and he pulled, he prayed, he begged pardon. Nay. Nothing worked.

How did he get out?

There was a mosque nearby. Before long evening came and an azaan sounded.

Ah!

Yes. The door opened silently by itself. He peeped into the mosque yard. A large solemn congregation at prayer. So he waited outside to see them emerge. Lo! None did. He peeped again. The yard was empty ...

Kamaal hai!

Yes. Strange things happen, Vakil Sahib. Amin Sahib never touches Afghani pigeon salan now, *wallah*! Another time Mahmood Sahib went walking down from Faizabad to Ayodhya. He passed the shrine of the maiden saint Kunwari Bi. It was on a Friday evening. Satin sheet on the tomb and incense all round. Also an earthen pot of delicious-smelling halwa offered to the saint. Mahmood Sahib picked up the halwa and brought it home. Thought: Must call Osman Bhai over for this treat. But, now hearken you, Vakil Sahib, when the pot was uncovered, it was empty! Gone the halwa! And that night Mahmood Sahib awoke to hear a thud on his tiled roof. A burly marauder—he wrestled with him, cried for help. Men came with sticks and stones and pestles and pickaxes— and beheld Mahmood Sahib, maddened, wrestling with nothing! Running a high fever! A maulvi came and he blew on him and muttered incantations, and blew and swept again and again, until the phantom left him a-swoon upon the floor. Ah, greed! What will it not do to a man, to what low shame will it not betray him?

So, just so, echoed Vakil Sahib. Now my maternal grandfather had such a reputation as an epicure. Famous for his gorging. He devoured—believe me, Osman Bhai, I speak only truth—two kilos of desi ghee laddoos. He had fourteen children. He gorged while his kids stared. To that he said: Why do you stare, little ones? You've got all your life—forty, fifty, sixty years left to eat. But your poor father, this old man here, has less, much less.

Osman Bhai laughed.

Every night he worked up an enormous bellyache. He rolled from side to side, huffing and hawing, burping and breaking wind, until he rolled off his bed and stumbled to his old mother. He fell at her feet and wept tears of pain: Forgive me, O Ma. This greedy belly shall never crave again. Only say you forgive me! Only say! And he, a grown man at that. Such a sight!

Then?

Then the old matriarch got up, heated some grains of asafoetida in mustard oil over a spirit lamp, squatted down by his side on the mat and massaged his belly till by the small hours of the morning the pain was quieted. But next morning there he was, busy devouring a huge leaf-bowl of kalakand. Such is greed, Osman Bhai.

The spicy scents from the chaatwala's griddle had grown more importunate by the instant. Osman Bhai twitched his nostrils distastefully and Vakil Sahib jerked his head backwards in unison.

Look! cried Osman Bhai, pointing. Vakil Sahib looked.

Now, what do you make of that?

Beats everything, chuckled Vakil Sahib.

The strangest of sights met their eyes. There seemed to have developed a sudden snarl in the traffic that even Nankoo, at the height of his delusion, could not control. A row of trucks had lined up, not in obedience to Nankoo's commanding halt but helpless before the imperious barricade of an elephant. Under whispered instructions from its mahout, the beast slowly pounded on the bonnet of each truck with its trunk, then on the windscreen, then stepped up to the side and held out its trunk in expectation of a tip. One by one, the truck drivers dropped coins into the insistent trunk before they were allowed to move on, the elephant saluting each with majestic aplomb. On his pedestal even Nankoo looked baffled, uncertain what traffic commands to give.

Ha ha! laughed Vakil Sahib. If constables can charge hafta, so can elephants.

Only our lorry drivers don't part with cash so willingly when it's a constable, no? An elephant is holy. Lord Ganesha, no?

There was a faint twinkle of laughter in Osman Bhai's voice. Vakil Sahib shared the joke heartily.

How it happened, neither knew. One moment they were laughing over Lord Ganesha's hafta, the next they were digging into twin leaf-bowls of chaat. Spoon by spoon, in complete and concentrated silence, the curd-lapped, chilli-hot, tamarind-tanged delight vanished. In great and absorbed gravity they paid up; in slow, sombre, segregate soul-searching they rose to go. They crossed the road in silence, entered the park. Halfway through the park, Osman Bhai collapsed on a bench. Clutched his forehead.

Toba, toba! *Lahaul vila quuvvat*! What has this miserable sinner gone and done! It is the sacred month of Ramzan, Vakil Sahib, and I ... I partook of that satanic abomination, that chaat!

Vakil Sahib too had had his tryst with soul-testing sin. For a long moment he stood, looking at his tormented friend. When he spoke it was in a voice hoarse with compunction.

I too, he whispered, choked with shame. I too, Osman Bhai. This year they have fallen together, Ramzan and Navratra. It is the holy nine days of the Goddess, our Navratra. My wife fasts all nine days, lives only on fruit and that at sundown. I managed ... for four days. But now ...

They stared at one another in shared self-condemnation.

You shall not tell the Begum, Vakil Sahib, pleaded Osman Bhai humbly.

You will not let slip this ... this thing before the mother of my children? asked Vakil Sahib nervously.

There was great and unimpeachable honour among thieves.

They rose to go, their elation of the morning punctured.

The Begum might not know, but, Vakil Sahib, from Allah's All-Seeing Eye what transgression can lie hid? Osman Bhai thought aloud in despair.

There is room for atonement in God's world, speculated Vakil Sahib sententiously.

I can always fast an extra day. It's permitted by the Book, reflected Osman Bhai.

I can beg the Devi for forgiveness.

Like your grandfather, no? prompted Osman Bhai. His essay at facetiousness failed.

It was in a chastened state of mind, their self-esteem shattered and their conscience clamouring aloud in their bosom, that they walked homewards.

I'm not talking theory, please. I'm not even qualified to do that. I abdicate discourse. I only wished to find out more about Vakil Mahendra Chandra and Osman and Masterji Hargopal Misra and Lynette Shepherd and Vani Kabir and Suruchi and Aditya and Swati and Kartik and Rubina and the acutely self-responsible old professor. I can't claim the dubious humility of saying I only know that I know nothing and earn my stance some accreditation. I know almost nothing, I say, except these people whose selves and circumstances I researched with almost manic energy. In their own ways, eleven people can make up a basic world. In them, through them, I think I've come to know fractured bits of a surpassing clarity. Like the first fine laser beam of pity going straight and searching through a turgid human heart.

Let me return to Shirin Ahuja.

Dipping into daydreams was for Shirin like Juswant tippling booze. A Sunday afternoon and Juswant safely asleep in the bedroom, she sat, idly browsing through the *Times of India*. Her eyes sleepily brushed over the headlines: Agitated Students Attack Hospital, Damage Property; Mulayam Blasts BJP, Cong, BSP; Tributes Paid to Lokbandhu; Five Killed, Twenty-eight Hurt in Jammu Bomb Blast; Gold Biscuits Seized; Affluent States Getting More Kerosene; CM's Hi-tech Gifts to Curb Crime; Madhuri Weds ... until she turned to page four and sat poring over the films' section. *Toota Teer* running at Darpan, *Himmat* running at Umrao, *Maachis* at Regal, *Border* at Palace, *Sarfarosh* at Plaza. More terrorism themes in the offing—she had tired of those. *Mission Terror*, another terrorism one coming at Rukmini, *Kya Kehna* at Manoranjan Mahal, *Honeymoon Hotel* at Ajanta, *The Nympho* at Lakshmi, *Elizabeth* at Chandralok. That last one maybe. But no point going to see a film alone. Let's see what's on Star Movies ... nothing promising today.

She put down the paper, yawned, looked around the room. Time was when she would fastidiously match her curtains with her moods. The colours of her walls had been records of mental states. The abstract paintings tortuous journeys into her confusions. The glass-topped table a monument to her small, tenacious clarities. Once she had been fanatical about this room. Now everything was old. A mongrel room. The curtains didn't rhyme with the walls. The furniture was scratched and stained. One cabinet had its plywood peeling, another heroically propped upright on a couple of bricks. All inconsistent. She had learnt to be tolerant with this tired room. Forgive its errors. A chair was now only a thing to sit on.

When she was alone, her mind reverted to the thought of him, lying in there.

So we muddled along, miserable together, but we didn't separate. Because all we had lost was our good manners, not our good intentions. Because in the pits we never quite forgot the peaks we had touched. (Clichés, clichés, her other mind scoffed.)

Over the years active emotion became rarefied. She had earned a sort of grace—protection from its shabby excesses, its indignities. Our quarrels became so much better in quality, she reflected ironically. Superior textured, stylishly clipped dialogue. No more blinded spells of desperate weeping. No sweeping furies blasting out her senses, no black, bitter words rotting around, stinking up her soul. Properly educated in the management of moods she had been—Grade A and passed with distinction. She could, for example, just sit quietly, aware of injury but far removed from it all. She had acquired the capacity to air out her head, let yesterday's nastiness just blow away. And she had learnt not to be bogged down by the muddy shadows of unlighted, sweat-sodden rooms, the stress stewing in the close air. Those odours of urine and vomit and booze. That heavy stench of hopelessness. Sitting alone on a spacious day, she could even think of sculpting an alternative self.

Three in the afternoon. He didn't snore any more. The psychiatrist had dosed him on tranquillizers. He slept. Earlier he would pace the floors like a caged beast, now his mouth kept slipping open, he kept dropping things, his speech came out all askew, spit-spattered.

Not that they spoke much. He was too weak. She was too exhausted. Housework, market, doctors, job, tuitions. Their exchanges were curt, workaday ones. They had no strength left for personal feelings. Though, of course, there were days when he seemed to derive pleasure from extracting service out of her. (Why did they always coincide with days when the servant didn't turn up and along with the other chores she also had to do the floors, wash the dishes and the clothes?) She wondered how she had managed to squeeze out the last ounce of energy. But he seemed blind to her fatigue. Press my calves. Rub a bit of oil into my scalp. Some days her poise deserted her and she felt she could still smell alcohol. Especially that special steamy rum-reek recycled as urine. Ugh! How it made her puke when she was pregnant. To the end of my life that stink won't leave me alone. If I'm squeezed out like a sponge, every pore of me shall give out that rancid, fermenting odour—I'm that saturated. In the early days she had made the mistake of telling her friends, and their well-meaning advice was: You're his wife. You should do something about it. Why don't you do something? She had stopped sharing her problem in disgust. She couldn't tell them of the abuses, the get-out-of-the-house-out refrains, the blows. The only witness was the little one, sitting up in bed, shrieking in terror, as she quietened him quickly, one hand patting his tiny back, the other rubbing the blossoming bruise above her right eyebrow where his clenched knuckles had struck her.

No, I am not calmed by time. God in his mercy did not give me grief. He gave me anger instead. Tricked me with the more bearable emotion. A slow, noxious rage that persists beneath all my smiling, bedside faces. So now he's worried if the tranquillizers have made his speech slur. I could say to him: You want to know what slurring is? It's the way you used to say to me—Out of the house! Out! Like this—she mimicked it aloud, sitting alone. Out of the house! Out!

Often, those days, weeks back, when he was still confined to bed, she would wake up with those words circling in her head. Then she vented her fury on him on the smallest pretext. Left him calling feebly after her as she raced two steps at a time down the stairs, out of earshot, out of the poison-zone, in high, gleeful vengeance. Returning ten minutes later when he had stopped calling and sat, waiting patiently, like a child for its punishing mother.

Where did you go? he would ask meekly.

Me? I'd just gone—Out of the House, Out!—you understand? she mimicked in vicious self-recompense. What did you want now?

Silently he would point at the uro-bag dangling at the side of the bed. It's begun hurting again—the needle, he would murmur plaintively and she would lose her head.

You bet, Jus. You bet it's hurting again. It'll go on hurting, Jus. And can't I go downstairs for a minute? Forgodssake! It's always your sickness, your digestion, cough, sleeplessness, blood pressure, haemoglobin, constipation! How 'bout me? Am I incapable of illness?

He would lie there, crushed, with frightened eyes. Then he would say, voice trembling: Are you angry with me?

And she would realize with a shock that her jibes were lost on him. He had passed out of reprisal range into a state of psycho-degraded simplicity where only the elemental things registered—tones of voice, textures of touch, vibes ...

Poor wretch, she thought, and was amazed at the thought. Increasingly she had started thinking of him in 'poor wretch' terms. What a price to pay! And could I be the one who's tipsy now? Have I been going around, intoxicated with my own fury? I no longer understand myself. I'm a stranger to myself and not an attractive one. The only quality I find a bit okay in myself is a certain persistence. All my life I've been persisting with something or the other. Adding up every lesson learnt, every illusion forfeited, all that I've bartered and fought for and saved and preserved. And who knows, I too was to blame for those dreadful days. An over-assertive, manic-depressive, nagging, weepy woman—a very trying person to live with. I was overworked beyond endurance, giddy, neurotic. I suspect my present blocked-up states have something to do with all those hours of back-breaking work, the bottomless despair. It's a very suspicious lapse of memory I sometimes suffer from. I just wonder if life's all over and there's only the growing old and dying business ahead. Is it too late in the day? Can a new feeling ever engulf me? Something undreamt of, overpoweringly sweet, that my exhausted, persevering soul might forget its chores of conscience? (Self-pity, self-pity, most negative of negative emotions, kick it out!)

Are you angry with me? Wish I could drive you home.

She would never be done sorting out her troubled feelings for him, struggling with those diabolical visions and voices in her head, hyperactive against her willing.

A man gone to seed. Deteriorated completely in ten years. The night she returned from Agra, he clapped an arm heavily round her shoulders, making her stagger. Oh hell, she said, he's in a dangerous state tonight. His mouth like a sewer. His voice— each word coated with oozy scum. The air faintly sour around him. Sweat-sour, puke-tainted. Lurching against the bathroom wall. The way he swayed on his feet, planted them wide apart, buckling at the knees. Showering the pungent, acid spray all over the wall, the floor, his trousers, his toes. Stumbling back, fly unzipped, his sorry dick shrunk to a foolish, fallen shred.

She had mopped it all up, meticulously, teeth set in a grimace. Catching a glimpse of her face in the bathroom mirror, she saw that the teeth-set grimace had come to stay. It had stamped itself, a permanent cast, on the mintage of her cumulative selves.

We've failed one another. What remains is dull mistrust. A lasting grievance.

Bloody bitch! Get out of the house! Out! I'll throw you and your bloody brat out!

The rum-sodden words sloshed against his teeth. The veins stood out on his temples. His pupils slurped about his bulbous, bloodshot eyes in sleepy affront. His swollen frog-lids lapsed in bags of mottled bat-skin. His face dark, inflamed, breath pumping heavy in his chest. That big belly.

Slut!

He hurled the key across. Go up, slut! No one's going to help you. Not even if you open up your filthy cunt and beg your father for his battering ram! Go! It's dark as hell up there.

Dark as hell.

Somewhere between the third and the fourth drink the viciousness took over. She had always been frightened by the depth and power of his unquenchable hatred.

Later, when he slept, his big, loose mouth popped open and shut, filling the bedroom with a foul, acid stench. With rumbling snores, groans, wheezings, whistles, broken mutters ...

He never knew who his controlling alter-ego was. In time she came to develop a reactive alter-ego of her own. In their rare good days they called these other two Brook and Ellen.

Four-thirty. She was roused by the sound of a flushing cistern. Tap running in the bathroom basin. A long time. She clicked in annoyance. As it is there's acute water shortage. (In the old days, Juswant would quip: It's Shirin's water therapy, yaar. She's drinking up all the water in the colony. And she would snap back: The less said about drinking the better, Jus!) Oh hell, he'll empty out the overhead tank ...

She went to look. He wasn't in bed. The bathroom door was ajar. He was standing, slumped at the basin. She sniffed.

What's this funny stink? And I *told* you not to mess around with my Camay again. What a mess this bathroom is!

He turned quickly like a guilty child, trying to hide something behind his back. He wore only his long cotton kurta, his squat, naked legs grotesque beneath the half-wet hem.

Then she saw he was trying to wash his soiled pyjamas at the basin. Saw the muddy stain. Placed the stink. Her eyes travelled from the Camay to the stain, to his defenceless nakedness, to his pleading, broken face.

I couldn't help it, he whispered. I can't hold it back. These medicines ...

He began to weep.

Standing stock-still, she saw he really didn't know Camay from Rin any more. She grew suddenly, uncomfortably conscious of her own power over him.

The tap went on running.

ten

When Shirin Ahuja died in the blast she was probably clutching a food packet. The guys at Ringo's, the fast-food joint across the road, said she had dropped in at a quarter to four on the twenty-second of March and had ordered a couple of pizzas to be packed. But when Masterji Hargopal Misra was mashed to pulp he was clutching his precious violin. Death's a chancy thing. The impact of the blast made the violin fly clean out of Masterji's grasp. It landed, without a single string disturbed, in the hibiscus garden some distance away, stayed in police custody for a while and was later redeemed by the Academy of Music where Hargopal Misra had taught. If the muse exists, I know her heart's in the right place. Out of two valuable creative instruments, the seventeenth-century Stradivarius and the old ungifted music teacher, she chose to take away the worthier one.

Master Hargopal Misra had no living relatives. He occupied a small rented room, twelve by twelve, furnished with a solitary charpai, a table and a chair. His cooking was done on a wooden plank bearing a stove and some basic kitchenware, his washing at a common wash-cabin at the end of a corridor.

You will wonder where I acquired these details but it hasn't been at all difficult visualizing the crackpot music master with the susceptible heart. I had more people to volunteer information about him than any of the other ten—neighbours, the milkman, the grocer down the lane, Mayank and other students and fellow teachers, the maestro, Raghunath Rai, and the Japanese lady, Mrs Masako Kawaguchi, who met him for just an evening. But most telling of all were the accounts of Sukhiya, the beggar. Sukhiya himself insisted, however, that the real authorities on the subject were the stray dogs of the lane if they could but speak. Now Sukhiya had undertaken the duty of apportioning a quarter of his day's takings for the dogs' Parle G biscuit supply. And all those who remembered Masterji tossed a rupee or two into Sukhiya's begging bowl for this communal effort. There were days when Sukhiya devoured the biscuits himself, unable to resist the temptation. But there were other days when each dog got a tiny share of what they had grown accustomed to since Masterji's days. Opinion in the lane was divided, there being cynics who believed that Sukhiya was playing up the Masterji trump card to pull at the neighbours' collective conscience and squeeze alms out of the most tight-fisted.

I found Sukhiya squatting beneath a sanctified pipal shrine where the lane bifurcated and turned towards the temple. He was only too happy to share his memories of Master Hargopal Misra.

How long have you known him?

Since the flood of '78 when they said the Buxi Bund had cracked, he answered.

How did you get acquainted with him?

A mischievous smirk flitted across his leathery face. I enjoyed—how you say—making him cross, he replied. The account that Sukhiya then proceeded to give me can best be reproduced in his own words.

I wasn't this way always, said Sukhiya. I had a proper fruit and vegetable cart. I pushed it down the lane shouting *kela albela hai* or *angoor angaare hain.* In the mornings I enjoyed opening my jaws wide and calling up the strongest belly-bawl outside Masterji's window just when he was sawing away at his fiddle or sitting at the harmunia. Then one day I had an inspiration. I decided to try it outside Masterji's window. I set my hawker cries to a film tune. No other cart-wala had thought of it.

So I sang outside his door as loud as I could:

> *Aaloo muhobbat wala*
> *Muhna main aisa dala*
> *Aaloo jo le le meri jaan,*
> *Ho jao ispar kurbaan.*

The sawing at the fiddle stopped and he came tearing out of the room, roaring: Sukhiya, stop your beastly howls this minute! Your aaloos shall tear out my jaan!

Try them, then say, I said.

Brainless dolt! he cursed. With a jingle like that, who'll risk it? Change your song.

You tell me what to sing, Masterji. What are you a music-wala for? I teased.

He thought a while, then said: I can't think of a single song for selling potatoes, Sukhiya. Onions maybe. For instance, pyaaz for riyaz. But that's nonsense.

What's riyaz, Masterji?

Riyaz means practice, daily music practice to keep the voice or fingers perfect, he told me.

The next morning I was there bawling harder than ever: Pyaaz for riyaz, Masterji!

He came bounding out. Brandishing a flute at me like a stick, shouting: Silence, Sukhiya. Take your onions elsewhere.

But you know what happens to so many of us, Patrakarji? said Sukhiya to me. Neither potatoes sold well nor did onions, neither albela kelas nor angaara angoor. Me, I became a rag-paper-tin-can-bottle-wala, a kabari. Now I would pedal my rented trolley down the lane and couldn't resist provoking him at the riyaz hour. I'd cackle: Little-old-bottle-big-old-bottle, old paper, old plastic, old tin-can-iron-wala!

He rushed out as usual, fretting. Stop your din, Sukhiya!

Then he noticed that I had changed my fruit–vegetable cart for a bottle–tin–paper trolley.

What's this? You've turned kabari? he asked.

As you see, sarkar, I said. Can you give me the right song for this sort of line?

He thought. I don't know any film songs, Sukhiya, but there's a bhajan my guruji taught me years back. It goes like this: *Clear the space of my heart, O Lord. All the world is dross, is trash. Let me burn it, throw it, expel it ...*

Here I interrupted: What's the use, Masterji, if the customers start burning or throwing? I'm asking them to sell it to me.

He saw the difficulty. Then he remembered his riyaz. Okay, be off, he said. I'll think of something else.

He was true to his word. The next time I went hallooing past he came out and stopped me. Oye, Sukhiya! I've found the right song. Only it's a bhajan again. I can't for the life of me think up any film songs for you.

Let's hear it, sarkar, I said.

It goes like this: *Barter all in your market square, O Master. Take my loves and my pains, my wants and my gains. Give me your light instead ...*

I didn't allow him to finish. Aha! I said. I can change that to: Sell your bottles and your pans, your papers and your cans ... but what's the tune, sarkar?

It's in Raga Khammaj. But whoever heard a kabari hawk his trade in Raga Khammaj. Anyway, this is how it should be sung.

And there and then on his doorstep he sang it for me and all the passers-by smiled, though a good many jeered.

I still couldn't resist having a bit of fun at his expense. Now I sang as I went past: *Barter all in this market square, O Masterji. Bring your bottles and your pans, your papers and your cans. Take my paltry paise instead and all that is this man's.*

It wasn't a game for him. He came storming out as usual, shouting: Sukhiya, what will you take to stop bellowing outside my door just when I'm doing my riyaz? Or shall I set Kurkuri on you?

That scared me. That Kurkuri was such a biter, she'd gouge out a half-kilo of man's flesh with her fangs if the mood took her. I meekly moved away and never went that way again.

Then one night I don't know what exactly happened. I was there in the gutter outside Masterji's door. I guess I was roaring drunk and all the grief of the world boiling inside me and blubbering their way out. In between sobs I'd cry out: May your children prosper, a paisa, sarkar. May God never lighten your purse, a paisa, sarkar. May your children live and be kings, a paisa, sarkar.

I sensed him beside me. I couldn't quite focus on him but there he was.

Sukhiya! His voice came from far away. Where's your cart? What's happened to you?

I went on wailing and I heard him say: A beggar and a drunk. Ah, poor Sukhiya who sang as he sold potatoes and sang as he bought garbage! Come in. Come, sleep in my room. It's cold out there, Sukhiya.

He helped me up, almost lifted me bodily and I found myself on a mat, food in a platter before me. I wouldn't touch it. I lifted my voice and frothed and babbled and bawled and muttered and cursed. And then he did something very strange. He picked up his fiddle and followed my howls and curses and aches on it in music of the strangest kind. I don't remember a thing after that for I fell asleep on the mat, Patrakarji.

Listening to Sukhiya, I couldn't contain my excitement. I could see the kindly old music teacher in transports of passion, discovering, in a man's broken bewailing, scales and octaves he had never known before. I couldn't help wondering if the violin he used that night was the one he had promised to play only hymns on. In all the anecdotes I unearthed about Master Hargopal Misra this one returns to my mind as though it is the essential soundtrack of his self. It accompanies my approximate scripting of another day in Masterji's life.

Even when the weather changed and the days became warmer, Masterji wore his old serge sherwani with matching boat-cap. Two identical tufts of hair sprang out from behind each ear and waved saucily in the wind as his moped sped forward towards Mayank's house. His piqued snout and puzzled eyes betrayed a disturbed state of mind.

That afternoon he had decided to sound Mayank on the snippet that Janardan had finally consented to let him have. He had spent the morning spelling over the lines of newsprint, considering the black-and-white picture inset of a girl in leather tights and jacket, exhibiting a violin:

Joanne Howson, a graduate of the Royal College of Music, London, displays a 1698 violin, priced at 700,000 pounds sterling (about $1.75 million) auctioned at Christie's. A Kreutzer Stradivarius, which sold last April, went for the world-record price of 947,500 pounds sterling.

After intense self-debate, he had decided to consult Mayank on the subject of safety. But, as it happened, Mayank was out. His mother welcomed Masterji into their smart drawing room, made him sit, offered tea.

Science coaching? enquired Masterji, pouring tea into her floral-patterned china saucer, blowing noisily on it.

I think so, she answered uncertainly. Won't be long now, Masterji. Said he'd be back by seven. Please wait a bit.

He agreed.

Pity he had to discontinue his music lessons, behenji, Masterji said. He was coming along excellently.

He funnelled his lips carefully into a beak and sucked at the tea. He drained the brimming saucer, poured another saucerful.

She looked a little unsure. What did he tell you, Masterji? she asked cautiously.

He said he's preparing for the IIT entrance tests so no time for music practice this year.

She looked relieved. Oh, I suppose he knows best.

Then she deftly changed the subject. That's a very ancient sherwani you're wearing, Masterji. Must be twenty-five years old, if not more.

Much more, replied Masterji proudly, finishing his tea.

But isn't it too hot for a sherwani now? she ventured politely.

To tell you the truth, behenji, I wear it because of its pockets. See here ...

He stood up to display the sherwani's multiple, capacious pockets. No point carrying a bag, he said. I'm sure to lose it. This left pocket holds my keys and my diary, this right breast-pocket holds my little towel and my glasses. This left breast-pocket holds my money. And this lower right one—ah ...

He patted the bulge fondly. This lower right one holds my three packets of Parle G biscuits!

She was amused. You're that fond of biscuits, Masterji?

He looked abashed. Not I, behenji. They're for the animals I meet, he said, sitting down suddenly, looking prim.

She began to laugh. Animals?

He grew confiding: Oh, dogs and suchlike. Strays. Pigs. Homeless cows. Buffaloes. Sometimes tired horses ...

They all like biscuits? She was disbelieving.

When they're starving they even eat polythene bags. Biscuits they love. There's an old bull in my lane whom I feed two kilos of flour every morning. To be honest, I wish I could do more.

He grew expansive. Have you seen a poor little pig strayed into the street? Trying to cross a busy highway full of lorries and speeding cars. He looks so like a baffled child. I look at him and wonder what he makes of it all, the lorries, the noise ... My lane's quite slushy, behenji, especially in the monsoon, but I let the pigs be.

She was getting bored and a bit disgusted. She had work to finish. She also hoped he had wiped his sandals well on the doormat before stepping on her carpet.

But he had warmed to his theme: I also feel dreadful for the goats that are led to the Nakhas Kohna meat markets. And the chickens in their mesh cages. Or stuffed into baskets. And why do these butchers hang chicks upside down? How agonizing that must be! Whenever I go past, I utter a small prayer—Oh Ishvar, be merciful to these poor unoffending babes. Oh angels of healing, holy masters, guardians, energies, circle them in blue light so that when the blade falls they may not feel it ...

He was now properly carried away. She was touched by the warmth of his ardour. You really love these creatures, don't you? she remarked lamely, looking at the clock on the wall.

It is music that has made me this way, behenji, he answered simply. And to make no secret of it, behenji, they too, these dumb beasts have fed my music. I'll tell you of a very private experience. Many, many years back I was asked to play at a music festival at the Samiti. Saraswati Puja it was, a big occasion. Now my colleagues there, behenji, they had earlier planned to humiliate me. Make me feel a prize fool. So, no sooner had I started than the coughs and shuffling of feet began. The laughs, the exaggerated ahs and wahs! And halfway through my performance they began to clap. You know what that means, of course. It means: Get out, you bore, we've heard enough of your trash! What could I do except bow and end? Then my scoffers took over and they played their instruments. Such fine, high-class music they played, so right, so perfect, so movingly executed! Ah, it hurt, behenji, it hurt. That they, mindless scum who had no fine feelings, should dare to mock a sincere artist! But such things can't be helped. I came home in a towering rage. I'm a mild man, behenji, but that evening I vented my fury on chairs and platters and wooden doors and electric switches. I abused everything in sight, even my little dogs. And when they came scurrying up for their nightly roti and milk, I did what I couldn't have dreamt myself capable of—I kicked them viciously out of the door, kicked each one hard. Ah, I shudder to remember it. They squealed and yelped in pain—and the look in their little eyes! Then I locked myself in and chewed over my wrongs. I'm nothing, I said. Just a fool. A clown everyone laughs at. I know a few stale thumries and khayals and the required number of ragas to get my boys through the exams. Real music's too high for me. Low-class art, that's mine. Fit only for petty tuitions—not even that. I fell asleep thinking dark thoughts. In the morning I unlocked my door and what should I see? My little strays lying patiently on my doorstep, humble and so hopeful. They came bounding up to me with little whimpers, still so trusting. And so very hungry. Can you imagine my shame? Ah, this misery was worse than the other one. That those low scoffers had reduced me to this! Made my innocent beasts pay for their smallness! I'm not ashamed to admit, behenji, that I shed tears. I brought all my strays in, patted and fondled each one, spoke to them, fed them well, and as the little ones gobbled at their bowls, Ma Saraswati herself sent me grace. I thought to myself, quite suddenly, as though someone, some gentle goddess, put the thought in my head: Well, that high-class music made unkind men of them, but my low-grade music at least made a kind man of me ... That was my experience of *anãhatnãda*, behenji, the unheard music, the music in the soul, the music beyond sound ...

She had had enough. She yawned and changed the subject again. But Masterji had unique political convictions. He rigidly clung to the belief that the Congress Party was the best and the Indian Congress Party was the mother of the African National Congress and the US Congress as well, opinions which made his hostess look extra closely at him, examining him for other undiagnosed symptoms of lunacy. Presently she rose from the settee and said: Forgive me, Masterji, I must see to something now. I'll switch on the TV for you. There's *Titanic* coming on AXN. Do feel comfortable. Mayank should be back soon.

And with that she swept out of the room, leaving Masterji puzzled by her brusque and speedy exit.

The film was half over. This was the scene when things begin going wrong in the grand banquet hall. Crockery careens across tables, cutlery skitters off, hubbub, hysteria, pandemonium. A woman beseeches the Captain and he turns away in distress, face tightly impassive. The musicians disperse in an initial getaway reflex. The conductor calls them back. Returning slowly, they take up positions, strike up a bleared, rheumy message. The frayed phrases jell together into nervous melody, a fractured continuity tenuously re-knitting itself in an artery of pliant sound.

Goose pimples erupted on Masterji's arm. What was this melody in the air? He sat bolt upright. What was this plangent, melting, searching strain if not ... if not, yes, yes ...

Ga re sa dha dha ... yes, yes ... *pa sa sa ga re* ... You had to be primed up by the troubles of a long lifetime to receive the vibes of this stirring music which slipped into the heart like some soul language or God's reasonings with man.

Open-mouthed with uncontainable excitement, Masterji slowly rose to his feet, receiving each note as it fell into his heart, starting the ripples. Then it lost itself in the greater melee of sirens, clamouring crowds, lifeboats, cataracts of spouting sea.

If Mayank would only return, he would ask him what that melody was. But no sign of Mayank still. It was already getting on to be eight-fifteen. He watched the film to the end, didn't care for it. Waited for the return of that snatch of melody and was disappointed. Waited a bit more till the end of the evening news. Impatiently glancing at the clock, the newsreader's words falling distantly into his ears:

A powerful explosion went off at New Jalpaiguri Railway Station this afternoon, killing eight persons, including three Army personnel. The bomb was set off at twelve-ten p.m. even as the jawans were preparing to board the Sikkim–Mahananda Express on Platform Number Two. The Army intelligence fears more such attacks in North Bengal, with the region fast turning into a base for foreign intelligence agencies and separatist organizations. The CPI-M has called a twelve-hour bandh in Siliguri subdivision tomorrow from six a.m. The Union Home Ministry is monitoring the internal security situation following the blast. Officials said they would wait for further information before commenting on the blast ...

Those fellows in the border areas are really having a rough time, reflected Masterji, and where the hell is Mayank? At nine he left, puzzled at Mayank's absence.

He stopped at a PCO and telephoned him. It was nine-twenty. Mayank was back, evasive, acting mysterious. Then, in a rush, he confessed: Arranging a musical soirée—especially in your honour, Masterji. Yes, at our house. There'll be lots of guests. Some NRI friends. Some of their friends—foreigners. All hot on Indian classical music. No, the date hasn't been fixed yet. You see, some of them are scouting for music tutors for their kids, so I thought ...

Hanging on to the telephone receiver, at a phone booth miles away, Masterji was too overwhelmed to speak.

So that's what you were doing all evening, Mayank! There was a strain in his throat. You have your IIT entrance exams coming. Mustn't neglect your studies, my boy.

Oh, that's no problem, Masterji. Everything's taken care of now. Cards—it's strictly by invitation, by the way. Refreshments. A journalist too. Photographer ...

Masterji thought he was dreaming. All this for me? He didn't articulate the question but Mayank anticipated it.

I've told most of the NRI guests about you. They're dead keen to hear you play your flute. Yes, since you're so versatile, a bit of vocal might not be a bad idea too—we'll work that out later.

Sitar? offered Masterji, still stunned.

No-o, Mayank sounded doubtful. Mustn't send across the wrong signals. Masterji knew his sitar playing had often been laughed at at the Samiti. But violin? he suggested. Suddenly he remembered the melody in the film, breathlessly told Mayank about it. Didn't hum it out for fear the PCO man might think him crazy.

Titanic? Ah, I think I know the one you mean. I've got an audio cassette of it. I'll drop it at your house tomorrow, Masterji. It's quite a well-known one.

That night, back in his one-room tenement, the strays fed, the lights off, Masterji had trouble falling asleep. The soirée and the melody competed for primacy in his imagination. And that adorable boy who seemed to make every impossible dream possible. His forthright eyes, his chiselled nose and sensitive lips, his creamy skin, his tidy, delicate shoulders, soft-moulded hips ... every inch of him built of angel stuff.

_____

eleven

This is getting to be too large a crowd of characters but that's just the point. Bomb blasts would be wasted if the crowd were small.

The first response to my ad regarding Vani Kabir came from her cousin, Mrs Vrinda Nigam. The papers, appointment diary, photographs and anecdotes about Vani did nothing to throw light on the reported tension in Vani's mind in February–March. I went through the appointment diary and in one entry I found scribbled the letters PC. The last entry was on the twenty-second of March: Lytton Street, 4 p.m.—that is just before the blast in Sikandar Bagh. There was a name too: Tandon. On investigation Tandon turned out to be a lawyer whose chambers were situated on Lytton Street. But he had never heard of Vani Kabir. I couldn't ascertain whether he was lying. Yes, he admitted, on consulting *his* diary that he'd had an appointment with a client, a lady who never turned up. Professional discretion kept him from disclosing the name of the client but, in any case, that was neither here nor there because the client did not show up.

I rang up Mrs Vrinda Nigam and asked if Vani's PC might hold some clues. We had access only to her official password and we spent a day going through files, folders, favourites, whathaveyou in her office computer and still found nothing beyond the expected memoranda and info that a women's activist keeps in store.

Then, out of the blue, a new informant turned up. She said her name was Parul Chopra, and that she was an old classmate of Vani Kabir's but they had lost touch for years until Vani paid her a visit in late January.

I fished out the diary and checked the date: the twenty-first of January. PC! Parul Chopra!

I read your ad, said PC. And if you give me an assurance of complete discretion I'll tell you what I know.

You were Tandon's client? The lady who didn't show up at four p.m. on the twenty-second of March at Lytton Street?

Yes, she said. Can I count on your support in preserving my incognito?

I promised and even in these pages have kept my promise. Her initials were PC all right but her real name wasn't Parul Chopra. I have randomly selected this name and certain others connected with her peculiar circumstances. For convenience's sake let her be Parul Chopra then.

When Parul Chopra's maid brought in the visiting card, she couldn't for the life of her place V.S. Kabir. The card mentioned no occupation, no address or phone number, nothing.

Tell him Sahib is available only after seven.

It's you she wants to meet.

She? A woman? How old? Parul questioned the maid.

About the same as you, didi, informed the maid.

Okay, tell her to please sit and serve her some thunda, I'll be down in a minute, instructed Parul, making ready to change out of her house gown into a fresh salwar-kameez. What a name—V.S. Kabir. Kabir? Kabir? V.S.? Could it be ... I don't know anyone else called Kabir whose first name starts with a V. Running a quick comb through her hair, rubber flip-flops discarded for leather chappals, Parul's mind circuited around the intriguing name, wondering if her hunch was right.

It was.

After the first astonishment and formal effusions of delight were done, after exclamations like you-haven't-changed-a-bit and me ... see-how-much-weight-I've-put-on! were over, Parul asked her old classmate: But why do you disguise your name? Vani is such a nice name. And V.S. Kabir! Ugh! Makes you sound like a CID inspector!

Vani was tall, savvy, faintly fragrant, power-dressed.

How do you know I'm not one? she quipped.

The initial diffidence was got over. Albums shown. Individual photographs of husband, kids, dogs. Holidaying in Manali. Dancing in Goa.

That's Manoj ... he's changed, hasn't he? Since you last saw him at our wedding reception twenty years ago. That's Sasha. He's got ninety-six per cent in his ISC. And this one's Katya. She works in Mumbai. Software engineer. It was too early but such a good job. Seventy thousand rupees a month and perks. But she's such a restless girl. She only wants to go to America ...

Sasha and Katya? repeated Vani. Russian names?

No. Sashank and Katyayani, said Parul, colouring a bit at Vani's smile. Vani Kabir had a small, surreptitious smile that left people feeling disquieted.

The next natural question was: So what've you been doing all these years?

I worked in an advertising company for some years. Churning out one-liners like Tu Cheese Bara Hai Mast-Mast for cheese companies and What Cannot Be Cured Must Be Insured for insurance companies. Okay while it lasted. Then I worked as a journalist spinning out reports like Government to Begin

Crackdown and Noisy Scenes in Lok Sabha. And Security Stepped Up in Border Districts.

Parul laughed at Vani's controlled self-mockery.

When the paper's official astrologer was late with his inputs, I flipped off universally adjustable weekly forecasts from Capricorn to Sagittarius. No, to be exact, there were four of us and we divided the stars between us. Virgo, Libra and Scorpio fell to me. I built up a store of all-purpose clichés: You'll be cheerful but intervals of depression cannot be ruled out. Or: A mixed week ahead, take care of your health. Or: Think before you take any financial risks. Or: You'll be a mine of energy but will be prone to occasional malaise.

Parul secretly marvelled that anyone could make a living out of that, but she chuckled.

Sounds great fun, she remarked politely.

Vani didn't fail to catch the flawed laugh.

No fun at all. All routine stuff. I quit. Presently I'm a counsellor at Shakti. Heard of it?

No.

Women's activist group.

Parul feigned panic: Oh, oh, a *feminist*. One of those!

One of those, confirmed Vani dryly.

You rescue burning women from dowry deaths and record their dying declarations?

Vani's face went taut. It isn't funny, she said. Yes, that's something I have done—at least thrice.

Parul corrected her tone but the temptation to merriment was irresistible: I read in the paper about two crimes which occurred simultaneously. A textile mill fraud case and a rape case in the same village. The police and the feminists got cracking. Eventually, the rapist was arrested for fraud and the impostor for rape!

At the back of Parul's mind there lingered some long-faded gossip about Vani Kabir having brainwashed her younger sister into walking out on her husband over an issue that could very easily have been patched up. But Vani Kabir, if she took offence, was good at keeping her cool.

We do our best, she said calmly. I'll tell you of a recent case I handled. A very strange murder. A man killed his wife. She just wasted away. The husband sent an SOS to her brother when it was all over. But the brother suspected foul play and came to us. Of course, no post-mortem was possible by then—the body had been cremated. We made inquiries and discovered a few funny things. This very tender husband was medicating his wife personally with the help of a doctor friend. But the doctor, when contacted, confessed that he had met the wife only once years back. He had witnessed a quarrel. The wife's hand was stuck in a door and the husband was trying to crush it by shutting the door.

Parul was appalled. Oh no! she gasped.

Oh, yes, persisted Vani. That should give you an idea of how tender this tender husband was. Her lips curled in an unconscious sneer.

So how did he kill her? Parul wanted to know.

Most ingeniously. He used to carry opposite accounts of her condition to the doctor who, in good faith, prescribed medicines which only aggravated her condition. We found the silver foil of used capsules. She was suffering from hypoglycaemia, hypothyroid and she was treated for diabetes, hyperthyroid and things like that. It took time but it worked. And no evidence—nothing that could be proved, if you know what I mean. So beware of these tender husbands is what I say.

Parul decided to joke around. What to do, yaar? This is something really worrying. Manoj is being extra tender these days.

Vani shrugged, despairing. You married women! Never content. I've had so many women complaining of their husbands' bad behaviour. You're the first one complaining of a husband's good behaviour.

That's just it—it isn't natural. Though she didn't realize it herself, Parul's manner had turned earnest.

Maybe he's got a girlfriend, suggested Vani. I'm told men are extra nice to wives when they're unfaithful.

So what does one do? What do experts like you advise? Parul had recovered her mask.

One tried-and-tested method is to work on the other woman's spouse, if she has one.

Pati patni aur woh ka pati! Parul could be funny in unexpected spurts.

Vani burst out laughing. The stiffness dissolved, they were both at ease. Parul sent for coffee.

Actually, said Parul, you and I are in the same boat. You're enjoying single blessedness and I'm enjoying single matrimony.

What's that now?

Most of my friends are well into what I call multiple matrimony. Me, I'm still a one-man woman. They really look down on me. Flaunt their affairs as proofs of a more ... more complex and mature emotional life, get what I mean?

We call your kind of case mono-man-ia, remarked Vani.

Your kind of life is a progressive moronizing of self, her face indicated. Parul understood, was stung, brushed the subject aside, and encroached slightly on a counter-attack.

Oh, you can talk! You *toh* don't have to bother with all this *khich-pich*. You aren't married. By the way, why didn't you marry?

Vani decided to shed her aloofness. I haven't ever told you about my parents' marriage, have I? My ammi was Muslim, my abbu a Hindu. They had fallen in love. Eloped. No, this isn't another art film. It's for real. They married in court. Later, when they returned to the city, Ammi's parents refused to accept the marriage as legitimate. No nikaah, you see. And nikaah meant conversion to Islam. Well, Abbu had never been fanatically religious anyway. And he was head over heels in love. He was quite willing to go through with it but Ammi threw a fit. Why must you convert? What's wrong with you? Do you have to bend backwards to prove how accommodating you are? If you do convert I'll never be able to respect you. Be what you are. He had to comply. You saw her when she was middle aged. But in her twenties she was really something. An impassioned beauty—no one could ever stand up to her. So her parents and the entire Muslim community refused to recognize their marriage. In other words I'm an official bastard—socially.

And the Hindus?

The Hindus. Didn't say a word. They simply cut my parents off. Made trouble in other ways. No one would rent them a house. All sorts of obstructions everywhere. My parents couldn't care less. Their marriage survived. So you see ... arranged marriage is out for me.

But what about love? pursued Parul.

Love? Vani laughed heartily. I've seen that. My standards of love are impossibly high, I'm sorry to say. My abbu was besotted with my ammi. They made a great twosome. He was mild, thoughtful, lenient. She was a livewire. A blazing beauty. All action and daring. I'll never come across a married couple as picturesque. Even when they fought, they were so fantastically complementary. And see what they named me—Vani Shahnaz Kabir.

But what are you now?

What do you mean?

Hindu or Muslim?

I'm Vani Shahnaz Kabir. That's who I am. Yes, I had a Muslim upbringing but kids inevitably follow the culture of the mother, no? So that's why I didn't marry. Having seen a great marriage like that, nothing could hope to match it. Satisfied?

You haven't missed much, said Parul, choosing to be generous. Look at me—so anxious about my husband's smoking, obesity, chest pain, overeating, hypertension, promotions, sulks ...

And tenderness, Vani joked.

Yes, that too, Parul said quite seriously.

They had come to the end of their resources. A long silence fell during which Parul could only fuss around with biscuits and chips.

Now have your coffee *garam-garam*, she urged.

Then Vani remembered something. Do you still write poems? she asked.

Parul flushed. It was a sensitive, vulnerable secret.

Sometimes, she confessed, guarded.

I remember that poem of yours. In school. How did it go? *Green pool. Satin flap of wave.*

Yes, said Parul. *Green pool. Satin flap of wave. Heron foaming past white flare of sun.* It was called *Japanese Print*.

I remember, said Vani. She also remembered how the class had made an ass of Parul on All Fools' Day by sending her a fake letter saying she had won a British Council prize. She knew Parul remembered too. A pang of preserved compunction came alive. Parul's face betrayed nothing.

Did you publish your poetry? Vani asked.

Yes. A privately done volume. I took a copy to Leo. Remember her?

Leo! Of course! English teacher, Miss Leonora Dodson. *Julius Caesar*, *Twelfth Night*, Tennyson, Hardy ...

Parul spoke on, remembering Leo: She's the one who took an interest in my scribbling. I took her my book. She's ninety now. She sat, holding my book. Kind of puzzled. Running her hands across its cover. Feeling its spine, its pages. Like a deaf person who's intently listening to music through her fingertips ...

Vani watched Parul speak. Suddenly she liked her, this private voice of hers, this persisting precious un-undermined self. Parul did not notice. She went on describing Leo: She sat so still. Sensing my book through her fingers. You could tell she had gone beyond books now but she could experience the spirit of the thing, if not the letter.

She stopped, self-conscious. Another long silence. Not of exhausted links but of recharging possibilities.

They sat. Parul said: Isn't this room a bit too cold? She rose and switched off the air conditioner. Then she returned to her chair. Have you noticed these layers of sound? she asked. When the AC stops, there's the ceiling fan. When the fan stops, there's the ticking clock. When the clock stops, there's your own heartbeat ... Her voice trailed away. She was surprised to find she could share such thoughts.

Vani didn't say, I like the way you speak, but her expression did. She rose to leave.

Well, I'll be off.

We must meet oftener.

Sure. What we need is a mutual morale-boosting club.

You tell me I've got unwrinkled skin, me tell you you've got nice black hair—that kind of thing.

How else is one to fight this midlife bug?

Uff! Midlife! Know what? I've decided to cultivate heart disease. A rational, considered choice. You see, I live in an area which has heaps of cardiologists. So convenient for the family ...

When they parted at the lift, they were still laughing. But once the lift began moving Vani's tension returned. No go! she thought. I couldn't even start questioning her. A super-flop meeting.

Parul went back to the flat, smiling, blissfully ignorant.

twelve

Late Spring morning in the park. Grated sunlight on Lynette's bench. Newspaper, spectacles, plastic basket, coffee flask, a chipped ceramic mug. She caught herself at it again:

Did it really happen that way or am I only imagining it?

That's what she had said aloud. She was watching herself with severity, exacting a penalty for each time she lapsed into the silly habit of verbalizing audibly to herself. Fighting the tendency by focusing on things around her.

The birds, for example. How busy the branches were. She paid close attention to each separate sound. Small, fluting twitters erupted overhead. Squawks and tricks of tune. Trills and spurts, whistles and shrill whoops, soprano octaves. Shurrings of breeze. Beneath it all, other sounds. Little saws working. Insect jingles. Snip-snap scissor chirps. Small engines jerking and revving.

Already a hint of mango blossom in the air. Concentrate, concentrate.

From outer reality to practical matters. Capsicum selling at sixty rupees a kilo. Sixty! Only fifteen rupees in the hills. The hills! She found herself slipping down the sheer slopes of forbidden recall. Darjeeling that September. Mist fumed around the guest house all night. The building was like a giant ship adrift in the clouds. The road in front rounded a bend and seemed to fold on nothing. She remembered the names of houses, cafes: Willow Glade, Glennery, Meghna Manor ... She had once walked into Glennery, announcing cheerfully to Brian: Let's sit there! Only to realize that the table she wanted was three strides deep in a mirror! She had raised a laugh in the restaurant. And that bench on the Mall. The mist came swaying and smoking through the sunlight. The green Second World War jonga jeeps. Crazy, steep red mountain roads and forests so dense, the sun didn't penetrate—like the darker areas of one's mind. And Tiger Hill at three a.m. A large patch of fog had come to cover it up. She had been bitterly disappointed. Then the fog cracked. A strain in the sky, felt rather than seen. Fiery liquid swelling, seeking an outlet, then a needle-prick of light, a thin cleft of gold, a crawling stream ... Suddenly the sky was in shreds. Pierced by a scalding ball that boiled round and round in a great, blinding ring of pulsing rainbow colours. Then, as one looked, massive smoking cataracts of flame appeared. Trees, high peaks, steep drops, falls tangled in a large web of light. Everything streaming with fibres of blonde light. Sunlight drained down the terraced hillsides and pooled in the blue-misted valleys beneath.

On the way back from the bus stop, Brian had stopped at the post office to pick up a letter. Who from? Jain, of course. Plain Jain, they called him in private. The GRP man, sturdy bum-chum, who had moved into their bungalow to look after Alan, Brian's dad, lying paralysed in bed, so that they, Brian and she, could take a break. Jain's just like one of us, Brian used to say. When Alan had that stroke, Jain shared night shifts in hospital, keeping awake while they slept. When Alan died a little later, Jain had taken care of half the funeral arrangements.

You're a truly Christian chap, men, Brian had complimented his friend.

Jain hadn't reacted. A sour look had come into his eyes. You could actually read the thought in his head: Thanks for the compliment. As if all virtue is something your Christianity holds a patent over!

Initially Jain seldom spoke. His face did his speaking for him. Later he opened up, came out with teasing quips, practical jokes. Like that Holi when he came with a covered dish of aromatic fried mutton, cooked by his wife. (A freethinker, this Jain. Had abandoned his vegetarianism long ago.)

Here's the Holi Gosht, Shepherd Sahib, he had laughed.

The what?

The Holi Gosht, Jain had guffawed. We cook it on Holi sometimes.

Brian had been secretly offended but Lynette had laughed.

Even as early as that, Lynette had had misgivings. Why must Jain write to you so often? she had asked. He can telephone, can't he?

Trunk calls cost the earth, men (those were the pre-STD days), and they need booking and waiting for hours. I told Jain to let us know how the old man's coming along. A letter's simpler and cheaper.

Brian had spoken fast. Lynette remembered that evening walk. A street light swung and the light wagged over the leaves. Then there was a blackout. A last scrap of light came fluttering down the poinsettia bushes and fell right through.

In Brian's trouser pocket she had found an empty envelope, addressed in a strange, rounded hand. But that isn't Jain's handwriting, she had thought.

That handwriting! She had come across it in letters, cards, chits, gift-paper! Pink paper, blue paper, ruled white. That handwriting set her heart jangling now and her head racing out of control. She couldn't even ask Brian because he wasn't there any more. She had grappled with the truth, hoped the pain would pass but it didn't. It hurt all the time. It was lying in wait for her when she awoke in the morning and by the time she had made her morning tea, it was gnawing away at her in full force. It reappeared in troubling inverted contexts in her sleep. That deep it went. That she had lived thirty-five years alongside a man, never realizing. She abhorred this long-suffering-wife role that had been forced on her. The sterling constant relationship, the strong enduring force behind a man, against which he might enact his occasional, pardonably small and shabby infidelities. The trusting little wifey to whom, after the escapade was over, he returned with guilt in his heart and gifts in his hands. It was a contemptible position to be in, and what more contemptible than to stay unconscious of the real situation—for years and years. Living in her fool's paradise! She had already spent months agonizing. She wondered why she clung to the pain. Because it overshadowed a bigger loss? Sometimes one unconsciously chose a lesser pain as an immediate protection from a larger one. One of the tortuous tricks one's cunning mind played on oneself to safeguard one's sanity from ultimate disintegration. Only now, sifting through old papers, putting old clues together, the full extent of the involvement with that woman had struck her with heart-twisting clarity. Three decades too late.

Retrospective injury, that's what it was. The shock of betrayal, thirty years after it actually occurred. Far more excruciating than current injury. Marcia Gosse's photograph and phone number. And Brian's seemingly casual remarks—so fresh in the memory now. Marcia Gosse used lots of perfume. Marcia Gosse liked wearing red. Marcia Gosse sang well. Marcia Gosse was free with compliments. She was pushy. Made a man feel a superman. Thought nothing of getting dead drunk in bed with a man ... And she, Lynette, unaware of anything amiss, waiting for Brian's return, the little wifey!

The photograph. A pretty, smiling, camera-friendly face with her head tilted in a practised posture. A wide, well-exercised, red-lipsticked smile. Her red and black dress flaring around her in a dramatic swirl. Marcia Gosse. Marcia Gosse. Thirty-five years too late her name kept replaying in Lynette's head in a devilish insinuating chant. Until she wondered if these were indeed the preliminary intimations of madness. Always a mistake to build all one's faith on a man! The whole world was so savvy, why was she so naïve? But what to do with this aberration now? Would ringing up Marcia Gosse help? Would it exorcise this torment?

But if she spoke to her, what would she say to her? I'm ringing you up to be able to expel you from my head ...

Dialling from a different PCO. May I speak to Marcia Gosse, please? A young woman's voice answered, melodious, lime-tanged. Sorry, she's busy. It stabbed her to the heart, set her stammering. She tried to connect it to the photograph. And put the phone down without a word. She's avoiding me. That was her. I just know it. The PCO man watching through a glass partition. Dialling again. The line sputtered, cracked, went dead. Lynette's voice hadn't carried at all.

The mob which stormed Sakina Bibi's kothi and wrought such havoc the day after the blast was made up of a large number of busteewalas from the nearby slum of Fatehpur Bicchwa. Sakina Bibi couldn't get over this fact.

The bustee supplied us with our servants for years, she told me. It gave us our cooks and washerwomen, our floor-scrubbers and dish-scourers. They were ordinary people who loved their precious TVs and stole electricity from the street electric poles. They had birthday parties for their kids. They copied film stars and starlets when they danced and tried hard to climb that difficult rung of the social ladder that divided proletariat from lower middle class. Who could have foretold that such a peaceable herd could be inflamed by such raving passion? What toxins of animus or vengeance or sheer beastly expediency could hibernate in their collective recall, to waken in their bloodstreams with such devastating menace? Yet, come to think of it, reflected Sakina Bibi, even on that day of the party at the bustee something ominous had occurred which went unnoticed.

I visited Fatehpur Bicchwa and walked around the lanes, skirted the tin shacks and leap-stepped the overflowing gutters, trying to visualize the party Sakina Bibi had described, the party which had held two fateful portents (one of them the reel of film the police later seized) though no one realized it then. Once an outlying village, the area had now sunk in civic stature and become a slum. Urban colonies had mushroomed beyond it, creeping steadily down the slopes to the banks of the Yamuna. Between dilapidated colonial bungalows on one side and pretentious medium-rise on the other, Fatehpur Bicchwa clung to its mucky little railway-line-backed strip, stubborn, straggling and slushy. Loud with TV blare and hooch-brawl, baby-squeal and shrew-shriek. A labyrinth of provisional alleys between mud, cow dung and bamboo structures, plastic-sheet shelters, asbestos, gunny and motley brick and mortar. Everything electrified with tangles of outlaw wire from a pole on the main road. Cows, curs and responsible pigs, busy at the garbage heaps and swilling gutters, kept the bustee air endurable to indigenous nostrils. The sound of the trains shuddering along the pebbly embankment behind submerged the din of twin loudspeaker trumpets on the pole. Banners from the previous elections, showing elephant or lotus or bicycle or palm-of-the-hand, now ragged from dust and rain, festooned between thatch and thatch, and TV antenna and upturned clay-pot totem pole, served as community clothes line and crow-perch.

No doubt Professor Mathur, elated by a cascade of creative insight into contemporary anthropology, found it all enchanting. I can just see him, accompanied by Munna, heading for the festive venue, making observation and discourse.

See that wall there, Munna, my son. That's what I call specimens of the famous Proletarian North-Indian Mural, circa 2000 AD. The UP School of Art. Material? Betel juice on lime wash, wah! Local stuff, readily available, cheap vegetable dye, colourful recycled waste. No need for brush or pestle. The human mouth as executor, the blank wall for canvas, all the world's a studio, hah! And listen you—that song, how does it go? *Queen Monsoon, rain, rain hard. Let not my beloved get away.* Do you know, Munna, my lad, I used to know a Sanskrit verse that said exactly that. Kalidas? Bhartrihari? Ah, this brain grows old and forgetful. Now, where is this party supposed to be? She said behind Hrithik Tailor Shop. Do you see a Hrithik Tailor Shop anywhere?

Munna was dressed in his swanky best. He swung a camera slung round his braceleted wrist. He had been invited to this Budday Pahty as official photographer. (Fo–taw–gra–fer, the professor insisted on correcting him every time he said photohgrahfer). Munna exuded cologne enough to confuse the curs of this slum but his heart was sick of the ceaseless corrections and effusions which his mentor tortured him with.

She said behind big hoarding board. There—that one, I am thinking.

The professor stopped before the hoarding, still enchanted.

I wondered why the Thums Up logo says I want my thunder. Now I know. Thunder was thunda all the time. A pun. A piece of Shakespearean wordplay. What was that word you used—funda? Short for fundamentals—no?

Munna maintained a despairing and stoical silence. More of Shakespeare and his fundas. Here we go again. From thundas to fundas. This old fogey's imaginationings!

They turned a corner and now there could be no mistaking the place. A festive spectacle. The slushy drains screened off by cheerful red and yellow marquee canvas, a canopy overhead, dripping with electric bulbs, streamers dangling in the breeze, even half-a-dozen old-stock Christmas stars and a couple of green gilt Christmas trees. On one side the words Hapy Birtday Pappoo formed out of a length of crêpe paper pinned and cello-taped on to the tent wall. And the indispensable loudspeaker.

Munna was charmed by the sumptuous display.

Are they Isaiis? he asked.

Why do you ask?

Those trees ... they're Isaii trees. Bada-din stuff.

The professor snorted. Isaii trees? He raised his eyebrows. Since when did trees start joining camps? No, not a single Isaii here. They probably got those Bada-din decoration things cheap. Off-season stuff. And can you name a Hindu tree, my boy?

The pipal, answered Munna.

The professor looked peeved. And a Mussalman tree? he pursued.

The date-palm, said Munna promptly. The professor's frown filled Munna with glee.

Outrageous, dismissed the professor, and Munna subsided in humble acquiescence.

They approached the festive tent, walking slowly down the coir matting laid on the uneven brick paving.

Lots of balloons they've hanged, said Munna in English.

Hung! snapped the professor.

Eh? Munna was at a loss to comprehend this mysterious show of spleen.

Only those sentenced to death are hanged, declared the professor irritably. Balloons never. Balloons are hung. Clothes are hung. Garlands are hung—

Parliaments too! put in Munna. He could be bright in spurts.

The professor lost his ill humour in a trice. He slapped Munna on the back, rumbling with subterranean laughter.

Parliaments too—though some of their members might deserve to be hanged!

They entered the dazzling party space and were immediately jostled from all sides by clamouring hosts. The entire bustee was playing host on Pappoo's birthday. And Pappoo's Mother—

for that was her official identification at all the houses where she swept and swabbed the floors and did the dishes—emerged, babe on hip, an ethnic Madonna in orange and gilt, her swarthy face wreathed in toothy smiles. Pappoo himself was all of twelve months old and wore a shiny smock above his thin, nude nether, and a paper party cap fastened to his well-oiled head. He saw the professor and burst into tears. The ethnic Madonna slapped him into silence, shrilling: Dirty boy! Who hit you? *Chup*! Then she turned on her bright, shark-jawed smile. Say jai to Babuji. Go on, say jai.

When Pappoo stolidly refused to do so, turning his tear-streaked face resolutely away from the professor as from an unbearably repellent sight, she coaxed: Achha, don't say jai. Say ta ta. Come on now. Say ta ta or you know what you'll get. Say ta ta to Babuji.

Pappoo's contorted countenance surfaced in desperate panic, he waved a tremulous baby paw at the professor, and his sniffling whisper sounded ta ta before he hid his face again.

A general outcry of pleased admiration from mother, hosts, guests.

Ta ta, said the professor genially. Clever boy, clever boy.

There seemed to be a hundred people present. Or else the narrow lane conveyed that impression. Women turned out in fluorescent greens, scarlets, peacock blues, shocking pinks. Much tinsel and pomade. Men in ironed trousers and bush shirts, lips reddened with paan. Kid girls in high-heeled sandals and net frocks and plastic beads, kid boys in polished shoes and long socks and oiled and parted hair. In the throng the professor spotted Sakina Bibi and Suleman, his fellow-lodger. Sakina Bibi was playing dowager queen. Suleman was sulking.

When Pappoo's Mother had come up to Sakina Bibi the day before and informed, Tomorrow is my Pappoo's Heppy Budday, and demanded a loan of three hundred rupees and a day off, there had been a bit of jhik-jhik between employer and employee. Now all rancour was buried as hostess and guest outdid one another in graciousness. Bibi had debated: To go or not to go? To go meant a cash gift she could hardly afford at this time of the month. (These little feudal ceremonies! When Pappoo's Mother came, armed with rakhis on Raksha-bandhan day and tied them on the wrists of Professor Mathur, Bibi, Suleman, even the cricketer lads outside, she collected a neat sum of fifty or sixty bucks!) But the show had to go on. Noblesse oblige. Besides, it meant no cooking one evening—that is, if Professor Sahib and Silent Suleman could also be persuaded to go along. Now here she was, the grand old dame of the mohalla, in silk and powder, and she had even dug out her kundan choker band and heavy wristlets.

Suleman had proved difficult initially. Such a sullen, unsocial one he was. All frowning concentration and abstracted silence. Writing, writing forever. She had said: Suleman Bhai, all work and no pleasure makes a camel of a man. One is not a beast of burden, nay, nor is life a sandy desert ...

When she spoke to him she lapsed into stilted pocketbook-Urdu-couplet metaphors. She felt she owed it to him to use his natural idiom. Out of deference to his exotic otherness as a poet. A creature of complex aches and mystic solitudes. There was in hoary tradition a lyrical poet–nautch girl nexus too to be sustained. Didn't Ghalib have that romantic complication with a dancing girl? The lostness of dancing girls and poets, belonging to no one, chained to the compulsion of their chosen art, ah, it was an old, passionate pact and it had its own vocabulary, its own convoluted code of coquetries.

He lifted his tired poet's eyes to her face. Reproachful. Ah, he hasn't forgiven me for prying into his book behind his back, she thought with a pang. Invading the privacy of his dark soul.

I have no use for vain mirages, he said curtly, predictably metaphoric.

No mirage, Suleman Bhai. A green waadi, she had continued, not to be outdone in idiom. Have you ever witnessed the fury of a camel? My ammi-jaan told me how once a camel had gnawed at her walid sahib's foot. Camels are bored and angry folk— all that tramping, tramping, all that sun and dreary sand and heavy loads. Now this camel just turned his long neck and grabbed my ammi-jaan's walid sahib's foot. And what did he do then? Quick as lightning, he dug his teeth into the camel's neck. Bit hard, hard. If another bites you, you bite him back. That's reality. There they stood, camel gnawing man, man gnawing camel. Until the camel let go ... You'll be as full of senseless rage as that beast soon, Suleman Bhai ...

He looked exasperated. He agreed to go to the party in the servants' bustee just to put an end to this old hag's chatter. She bored him to death with her endless needling, her endless spying into his notebooks, his scripts, his papers. She hadn't known where to look that day when he had surprised her in the act. He had stolen in stealthily behind her and she had started, almost dropped his script. She looked moved, her eyes dope-dewy, stirred, excited. Also embarrassed.

I meant no harm, Suleman Bhai. I had come in to put your gosht-chappati on the table and I began reading what you're writing. You write so beautifully. Almost as beautifully and simply as Mir Sahib. Come now, she had cajoled, dainty nautch-girl to poet again, if you don't like me reading your work, I shan't. Only it's irresistible. I read a line, then my eyes thirsted for the next. And the next and yet the next—how the hour has flown, Suleman Bhai!

She smiled a winsome smile, bags of loose flesh creasing on her jowl like cloth on a pulled drawstring. That's right. Applaud a writer and he's won over. Her ammi-jaan's walid sahib, the same as quelled the biting camel, was a poet too and such a one as stopped people in the market square and accompanied them home, be it miles away, reciting his verse into their intimidated ears. Only for the payment of a few courteous *kya khoobs* and *wah-wahs*. But this one didn't take kindly to her interest in his novel. He obviously did not share her enthusiasm for himself.

I shall be obliged if you don't examine my work again, he said, brusque.

Rest assured I won't, she had promised. He knew she didn't mean a word of it.

That was two days back. Now sitting beside her there was this difficulty between them still.

Meanwhile the party.

Now that the guests had arrived, the birthday ritual ensued. The loudspeaker went silent, a tiny table was placed in the middle of the clearing and a small cake, pink with cheap icing and impaled with a red, beribboned candle was triumphantly produced, lighted and duly admired. Munna stepped forward and clicked away at the cake with his dinky camera. Then Pappoo, brought in on his mother's hip, shrieking in terror at the sight of the knife, the crowd, the blinding flash of the camera. The guests encircled the cake, sang a line of Heppy Budday Tooo Yooo, and, happily unmindful of any subsequent lines, began to clap. Pappoo gouged at the cake. Balloons burst and a shower of silver dust descended to baptise his head, choke his nostrils and set him coughing. He coughed, spluttered, howled louder, tears rolling down his brown cheeks, streaking kaajal all over. Everyone cheered at this spectacle of active infant participation and the loudspeaker started again. Hayloh, one-two-three-check, hayloh! The guests milled around, gifts in hand.

The employer-log had been honoured with armchairs to sit on and a table-fan rotating behind. Sakina Bibi grandly produced, out of the interiors of her ample bodice, a small sequinned velvet purse. She had stitched it herself that afternoon, remembering how, in the good old days, great seigneurs bestowed largesse on their lowly serfs. She had filled it with cashew nuts and walnuts and raisins and a small, folded twenty-rupee note. Beckoning to the ethnic Madonna, she laid a beringed hand on Pappoo's head, closed her eyes, murmured a benediction and put the velvet purse in the child's hand. The child tried to chew it, was violently prevented by his shrilling mother. Professor Mathur offered a Hindi primer and Munna, a bar of Amul chocolate. And Suleman, baffled, unpleasantly out of his depth in a situation he hadn't anticipated, grew confused, reddened, thrust a hand into the pocket of his long linen shirt and pulled out a hundred-rupee note. With a gruff monosyllable, he tucked it into the neck of the child's smock and was rewarded with an extra flash of teeth from its overwhelmed mother. Bibi looked on, awed, touched. Oh, these poets! Thorny outside, tender within. He's not rich, I know. Earns nothing. Lives such a spartan life, but put a wee child before him and he melts, gives more than he can afford, good boy! I always knew he was an unworldly romantic for all his surly airs.

Group photograph. (Not fo-taw-graph but foh-toh-graph with the stress on foh, whispered the professor, fairly driving Munna up the wall.) Mother and child in the centre, all family kids squatting in front, neighbours in back row, other guests in next, and, sitting in the middle row, the employer-log, Bibi holding Suleman firmly down to his chair, thwarting his bashful attempt to slip away. Oh no you don't, my lad, and with that nice face too. As handsome as Yusuf, beloved of Zuleika, whose handmaidens cut their fingers, slicing lemons, when Yusuf appeared—so devastatingly handsome he was, a woman forgot what she was doing! Oh yes, I mean it too, my young Yusuf. She sustained smile and chatter and iron grip on his arm in one masterful act until the flash blinded their eyes and Munna said, Okay, thank yooo, and rose from the ground where he had knelt.

Then there were songs. *May You Live Thousands of Years*, sung by Pappoo's aunt. A girl performed a Madhuri Dixit dhak-dhak dance. A young fellow breakdanced to general rapture and another did a Govinda mimicry. Then, while plates of food went round, Pappoo's other aunt, a young lady of sixteen, much sought after by the bustee swains, read out her poetry. The professor listened, entranced. She read it in a meditative mode:

> Myself writing with this pen
> And writing, writing, fallen in love.
> This lane going where, I ask.
> I ask if I will reach my *manjil*.
> The night so dark
> I will fight because I am right
> And the fighter *hamesa* wins.
> *Yehi hai right choice*, my friends, to fight.
> There is something spesull in us all
> Know this—this is our big Super-Sakti.
> For the Complete Man there can be no fear.
> Doors will open.
> My sari will be whiter, this sari of saris.
> My skin will have the freshness of limes.
> My hair my crowning glory.
> My teeth like pearls.
> The soles of my feet like a queen's, uncracked.
> Walking, walking,
> I too a princess in the play
> With *taazgi* and *atma vishvas*!

While the audience roared Jiyo! and Wah, Professor Mathur appreciated the young woman's subtlety and irony in using popular TV ads. Then, with surprise, he realized she had meant everything literally. TV had given her a new thought-code and he asked her instead what her *manjil* was.

What do you want most? he asked.

A gas connection, Babuji, was the prompt answer.

He was nonplussed.

Here Sakina Bibi interrupted. A gas connection? Oh, get on with you! Your electricity poaching wires are so cheap. Nothing to pay. What do you want a gas connection for?

So convenient, Bibiji. So many power cuts. What to do then? Suppose I want to make Maggi in two minutes, I have to light my kerosene stove. My Chunnoo, he like Maggi ...

Why not shush him up with Ingliss Marie Biskut? suggested another neighbour. When my Lallu ask for Maggi and there is a power cut and the heater can't be lit, I always give him Ingliss Marie Biskut.

The professor realized he had sparked off a contest between two upwardly mobile Joneses. The situation was resolved by Sakina Bibi, who snorted and said, As for me, my betis, Hindustani Marium is good enough for me. They laughed politely, at a loss to understand.

The antakshari began. The employer-log had finished eating and had genteelly hidden their plates under their chairs. Paan and aniseed and lump sugar went round.

Bibi enjoyed antakshari. The alphabet-song match. A bit like a qawwali, no? she whispered to Suleman. Only in a qawwali you make up the words on the spur of the moment and in an antakshari you just pick up the last letter of a film song and start your answer-song with that ...

The young men and young women of the bustee competing. Two groups facing one another on the coir matting, the loudspeaker amplifying it all. Flirtatious, foot-tapping songs:

> *I stood in supplication at your gate, beloved.*
> *You passed me by with never a look.*

And

> *You could not break the silver wall,*
> *You broke my heart instead.*

And

> *Hum bhi hain josh mein*
> *Batein kar hosh mein.*

No one knew exactly when things went out of control. The girls' group had sung out:

> *This love is a vengeful game, dear heart.*
> *For the sleep you stole, I shall have your*
>   *sleep.*
> *For the tears you drew, I shall draw your*
>   *tears.*
> *For the heart you smashed, I shall smash*
>   *your heart.*

And the professor was cynically thinking, Ah, yes, for the arm you twisted, I shall twist your arm—what a neat truth of history! And Sakina Bibi had just said to a young woman beside her, Only two children, beti? Have more. Nonsense. Children are God's gift. Have no worry. He gives and He shall provide. It was then that the old drunkard who had swayed in a while back, reeking of hooch, started shouting abuse. In the beginning it was all garbled. Something about the MLA who was dragged by the busteewalas into a slush-pool when he came campaigning. Something about saying to him, We will strip you down to your saffron langoti! Something about we will make those Brahmin and Thakur pups wash our dishes and scrub our floors and lick our leavings, these screwers of mothers'/sisters'/daughters' narrow-tight-loose-slack-stale cunts—and the loudspeaker amplified the hullabaloo and some voices were heard pleading with the old one to shut up and remember there were guests present and the old man shouting louder and others trying to shout him down, and everyone starting to leave at once, until some bright spark hurriedly put on the *Hum bhi hain josh mein, baatein kar hosh mein* song and turned the volume up and people clapped their hands to their ears as they rushed away. Sakina hailed a rickshaw for herself and Suleman, the cricketers picked up their bikes, and the professor and Munna walked, leaving the hosts to wrestle with the gatecrasher who had disturbed so lively an evening.

Then it was that Munna discovered that his camera was missing. He was upset. They went back to look. Told their hosts, who were hurt, offended. What do you think we are? Pickpockets? their eyes demanded. The professor hastily withdrew, Munna dejectedly muttering imprecations against these bustee-log!

Pity, said the professor. Such a good camera. All the photographs lost too.

Munna felt in the pocket of his denim jacket. Took out the reel.

Here it is. I took out reel after fohtoo. Now all fohtoos here.

He deliberately said fohtoo to spite the professor. The professor took it without comment and slipped the reel into his trouser pocket.

I must remember to hand it to Bibi to give to Pappoo's Mother, he said aloud. She'll pay you for the reel though the camera's gone. I'm sorry about that.

They walked back, sombre, mulling over things.

fourteen

As far as I am able to make out, for both Suruchi Chauhan and Vikram Aditya companionship was qualified loneliness and they made what they could of it. They were of an age when sex ceases to be an appetite and becomes a language and if a relationship developed between the two it seemed like a piece of retrospective indemnity on destiny's part. But all that shall come later. At this point in my narrative they were advancing cautiously, Suruchi impelled by a fascinated frisson of mystery, Aditya by a wary trial of indefinite possibility. Aditya's maidservant supplied some of the details of their second meeting when Suruchi came to visit Aditya. My imagination did the rest.

Suruchi Chauhan had pursued the case and now that the papers were ready, she picked up her car and, on an impulse, drove down to the address he had left three months back. They had spoken briefly on the phone a couple of times but she had discouraged him from coming again.

No more Amarnath treks, please, she had commanded. You'll make me very uncomfortable if you come. When your lease renewal papers are ready you'll receive them. But she hadn't planned to drop the papers personally. It was a last-minute decision, followed by a quick phone call.

A longish drive. The last lane off Shivaji Marg. Past a shopping complex, a hospital, a statue of Shivaji, a park, a movie hall and across a flyover and yes, it ought to be here. Number 142. But there was only a dismal row of garages here, a general merchant's, a chemist, an auto-parts ...

Suddenly she spotted it. Concealed behind a dense clump of neems, just behind the row. Another crumbling old British bungalow that had surrendered its ample gardens to the brash demands of change. Now there was no lawn left, no rose garden or flower patch, no greenhouse or side-orchard or corner well or outhouses. All that had been converted into shops, behind which the tiled yellow bungalow with its square porch and deep, shady verandas dozed in its transformed space.

She parked in the lane and walked. The rusty gate clanked. A dog barked. The old servant who opened the door looked as though she had been recently unpacked and aired.

She was expected and a welcome prepared. Vikram Aditya Singh had dressed in a Van Heusen shirt for the occasion and the mouldy, sprawling sitting room carried a whiff of room freshener and men's cologne. She was flattered, he was a trifle tongue-tied. She took control of the situation, sat, made small talk, gave him his lease renewal papers.

You'll now have to visit the district court once—with two witnesses. That's all.

He thanked her for her trouble.

I read in the paper about that problem in your offices, he said. I was quite worried.

She laughed. Oh, those mafias. They're the ones you should've been worried about. All in the day's work for me. Years of experience.

She told him how she had handled them.

There they were, sitting on either side of the tender box. Looked like ordinary college students to me. A handful of them more on the main staircase. When the hullabaloo started, I walked out of my cabin. They were pushing and pulling, roughing up other parties who had come to cast their tenders. This was a three-crore project. I had expected trouble. In fact I had told the DIG of the Special Task Force of my apprehensions and he had sent over some of his plain clothes commandos, feigning to be architects. That's it. A dozen fellows arrested. We had to cancel the tender, of course. My immediate superior, Mr Yadav, wanted to ask for a legal opinion before cancelling the tender but the last time he played that card, the expected thing happened. A lawyer gave an opinion that the mafias dictated at gunpoint. This time I said I would have none of it. Each case carries its own lessons.

He listened respectfully, so clearly in awe of her that she was abruptly embarrassed at her own biceps-flexing in the face of his incapacity. She spoke, instead, of her lost promotion, her complaint, the case she had filed. Then it struck her that, true to her instinct for professional dominance, she was doing all the talking, and she asked what he did.

He was laconic. I help out in an income tax lawyer's firm.

Does he pay you well? She instantly regretted her interrogator's tone.

Enough for my needs, he replied. I also own those shops in front. The rent comes in.

So what're your working hours?

No fixed hours. My employer's an old friend. Sends work over when I can't go.

There was a silence. The servant brought tea and salted cashew nuts, biscuits, burfis. She admired the ancient tea service, the polished silver spoons.

My grandmother's, he said.

That turned the key. The inhibition unlocked. She took the envelope of faded uncashed cheques from her smart leather bag and placed them on the table.

These you should keep, she said.

No, I don't need them. You can keep them. Preserve them, destroy them—do as you think fit.

Now that he had mentioned his grandmother, she wanted to probe further.

Is this the house she lived in?

Yes. She bought it from a Parsee landlord who bought it from a Scotsman.

When did she buy it?

The fifties, I imagine. She was posted here then.

As what?

Inspectress of Secondary Schools.

Finally the long evaded subject: When were those cheques sent?

She watched the voltage fluctuation in his face.

That was much earlier. Say late thirties and early forties. She used to be in Meerut then. Then he added: By the fifties your grandfather's practice must've boomed.

She decided to put her perplexity in words: What I'm trying to figure out is why he needed money. My dadi's family was filthy rich. Had a title and all. So why should he have run up debts? The amounts he sent aren't all that big ...

He shrugged. Just one of those things—gaps in history. Maybe he had secret expenses that she supported. Maybe she had sold him something and he paid her in instalments later. All we do know is that for some mysterious reason she did not encash those cheques he sent her.

There was a beep of understanding in her eyes: She didn't want his money.

Who knows?

She took a deep breath and asked the central question: What exactly was the *relationship*?

So far they had both hesitated to state the relationship. Now she stressed the word as though her voice had run out of ink and she had to rub the words hard to make them flow again.

I told you. Your grandfather, Gajendra Singh Rathor, was a rich barrister's son. My nani was his father's munshi's daughter. The munshi died. She and her mother and sisters were dependants at your great grandfather's household. So-called poor relations. You must've heard stories of those huge extended families in which one affluent man supported fifty ...

His voice tailed off.

She did not say anything but they were both thinking the same thought. An affair. A little in-house, hole-and-corner liaison.

Did she give you the uncashed cheques?

No. I found them in her papers much after she died.

She was aware that she was beginning to sound like a cross-questioning counsel but there were matters which seriously vexed her.

How did you come to connect Gajendra Singh Rathor with me?

He answered, patiently sipping his tea: One of my surviving aunts—she's in Agra now—slipped across some hints. I once wrote to your father about my grandmother's papers left behind in Meerut. Oh, bits and pieces here and there—you know how it is. Scraps of information.

Still the unsorted mystery. The exact relationship. Neither of them would risk spelling it out. As though each was apprehensive of entering a context of connections awkward to both and vaguely threatening.

As I see it, he said, divining her thought, at some point of time while he was a student at Allahabad, he needed money. In the early thirties he must've been a law student, still unmarried, supported by an allowance from home.

And she?

She used to receive a government scholarship—this I know for definite. She was very bright and very thrifty. And she used to do a bit of sewing and tutoring. She managed to put by something in the bank. Later, she landed a government job as assistant mistress in a Normal School and left Meerut.

Didn't your surviving aunt know anything more?

He seemed reluctant to tell. Just one thing more. After your grandfather married into your titled grandmother's family and all the rest, my nani, it is said, slipped and fell off the terrace. Broke her femur and smashed an arm. She had a limp right till the end of her days. She was married when she recovered. Somehow the family seems to connect the two things—I don't know why ...

Do you have a photograph of her or something?

There's one. I'll have to look.

He raised himself with slow concentration, took his stick, went in. He returned a few minutes later with an old, discoloured album. She looked at the sepia photograph. A washed-out face. Plain, tired, with a suggestion of prim severity. Missing beauty by inches. She stood in a graduation gown, her hair in a bun, holding the back of a chair. The paper was yellow, the background a nicotine haze. She shut the album, put it down.

You really don't want those cheques?

What would I do with them now?

She stood up to go. Thanks for the tea.

Thanks for your help. How did you come?

I drove—my car's out in the lane.

You could've brought it in.

I didn't know if there would be reversing space.

Okay, see you then.

In case you need any further help, just call up.

Thanks, I will.

She drove home feeling unexpectedly disturbed.

At home she took out the cheques, laid them out on her dining table, arranging them serially, looked closely at them, compared the signatures, the relative fading of the ink. She had a limp right till the end of her days, she thought. And he's been born with one. She wondered what to do with the cheques. She wanted a function worthy of their history. Something significant and seemly.

In her office the next day she stood at her eleventh-floor window, off and on, trying to diagnose the disturbance.

Four days later she stapled all the cheques together and wrote a brief prose-poem across them, two lines to a cheque.

Death-browsing
At my eleventh-floor vantage

Shall I chance it?
A micro-second's flight?

Like a slipshod trapeze flyer
Let go my grip?

I might just remain
Imperfectly caught

In a mesh of rebounding
Intersections,

That crucial connection
Missed.

Panting up hillsides might be your portion.
Death-surfing at windows might well be
      mine.

Who compels us?
Instructions from above,

A mislaid file,
A faded shred of pain.

There's lots to audit, settle,
Despatch, reimburse,

Something left to expiate,
Another pending lease to renew?

She signed it Suruchi. Put all the cheques in an envelope and posted them to him.

A week later she received by courier an envelope containing a single blank cheque. State Bank of India. Shivaji Road Branch. Account number 40887. Signed Vikram Aditya Singh.

She could not concentrate all afternoon. Kept taking it out to look at it. A blank cheque. Signed. She was overcome by the reckless poetry of the gesture, the unguarded ultimateness of the offering. And the common language of their signals.

Before leaving office she telephoned him.

Thanks for this thing you've sent.

Do you accept it?

Who'd refuse a blank cheque? She laughed a social laugh. But you've forgotten to put the date.

His voice was steady, careful.

The date, he said, is to be fixed by you.

fifteen

This totally ridiculous thing, fretted Lynette Shepherd, sitting on her park bench. It's stirred all the hidden centres of pain in my memory. Marcia Gosse wrote her letters in a gaudy gush ... Oh God! She's in my head again! Too many grievances tossed into that lightless bin. The thoughts hurt almost physically. Garbage emotions generating strong fumes. They lay around in her brain, a disordered mess. A cramping ache furrowing down the middle of her skull. No getting rid of it—not with aspirins, not with sedatives. Compulsively she rooted about, seeking each lost offence, shaking it out, examining it closely, grieving over it. She strove to stop them but the thoughts accelerated in her head. She found herself unwittingly repeating sentences, then whole paragraphs out of Marcia Gosse's letters until her heart began pounding like a drum and her throat went dry. That woman. What the hell went on between the two of them? Such a dizziness in the head that even coffee couldn't quell it. For years she felt: If I meet that woman, ever, it'll be an unmitigated disaster. I might even have to go to a shrink. Why won't my mind shake it off? After all, it was thirty-five years ago. I thought I'd wait—give it time. Like a time-bound virus this pain shall auto-destruct. The words might lose their charge, grow disempowered. But how much time have I got. This problem looks like it might outlive me. Strange thought. That people died, their aches and angers lived on.

Depression. Insomnia. What would she tell the doctor? I'm obsessing over an affair my late husband had thirty-five years ago, that I only just managed to comprehend. I was going through old letters and then—this thunderclap! That dumb I was. The clues were all there, staring me in the face. Really, she would have to seek a medical solution. Her racing brain had become a serious problem. No way of thinking herself out of the situation. She was irked. Losing appetite, weight. Constipated. Her piles inflamed. Why can't I live peacefully with this knowledge? But it looks like it'll cut into my heart till the very end.

When things came to such a pass that she couldn't look at a TV or magazine ad without comparing the model's face with Marcia Gosse's, when she sat poring over road and railway maps, tracing the distance between their place and Marcia Gosse's, Lynette knew she needed help urgently. The Birla Institute of Advanced Clinical Psychology and Occupational Therapy.

The counsellor's even voice: Every time you return to a negative thought-content, you nourish it. You've got to learn to play thwarting games with your own mind. Give it counter-thoughts to repeat like a parrot. Cut off energy supplies to your negative thoughts. Starve them. Firmly wrench your mind away and think of something else. Especially in the first hour of the morning after you wake up. Think of one particular symbolic object that'll open the gate to positive moods. She had chosen her pearl rosary. It helped to turn her counter-thought exercise into a chant. Eyes closed, she began whispering to herself: Jude, O Holy Saint Jude, great in virtue and rich in miracles, near kinsman of Jesus Christ, faithful intercessor of all who invoke your special patronage in time of need, to you I have recourse from the depth of my heart and humbly beg, to whom God has given such great power, to come to my assistance. Help me in my present urgent petition, in return I promise to make your name known and cause to be invoked.

After this she said three Our Fathers, three Hail Marys and three Glory Bes. She finished with the last supplication, adding a little appeal of her own: Saint Jude, teach me to forgive, teach me to make peace with my memories, teach me to sleep well again. Saint Jude, pray for us and all who invoke your aid. Amen.

This novena had to be said for nine consecutive days and had never been known to fail, her mother had taught her. She noticed the knot in her rosary. The pearl necklace broke this morning. The chain can break at a hundred and eight points. No, a hundred and nine. But it doesn't need a jeweller to put it right. The joints are made of such fine, twistable gold wire that you can just twirl it into a knot and it's whole again in a jiffy and nobody can tell where the break had been. I used to be like that myself. You couldn't tell how often I've come apart and where I've put myself together again. I could do it as often as necessary. That's how I used to be. Wired in gold.

Or Humpty Dumpty in reverse. That jingle the children chanted, forty years back (think of something else).

Humpty Dumpty charh gaya chhat.
Humpty Dumpty gir gaya phut.
Raja ki paltan, raja ke ghore
Koi nahin Humpty Dumpty ko jore.

How absurdly cute! The words still fresh. For a moment she forgot Marcia Gosse. There were half a dozen others in her memory. Hickory Dickory Dock was one.

Dekho re, dekho re, dekh.
Ghari bajaegi ek.
Jab ghanta hua,
Toh kood para chuha,
Dekho re, dekho re, dekh.

What was his name now? Big something. Big-Ears? She giggled like a girl. Big-Nose? Bignold. T.F. Bignold. Senior ICS man in the 1860s. Balasore, Orissa. Gave my great grandpa his railway job. Used to scribble these dinky translations in the margins of files. Cartoons too. Funny that she had forgotten these jingles for donkeys' years.

Sitting in their Cawnpore veranda once, she had recited some of them for Brian and Gloria. Gloria had been six at the time. Jain visiting. Brian had twitched his nose. He disapproved of this going-native business. A pucca sahib, Brian. Chutney-kedgeree-pea-pilau type. He wasn't amused. Bignold's translations were portents of mongrel vulgarities which the barbarian hordes, if vigilance was relaxed, might perpetrate on his intensive, acquired Anglo-Saxon authenticities.

What to expect now, men? The bania-log will soon start teaching our nursery rhymes in babu-English.

It had been a particularly unfortunate morning, Lynette remembered. There was Gloria sitting on the mat, playing with Jain, Brian smoking his meerschaum pipe, she copying a pattern out of *Woman and Home*. Gloria chattering to herself, crayons littering the mat.

Now give me the names of five flowers, she commanded Jain. And didn't wait for Jain's answer, lisping triumphantly: rose, lily, marigold, jasmine, lotus. Now five towns: Goruckpore, Fyzabad, Bar-elli, Cawnpore, Alabad. Now five birds: crow, swan, robin, cheel, koel. Five games: cricket, football, hopscotch, chor-chor, kabaddi. Five gods: Rama, Krishna, Shiva, Ganesha, Hanumana.

Brian had frowned, taken his meerschaum out of his mouth, grimaced, disgustedly blown a puff of smoke like one of the steam engines he drove. Gods? he exclaimed. You're mad or what? He turned to Lynette. What've yawl taught this-one? Has she been playing chor-chor with those beastly chokra-boys?

Out of the corner of her eye Lynette saw Jain stiffen. As a rule Jain did not react when Brian committed his social indiscretions in his presence. He practised a more oblique kind of rebuttal. Usually a cranky quip or a funny story. Like the time when Brian asked him what to take along to a bereaved Hindu colleague's home. What's the done thing here, men? Does one take flowers or something? Jain had uttered a short laugh and jeered: Born and forty years camping in this country out here and you still don't know what the done thing here is! Like the story Jain wickedly narrated about his brother's branch manager at the bank.

You haven't met my elder brother, my Pramod Bhai-Sahib, have you? Giant of a man, all of six feet, a wrestler's body. But a private sort of a man, quite a thinker, a voracious reader. Was in the Army, took retirement and now working as security officer for State Bank. Pramod Bhai was once assigned a tough job. The toughest in his life, he insists. No, sir, no hold-ups or sensational bank robberies to prevent. This was a tiny mofussil branch—a staff of ten in a single hall in kasba Inayatganj. Pramod Bhai had to protect his branch manager from a rioting staff. Reason: His manager was an overzealous man of the faith. He'd handed out a few pamphlets to the Dalit staff at Easter time, made a few off-the-cuff speeches when business was slack.

In the beginning the staff laughed and joked. When he gave Chhedi Lal, the sweeper, a pamphlet, the rest of the staff harangued him: Oye, Munejar Sahib, when Chhedi here converts, what's his new name going to be?

It'll have to be as close to his original name as possible. Now *chhed* means hole, na?

If he becomes a Muslim, his name will have to be Soorakh Ali, laughed a wag.

And if he converts to Christianity, it should be Mr Hole!

The branch manager was irritated. These uncouths! he all but declared. Soon afterwards he put up a text on the wall which stated: When He Was On The Cross I Was On His Mind.

Next day someone put up a cartoon of little Mr D'Souza in his baggy pants and checked bush-shirt and Bata sandals, complete with mahogany face and toothbrush moustache, hanging on a cross—with a comic-strip balloon above his head showing the rabble of Inayatganj Branch teeming in his thoughts. D'Souza was mad as a hatter as he tore down the poster. But Pramod Bhai, who was responsible for security, began to get a trifle worried. He tried to sound a delicate warning. D'Souza grew still more obstinate. Pramod said: They're not reacting now, Manager Sahib. They've gotten used to suppressing their reactions during two hundred years of Angrezi sarkar. But one day they might just blow a fuse. So D'Souza began directing his evangelical efforts at Pramod instead. The situation was pretty comic to start with. Pramod Bhai was helpless. D'Souza was a diminutive four-feet-seven-inches mite of a man, all conviction and energy, and Pramod was a mild giant of over six feet, and Pramod had to protect D'Souza from molestation and D'Souza was determined to convert him. This went on a while until on Republic Day the inevitable happened. After hoisting the national flag, D'Souza spoke of rights and duties and freedom and sacrifice, then one thing led to another and he began speaking of divinity. God is one. He is not a monkey or an elephant. He does not have four or ten arms. He does not ride rats, owls, bulls, tigers, swans or peacocks. I have gone through your book. First it says: Fight. But without emotion. How can you fight without emotion? You fight with a hymn on your lips, you go to the lions with a song of praise. It says fire cannot burn you, sword cannot cut you, water cannot wet you, wind cannot dry you. I say that is false. I can strike a match and burn you right now. I can cut you with a knife, if I spill this glass of water on your shirt, of course you will get wet and the fan there shall dry you. Verily, verily, I say this to you—here his voice rose in rhetorical authority—he that does not believe in the One True God and in the risen Lord, shall burn in the eternal fire, yea!

There was no stopping the little man's missionary zeal. Pramod Bhai had a tough time rescuing him, throwing the office duree on him, lifting him like a child and rushing him in and telephoning head office. In hospital he was pronounced out of danger. He was calm, determined. Forgiving all those who knew not what they did, and committed to the cause of loving and trying to make them see the light by his unremitting efforts. Pramod Bhai said he almost admired the little man. So inflexible, so fixed in his own unrelenting certainties. While he lay in hospital, Pramod comforted him. Spoke of the Dark Night of the Soul and Christian Suffering. Said: I have a very personal love for Isamasih, Manager Sahib. I understand what He stands for. I think of Him as a radiance of holiness and mercy. Soul-transforming. Like the Buddha— but somehow more human. The Buddha feels a cool presence but more detached. Isamasih feels warm. But for all that I am a confirmed Hindu. But look, you, Manager Sahib, if you must love your neighbour as yourself, you must respect your neighbour's faith as your own, no?

The little Manager Sahib was suddenly infuriated. He resented Pramod Bhai's homily. Are you here to help or are you here to show off your knowledge? he demanded wrathfully. So what happened? D'Souza recovered, was transferred back to Mangalore or Vizag or wherever he came from. Pramod Bhai was suspended, charge-sheeted for failing to ensure D'Souza's safety.

That was the longest Jain had ever spoken and Brian forgot himself.

I don't believe you, men! Brian had snapped. I refuse to believe that your brother was suspended. Over the safety of a mere Christian! That sort of thing doesn't happen in this benighted country.

Jain was composed. You're right, Shepherd Sahib. But those days it did.

Do you know—can you ever imagine how it feels, being a member of a minority community? Brian exploded.

Why, Shepherd Sahib, what's wrong? asked Jain with typical Hindu guile. Did I say anything that offended you? I'm very, very sorry. I was only remembering my Pramod Bhai-Sahib's experience and his manager ...

Was there, even then, a faint note of menace in Jain's voice?

Sitting on the bench in the park, Lynette shuddered. What had been a stray incident then was a gruesome reality now. She couldn't get over Staines's horrific death and what made it still more shocking was those two little mites. She had seen their faces in *India Today* and they haunted her sleep. What monster could do such a thing! A beast in human shape! To burn human beings alive! Innocent kids! (But that was just what the Holy Church did right through the Middle Ages, no doubt those discursive Hindus would say!)

And that poised Australian woman, Staines's wife. Her heart went out to her. How had she made peace with her situation? Lynette had preserved a newspaper cutting: *Staines' Widow Forgives Killer Dara.*

Lynette had started a forgiveness file and she already had three snippets in it. She read them often. Her counsellor at the Institute had suggested this bit of self-therapy. Lynette read through her flimsy scrapbook every other day.

Nov. 19

Gladys Staines, widow of slain Australian missionary, Graham Staines, says she has forgiven Dara Singh, her husband's alleged killer. 'My thirteen-year-old daughter, Esther, asked me as to why people cannot forgive.' Staines is in the Capital to garner support for the proposed forty-bed hospital for leprosy patients in Baripada in Orissa in memory of her late husband and two sons, who were burnt alive in January. To a question about the psychological state of her daughter, Esther, who is studying in Ootacamund, she said she is coping well, 'but, after all we are human beings'. To a query whether she considered India a tolerant society, Gladys said on the majority, yes. 'I have received thousands of letters from people other than Christians who said they were ashamed of what had happened and that it was not Hinduism.' Asked what kept her going, Gladys said the source of her strength is God Himself. 'I usually do not involve myself ... I have left it to God to act. He will deal with people as He deems fit.

The second snippet was: *Has Sonia Pleaded Mercy For Nalini?* Nalini had been one of her husband's killers. The third snippet in Lynette's file read: *Woman Helps Free Lover Who Gave Her Aids—Unexpected New Year Pardon*. Lynette thought of each of the three women by turns as part of her self-discipline. Compared the magnitude of their situations with the ignoble meagreness of her own problem. Sonia Gandhi had urged President K.R. Narayanan to commute the death sentence awarded to Nalini to save her eight-year-old daughter from being orphaned by an act of State. And Janette Pink had appealed that her Cypriot boyfriend be freed from Nicosia Central Prison on behalf of his four motherless children. And Gladys Staines had stated that she felt no animosity towards the people of Orissa.

And now that one thought of it, what had become of Orissa? Lynette had travelled across Orissa in a bus, crossed a small river, which the guide said was named Daya—mercy. She remembered the local guide's odd English:

In Kawlingaw war—ancient time—King Awsoka conquer Kawlingaw, which is ancient name for Orissa.

The guide said Awsoka for Ashoka and Kawlingaw for Kalinga.

Then this river rawn with blawd instead of awter and make King Awsoka reepent. Memsahib know what happin then. King Awsoka, he ask why so much blawdsed among the pippull of the warld. King beecaam Buddhist, forsake war and blawdsed and voilence, eat no non-veg, build monahstrees and stupas. We will now stop for ten minutes break so you can take your photos and aalso fresh yourself. Tea aavailubble in shop there and plenty bushes aall round.

Travelling around Orissa with Brian, she had done Udaigiri, Khandgiri, then various temples to, dear me, phalluses, as their names implied! Then Puri, where they stayed two nights. At night the sea raved in the dark, devoured the beach, went tearing away with a hiss. A thin spray constantly dashed against their windows. But when dawn broke, it had subsided to smooth, grey, unscrolled waves, like brand-new wall calendars. Curling up and springing into foam and light where they met the shore. She had hired another local guide, bought a tourist booklet. She was surprised to learn that

Lord Jaw-gaw-naw-thaw, as the guide pronounced it, was no different from Juggernaut, on whom Lord Macaulay had had lots to say. Lord Maw-kaw-lay on Lord Jaw-gaw-naw-thaw, she thought, amused. They could be two phlegmatic peers in the House of Lords or two Asiatic deities in a chant-filled sanctum. The same Juggernaut, beneath the wheels of whose chariots feverish Hindoo heathens flung themselves to be crushed. And this guidebook said Juggernaut and Krishna were one and the same. All very confusing it had been. In Puri, Juggernaut had a couple of aunts too, one his mother's sister, one his father's. He came to pay them polite annual visits. He even had a garden with a swimming pool in which he sailed in a boat. Even their gods live in huge joint families, was Brian's jocular observation. Aunts and mothers-in-law! Isn't there a Hindoo temple to God's mother-in-law, Lyn? he pulled her leg. Brian never took her curiosity seriously. He would go off on jaunts of his own. Only, there wouldn't be just one mother-in-law, he had said on an afterthought. There'd probably be a million—the number of wives their gods have! No such thing as one-to-one Christian marriage.

Sitting on the bench, three decades later, Lynette clearly heard Brian say that and she felt her head begin to steam with negative thoughts. One-to-one Christian marriage was it, laddie? And that woman there—all the time ... he had the gall to say that! Her breath came short. Too late she realized she was losing her foothold, slipping. She stretched out a hand, gripped the bench, steadied her head, violently flung the thought out and determinedly went back to what she had been thinking.

She still had that guidebook somewhere. You had to allow that some of the stories were rather sweet. There was a temple to Sakshi Gopal. An ebony-glossed image with eyes of gold. The book said it was dedicated to God as Witness. No one would bear witness to a young man's claims that the old man he had nursed in Vrindavan had promised him his daughter's hand in marriage. The entire village panchayat thought he was lying. Because the only witness had been the idol of Krishna in a Vrindavan temple. Go, bring your witness here and we shall believe you, said the elders. The young man, in despair, went all the way to Vrindavan, pleaded before the idol: You alone know the truth. Come with me and tell them. Be my witness. Don't fail me. And Krishna consented. Walk ahead, he assured, I follow. Only do not look back. Do not doubt. Have absolute faith. I shall be there behind you. I shall bear witness to the truth. But how shall I know you're there? asked the young man, still doubtful. You shall hear, from time to time, the sound of my anklet bells, said God. Then you can be sure I am right behind you. They set forth on foot. From the north to the south-east, across fields, rivers, dense jungles, mountain ranges. Every few hundred miles a soft tinkle assured the young man and he said to himself: Ah, I am not alone. The Lord is with me. But, sad to say, the mind of man is fearful. Puri is a sandy area. The Lord's ankles sank into the sand with each step, muting the sound of his anklet bells. Terror awoke in the young man's heart. He has abandoned me. He has left! So alarmed was the young man that he forgot his part of the deal and he turned to check.

Lo! said the guide. What he saw? A pillawr of stone! A statue of Krishnaw. This tempull here built on that very spot. To tell peepull: Do not doubt. I yam there, vitnussing awl. Seeing awl.

That was a cute tale, you had to grant. Some of the stories sent funny reverberations through her mind. She told the guide she liked that story and he, flattered, told her another.

Lord Krishnaw, He everyvunn's friend. He playmate to lonely child, he lawver to voomunn, he ... The guide paused, at a loss, hunting for a word. Then he said: He driver to Awrjunaw's car, teacher to awl. He lawv to joke and play and tease baht he very wise and kind. Wawnce, in the midull of Kurukshetraw battull field, a litull bird come to Krishnaw and say: Lawd, you mighty beings fighting-fighting all around. Big matters, big armies. I, litull bird, so fearfull. My nest is in the midull of the battull field. My litull childun in it. What will happunn to me, Lawd. The Lawd said: Never fear, litull bird. There may be big matters going on and big armies fighting baht your nest shall be safe. So saying, he put a big bell over litull bird's nest. For eighteen days the batull raged. Manny miscreants, manny casualties. Awll the heroes killed or hurt. But the litull bird safe because of Lawd Krishnaw's mercy.

Then, seeing her growing interest in the stories, he told her of the one in which Krishna became a little child to give company to a lonely little boy who had to cross a dense forest and had no one to play with. Finally he took her to see the temple of the manacled Hanuman.

Manacled? You mean handcuffed? Those things policemen put on fellows who're arrested?

He nodded. Sawmtimes evunn God's hands are tied.

But that's blaspheming, she said. We've always been told God is all-powerful.

Wahn momun, said the guide. God's hands are tied because God will naht break his own lahs. God's hands tied by man's kormah.

For one moment Lynette thought he meant that goat-meat dish the bawarchi cooked so well: korma. Then she realized he probably meant that thing they kept harping on: karma.

Lawd Jaw-gaw-naw-thaw, he keep Lawd Honumana imprisawned in this tempull.

Why?

Because awnly Honumana can keep the ocean tied. Honumana wanting to rush back to his master, Lawd Rama. So Lawd Jaw-gaw-naw-thaw bind Honumana's hands and lock him here. So long as Honumana stay here, no cyclone, howsoevahr voilent, has brokunn Jaw-gaw-naw-thaw's tempull. Sahm force holds the ocean back ...

She had studied the small stone structure, intrigued. Behind it, the sea was a blinding fish-scale silver. Years later, just last year, in fact, she recalled that sea, heard the evening news on the TV. Eyewitnesses said the sea roared like a missile just test-fired, trees crashed down and cries of helpless victims rent the air as the port town of Paradip was devastated by the cyclone. It lashed the port town with a gale speed of two hundred and fifty kilometres per hour. A little before noon, water from the Mahanadi river inundated the port area and within two hours the water reached up to four feet. Port employees had to literally drag the women and children into the building. Trees were falling all around and cattle were washed away. Saline water from the sea rushed in at nineteen hours. By then there was no power supply or water. Telephone lines had also snapped. The major rivers in north Orissa wrought havoc in Balasore, Bhadrak, Keonjhar and Jajpur districts as the entire coastal stretch from Balasore to Paradip turned into a vast sheet of water.

Lynette kept track of the newspaper headlines. Relief Teams Battling Against Heavy Odds in Orissa. Gastroenteritis Breaks Out, Government Denies Report. Paradip Prepares for Mass Burial. Gruesome pictures in the press. Decomposed bodies floating in murky ditches. The army and navy teams struggling in the Kendrapada and Jagatsinghpur areas. Earthmovers and dumpers moving stinking corpses to yawning trenches. Hungry hordes looting stranded relief trucks for food. Starving men coming to blows for air-dropped packets. Then she had thought of the Witness God, the Sakshi, who had avenged the murder of Staines and his innocent kids, and how Hanuman had unleashed the waves. And whatever happened to the guide? She hoped his nest was safe—he was a Paradip man. At the end of it all, why was retribution inevitably visited on the heads of other innocents?

But anyway, she hadn't thought of Marcia Gosse for thirty whole minutes. She came to herself. A whiff of raw mangoes in the breeze. Crystals of chipped ice seemed to clink softly in the air. The morning so fragile, the merest disobedience of its laws would smash it to bits. The bluish smoke of distant diesel fumes suspended in summer's haze rose from beyond the circular rim of the park. Thirty minutes of freedom! she thought with some relief. One phone call and I'll be cured. She rose to her feet and picked up her basket.

sixteen

Out of all the persons I interviewed, the one who had actually witnessed the blast was Neelesh Trivedi. When I questioned him I found his responses uneven. He appeared shell-shocked by what seemed almost personal guilt. When he spoke it was in jets of spasmodic revelation. He was torn between relieved thanksgiving at the miracle that had saved his life and remorse at what half his mind regarded as culpable absence at the time of the explosion. He had left Swati Maurya and Kartik Goswamy in the lawns of Sikandar Chowk Park and crossed the busy road to the shopping arcade in a further block.

How long before the disaster occurred? I asked.

Scarcely ten minutes, he said.

Where had he gone?

To an ice-cream booth, he answered, his face rigid.

Was the ice-cream for *them*? I pursued.

Yes, for all three of us.

He was in the act of crossing the road again, balancing three cones of Tuti-fruity ice-cream when a massive detonation like a thousand thunder-bursts split the air. In the dire commotion of the moment his first thought was to save the ice-cream. Then, like a piercing reverberation came the soul-deafening thought: *they* were right where the bang came from, where bolts of smashed brick and metal and branches had crashed and the black smoke was lifting in dense billows up to the sky.

What was the relationship between the three of you? I asked.

We were ... sort of ... tutors to Kartik, he answered. We'd been hired at first to pose as his parents at the admission interviews of some schools. Later we'd all become ... sort of ... friends.

Did the impersonation work? I pursued.

It did but the kid didn't ever make it. We tried several times. This was as weird as it was incredible but it had actually been that way, he said.

We carried fake certificates and all, he added.

Even my fertile imagination can recreate the circumstances with some effort. Let us accompany the three of them to the kid's home for one such bizarre briefing.

Last time even she paid me less than she paid you. This time *toh* I shall protest, Swati Maurya told Neelesh Trivedi in the lift. After all, I did all the talking but she said: Your signature did not appear anywhere but the Papa-person's signature did. His risk is bigger, so ...

They had been summoned urgently by Kartik Goswamy's mother. The admission lists were out. Kartik's name wasn't there. There was another school belonging to the same Mission and it hadn't yet completed its interviews. Maybe Kartik stood a chance there.

The same pair of make-believe Papa–Mama had to go— the boards of both schools had some common members and one never knew ... The same rate of payment as last time, though why she was paying them at all when they had no fruitful results to show ...

The scene in the Goswamy's drawing room was a stormy replay of the last one. A shrill phone conversation with Kartik's father in Dubai, Kartik sitting slumped in an armchair, his feet dangling well above the carpeted floor.

Bhagwan only knows what is the matter with this one! Just won't study! I know Vijoo will qualify in IIT in his first attempt and go off to America or something, but this one will surely be a barbaad sort of fellow! Wasting his parents' hard-earned money. What will people say? I don't know what answer to give when friends like the Guptas and the Srivastavas ask: Has Kartik got admission this time?

Looking at Kartik, Swati felt a pang of compassion. Kartik's involuntary response to the tirade had been to hug a cushion close and put a thumb in his mouth. Swati had an overwhelming impulse to slap the woman silent.

There was another briefing session, a bit of question–answer practice, a bit of counting, some spelling and a severe maternal talking-to. Then they went off to perform in the second act of the peculiar skit they found themselves so bizarrely trapped in.

The interview was a disaster. This time Kartik clammed up completely and only answered once. What is your name? asked the lady principal. Also, he said, so softly that she asked him to repeat.

They waited in the park, as before, for Kartik's mother to finish her shopping round in the Civil Lines market. Neelesh tried being jokey with the subdued kid: Also eh? At the clinic I work in, there's a fellow we call Billy Reuben. Chronic jaundice case. Gets his bilirubin tested every ten days.

Kartik wouldn't respond to these overtures. His terror was pitiful to see.

I wish I could just disappear with this poor kid, thought Swati. What an ordeal. School after school. Rejection after rejection. And that shrill harridan of a mother!

The woman was late as usual. More than an hour. The kid might be hungry or thirsty. What to do?

Neelesh bought him a bottle of mineral water and some churmura off a cart for himself and Swati. Swati got some vanilla ice-cream for the kid. Half an hour went by. Neelesh finished munching the fluffed rice and gram, unrolled the cone of newspaper and said to the kid: Come on. Let's see you try to read this.

Kartik bent low over the sheet, his stubby forefinger underscoring the lines: Car blast kills ele ... ven in Sri ... nagar. Eight c-cops, lens ... man among vic ... tims.

Good! said Neelesh. Read on.

A power ... ful car bomb ex-plo ...

Explosion, prompted Swati.

—in the heat ...

In the heart ... corrected Swati.

... in the heart of ... the cit ... y this after ... afternoon left eleven pee ... people in ... in ...

Including ...

Includ ... ing eight police man ...

Policemen ...

Policemen and a pho ... pho ...

Photojournalist. A photojournalist is a man who takes pictures for newspapers ...

Dead and twenty-eight wownded ...

Woonded. Woonded, corrected Neelesh.

The kid refused to read on and Neelesh strove to draw him out. There see, how nicely you can read. So why did you go dumb in the school just now?

Kartik gave Neelesh a sour look.

Swati took out the *Amar Chitra Katha* comic she had picked up from the footpath magazine stall outside the park. A lucky buy it had been—the mythological story of Kartikeya, the fourth child of Shiva and Parvati.

Here, my little Also-ji—she waved the comic before his expressionless face—the story of your namesake. Let's read it, shall we?

They flopped down in a shady patch of grass beneath the giant laburnum. Neelesh stretched himself out full length, staring into the branches, the copious canary-yellow spate of bloom glutting the sense in a lavish swarm of satiety. The kid sat cross-legged between him and Swati, looking at the pretty, coloured illustrations as Swati read out in Hindi.

Shiva and Parvati once asked their two small sons, Ganesh and Kartikeya, to run a race round the universe. Kartikeya set off laboriously but cunning Ganesh ran round his parents, declaring that they meant the entire universe to him. Shiva was pleased and blessed Ganesh. When poor Kartikeya returned, tired and sore, he learnt that his brother Ganesh had already won the blessing. He was sad and went off to the Himalayas to meditate. Meanwhile, Parvati worried about him because she felt Ganesh had been favoured ...

Here Swati stopped abruptly. The expression in the kid's face frightened her. His eyes were large, unblinking, in their speechless understanding of the situation. She read on hurriedly: Parvati persuaded Shiva to accompany her and together the parents set off in search of Kartikeya. After many wanderings they found him in his lonely mountain cave, thin and pale, practising severe austerities. Look, here he's standing on one foot with his eyes closed.

The kid tried standing on one foot with his eyes closed. Swati laughed, pulled him down.

Parvati begged him to return but he refused ...

The kid looked self-important, pleased.

Then Parvati touched a rock and a jet of clear water burst forth. And Shiva threw his trident into the stream and the water turned to kheer! So now Kartikeya had food and water and the spot came to be known as Kheer Ganga—the river of kheer. In the sattva yuga, when everyone was good and right, real kheer flowed from the rocks. Later, when the world grew sinful, the milk turned to water. Imagine, Kartik, a river made of kheer.

I like ice-cream more, said the kid. And I like this bottle water. He looked from Swati to Neelesh and suddenly the extent of his identification with the story struck them, together with their own place in it. The implication left them confused, startled. It made Neelesh turn gruff and Swati deeply moved.

In the Himalayas that kheer might have tasted just like ice-cream. And your Papa–Mummee might turn up with kheer and water, no?

I like this ice-cream and bottle water, said the kid stubbornly.

Swati gazed at him in silence. Know what I'm thinking? Just a wild idea. I wish we could get away with this kid.

Only it'd be called abduction, Neelesh remarked dryly.

I could buy a typewriter. I could open a coaching institute or a primary school ...

I can step up my blood donation quota to two litres a day, Neelesh mocked her. What would we live on? The Times of India Frauds' Relief Fund?

But though he punctured her crazy imaginings, she noticed that he stepped into the enchanted circle of her impossible dream, a temporary but willing participant.

I never had a child, she spoke up involuntarily.

He propped himself up on an elbow with an abruptness that startled her. You're married? he asked.

I used to be, she answered with such discouraging curtness that he debated with himself whether to ask her anything further. He decided against it.

When the beep of the Santro outside the gates of the park broke into their reveries, they scrambled up in haste. Also clutched Swati's hand so tightly that she felt his dread like an active internal bruise and at that instant she made up her mind. Nothing fantastic or impossible but something practical—that's what it was going to be.

seventeen

Hearing Parul Chopra's account I felt I was something between a Father Confessor and a psychotherapist. It was obvious that she had been through a harrowing trauma and to our mutual discomfort she broke down twice while narrating the events.

She had only later discovered Vani Kabir's motive for visiting her and to her it had seemed an act of the greatest treachery.

The chain of events reproduced below fell in place only after repeated questioning on my part and recurrent distraction and distress on hers. She had no choice, she said, save to confront Vani. Fortunately, there was the visiting card with the phone number.

* * *

Parul's voice had been hysterical on the phone.

So that's why you came, Vani? You sat there, didn't breathe a word. Just sat there, talking of this and that, pretending. How could you? No, don't even try to explain. It's no good. I know what you're going to tell me. Please, for God's sake, Vani ...

It had taken Vani all her professional tact and counselling experience to calm Parul down. We can't discuss this on the phone. I'll come over. I'll be there in an hour and we'll get this mess straightened out. Just hang on.

Parul's face was blotched with tears. She was still in her house gown, her hair draggled. The table was littered with local newspapers. She was sharp with the maid and sent her off to make tea.

You knew! You knew all the time! And you didn't tell me anything! Parul accused Vani. She snatched up a sheet of the *Hindustan Times*. Will you please tell me now what this is all about? Exactly what is your wretched activist group hounding my husband for? You can't ... you can't expect me to believe this. This says it's a case of sexual harassment at the workplace. This other paper has the impertinence to use the word 'molestation'. It's all so vague. What is Manoj supposed to have done? And who is this female? I've never even heard her name!

Vani took one look at Parul's working face, her shrill eyes and trembling lips and she grasped that the situation was going to be an impossible one.

Calm down. Just relax. Sit down, will you, and let me explain. Now pull yourself together. Come on now, compose yourself.

It all sounded so trite, fake, in the face of this poor wife's distress.

It says it happened in a car! Parul was beside herself with frenzy. What happened? What did Manoj do?

Vani steadied her, made her sit on the sofa. Parul hid her face in her hands.

It's all lies! I won't believe it! she sobbed. And he isn't even here. He's in Mumbai. On tour. The poor fellow doesn't even know this filthy mud-slinging's going on.

Vani didn't tell Parul that she and other members of Shakti had met Manoj three days back, that Manoj had been strategically whisked away to a secret destination in Mumbai by special orders from his company's chairman.

When did you last speak to him?

He hasn't rung up in the last two days. But he will today—definitely. What's funny is that even Katya didn't seem to know Manoj was in Mumbai. He didn't go to her place or ring her up!

There was a hysterical sob in Parul's voice.

Who is this Neeta Surendran that your group is supporting?

Look, can you listen calmly for a moment?

A subdued assent from Parul.

This is the woman who lodged the complaint. Members of Shakti went over to the office and demonstrated.

Yes, I've just read all about it—in this rag! You made a big tamasha. With slogans and banners and the press clicking away! Parul was having trouble speaking. You must've been there too! She looked Vani straight in the eye.

Vani made no reply.

And that day you came to get my side of it. That means much before you staged that demonstration in Manoj's office, the matter had started.

Vani kept silent. She knew she would now not have the heart to tell Parul exactly what had transpired. That she had met Neeta Surendran thrice. Twice at the Shakti office, once later. That Neeta Surendran was twenty-five, pert and very pretty, the office beauty, and that she had alleged that her immediate boss, Manoj Chopra, who was technical and marketing manager at Wycliffe's Electro Conglomerates, had been sending her first sentimental, then lewd messages by email, writing suggestive notes to her, putting porn magazines in her desk drawer and had finally molested her while the two were on an inspection tour. 'Molested'—a word suggestive and inexact enough, but containing a dangerous potential for extravagant inference. She felt sorry for this poor, ageing wife, struggling with the multiple and ever more horrendous and fanciful connotations of that translucent word. She knew she wouldn't disclose to

Parul how Surendran came fuming to Shakti only after the police refused to lodge her FIR under some mysterious pressure. Shakti had tried hard to procure a magistrate's order to the police to lodge the FIR but couldn't because a Sunday intervened. Surendran had contacted them again early on Monday morning, stating that an out-of-court mediation had resolved the issue, that the chairman of Wycliffe's had negotiated from the Delhi office and that she had been transferred with immediate effect to Coimbatore. Manoj too was missing and all that had been gained from the entire exercise was an outcry in the press and some clippings and photos for Shakti's files. She had been severe with Surendran for her volte-face, for not standing by her charges, but obviously considerations of career advancement had outweighed all others in Surendran's priorities. Vani hadn't wanted the case hushed up. She had thought of making of it a precedent issue and had called on Parul the last time in the course of her investigations. But Parul's complete obliviousness of the sordid matter and then Surendran's withdrawal of charges had confounded the whole situation.

And now here was Parul on the brink. Vani tactfully removed the newspapers from the table and surprised herself in the act of mouthing the very idea she so much scorned: It was nothing much. Just forget about it now.

Nothing much! Parul jerked upright. Character assassination of a decent family man, mental trauma to his family, and you say it's nothing much. Some slut goes squealing to you and you frustrated feminists, who want nothing better than to wreck normal homes and score a point against the male sex, you go around shrieking blue murder and disgracing innocent people!

Vani heard her out quietly.

Let me just get through to Manoj. Let me just get the facts and then wait and see. I swear I'll bring a defamation suit against the lot of you. Defamation and mental torture. Just wait. I'll sue your pack of perverted bitches and I'll sue all these newspapers here ... and I'll sue this bitch, this Surendran! Tell me—Parul's eyes were feverish—tell me ... you didn't meet that bitch. No? You couldn't have! Did you meet her? Did you?

She gripped Vani's arms. Her hands were hot, tears rolling down her face, splashing down her lined neck.

No, said Vani, very low. She could not meet Parul's eyes. Parul's hot hands fell away. She took a deep breath, relieved.

I knew it, she said. I knew it's all a mix-up. Let me just get through to Manoj and it'll all be cleared up. A fresh thought seized her face. When I do sue your group and these papers, can I count on you? Can I count on you to stand up as a witness and declare how irresponsible you've all been?

Her eyes seared Vani's face. Vani looked at her, vexed. She saw a woman half crazed with grief, her defences down, her expensive patina of artificially sustained good looks nakedly crumbled. Utterly useless and without the grit of the poor and devoid of the socially careful endurance of the middle class. Other than keep a good house and supervise a classy kitchen, other than write poetry and passively bring up problem-free achiever kids, unfit for struggle and unfit for flight. All she could fight for was her present protective delusions. She found her as pitiful as any woman suppliant who came, wrecked and psychologically maimed and seeking redress at Shakti. In some ways she was much more to be pitied than Surendran who had made the charges against Manoj.

Can I count on you? Parul's voice had sunk into a heart-wounded hoarseness.

Speechlessly Vani nodded.

She went back that day, her head tight with stress.

She telephoned Parul early next morning to ask how she was feeling. Parul sounded faint, ill. She had kept awake all night, dialling and dialling till her fingers ached. Trying to get through to Manoj in Mumbai. Without any luck.

Take a Valium or a Calmpose and try to get some rest, suggested Vani.

Two hours later Parul rang back. She had tracked Manoj down at a colleague's. She sounded more composed this time, quite reassured.

He says it's all right. It's all an office conspiracy—this girl hadn't got promoted and this is her way of hitting back. He says he'll be away for some time more but I mustn't pay any attention to this hoo-ha—it'll die down soon. But I'm not going to let this die down. Vani, are you there?

Yes.

I'm going to file this defamation suit. And you're going to help me. Vani, why don't you say something for god's sake?

I'm right here.

Good. And Vani ... sounds funny saying it, but even though we haven't been in touch all these years, I wanted to tell you ... it feels good to know that ... that you're right there and you'll back me up.

If that wasn't what a group like Shakti was meant for, to foster just that shade of feeling in distressed women, what was it for? thought Vani wryly. Only Shakti hadn't handled anything quite so ambiguous so far. Just my luck!

She hoped the storm would blow over, that Parul would be overcome by upper-class lethargy or would find some other distraction to dilute her determination to pursue the case. She hoped Manoj, when he heard and no doubt for reasons of his own, would discourage the scheme.

It was Vani who had to doze herself on a Valium that night, hoping for sleep. Not a chance. Early next morning, Parul turned up at Vani's flat. She had come in a taxi and had stopped half-a-dozen times and asked the way. She stood, drenched in the rain, looking just awful, with a charged obduracy sparking in her crazed eyes. Vani felt cornered.

Parul moved and sat with a strange, stiff deliberation. She spoke in the same stilted mode.

I spent the night rummaging in Manoj's cupboard, she announced in a strange voice. He keeps it locked—I had to get someone to break the padlock. Funny things I found in it. Girlie magazines, copies of *Playboy* and *Fantasy*, postcards. Even a ... a directory of sorts. The oddest thing. Ads put out for threesomes, foursomes, groups. I don't know why he stores these things. And Vani. I checked our bank papers and found an FDR missing. I'll have to ask Manoj where he's misplaced it. I don't know why I'm telling you these things ... I just need to tell someone.

She looked searchingly into Vani's face.

Tell me what she looked like—that female.

Vani spoke in an uneven voice: I thought you and I agreed that I hadn't met her.

Parul bit her lip. No, of course you haven't, she said, her jaw set.

And a line came into Vani's head, a curious travesty of one of Miss Dodson's sentences. The willing suspension of disbelief that constitutes marital faith. She felt intense pity for this woman. Are you trying to do a Hillary Clinton, my dear? she wanted to ask her. And after you've out-shouted the papers and out-shouted your doubts, how will you confront that man? With a fierce stillness that will probably last you all your days. Unless you crack up and begin babbling. Or will you learn not to care?

But can I honestly tell her: leave him. Walk out. Yes, she can go and live with her daughter and maybe pick up a professional degree. But will that guarantee a job for her with so much unemployment around and she such a hothouse product.

Have you thought of moving in with your daughter? she suggested tentatively.

Who's to look after my son then? asked Parul in a subdued voice, before she realized that she had betrayed more of her mind than she cared to.

Can't he move in with you? pursued Vani.

And despite herself Parul answered: He's just got admission in a good college here. Can't be disturbed. Too late for a hostel. It's just not feasible at the moment.

Will it ever be feasible? asked Vani.

Parul's face set in a stubborn line. First this defamation suit that I'm going to file. I'll prove Manoj is innocent. See if I don't.

_____

eighteen

After Vakil Mahendra Chandra's death in the blast and shortly after the riots, Osman Bhai's family moved to another apartment in distant Rasoolabagh. Vakilin told me she had tried to dissuade them.

I asked them: Why are you doing this? They gave me a whole lot of reasons. This house is getting too small for us. There's too little closet space. Too many stairs to climb. Water problem. But I knew they had bought the flat in Rasoolabagh because it was situated in a Muslim pocket of the city. And they knew that I knew. Osman Bhai even said: Besides, Bhabhi Sahib, *he* isn't here any more. We both remembered that amazing secret Vakil Sahib had thoughtlessly let out that evening the Pakistani guests came though neither of us said anything. From Rasoolabagh they went off elsewhere, who knows where, though it is rumoured that they are in Canada now. Personally, she swore, both she and her son Manik missed their little tiffs and if *he* were alive he'd never have let Osman go, that close they were.

But let me go into certain background details.

When Osman Bhai proposed bringing his visiting Pakistani cousins for a Hinduana dinner, Vakil Sahib had readily agreed. He enjoyed playing host and he conferred seriously with Osman Bhai about the items he desired to be served. Things authentic and ancient and improved by centuries of preservation, as he told Osman Bhai. Osman Bhai did think Vakil Sahib overdid this authentic and ancient and centuries business a bit. As though he had stored things in some state of cultural refrigeration for ages. But he didn't say so. Kachowries, raita, stuffed ladies' fingers, spiced jackfruit gravy, karhi (did Osman Bhai think two curd preparations amiss? No? Good), bottle gourd koftas (again two gram-flour dishes? No problem? Fine), spinach and cottage cheese, pea pulao (the peas were off-season though—no succulence in them at this time of the year).

Vakilin, who had her ear suspiciously trained on her husband's phone conversations lately, was mystified. Did he discuss only food with these shameless young women? Or was this a code for some advanced form of promiscuity? Her first reaction to Vakil Sahib's timorous announcement of the party was ire. He had expected that, of course. Pakistanis? she snorted. I long ago realized the Chinese are far better enemies than those Pakistanis, she declaimed. The Chini are so tolerant and adapting. There's a Chinese temple in Calcutta where the Chinese worship our very own Kali and serve chow mien as prasad. But Muslims?

Why, Nirmalaji, Muslim women in Bengal wear sindoor in the parting of their hair and conch-shell bangles too.

She ignored his interruption. Besides, I can't help remembering that other party of yours seventeen, no, eighteen years back. These goodwill parties of yours have a way of ending in disaster.

He groaned. He had once invited the class four staff of the district court for a Republic Day feast and he shuddered to recall what had happened. The barber class, weaver class, washerman class had refused to sit down and eat with the tanner class, the sweeper class and the swineherd class. They had had to eat in shifts. As for the stray Brahmin or Thakur—they politely declined even a drink of water. But that was years back, he protested. Hadn't he proved he was ahead of his time?

His spouse was rancorous. She had a special dislike for Osman Bhai. Osman Bhai lived in the apartment just above theirs and Manik, when he was little, spent hours in their house. One day he came back, thrilled. There's whale meat in Afzal's fridge! he cried. I saw it!

Vakilin was frantic. I hope you didn't try it?

I wanted to but they said it wasn't for me.

Wanted to, eh? (*Slap slap*.) Must be beef. Listen, you saliva-drooling starveling, you! You're not to touch any meat in their house—shark, whale, dolphin, bat or crocodile!

The two families had a common history of constant sugar-borrowing, fabric-comparing, combined shopping, doctor-summoning, medical advising, food-exchanging. But a little hillock of silent grievances had piled up too. One Bakhreid day, six-year-old Afzal took five-year-old Manik up to watch the sacrifice. They had gathered leaves for the little goat the previous day, and fresh grass from Sikandar Chowk Park, and had fed the goat with shrill whoops of delight. Manik came down, white and ill, and vomited all over the terrace. Afzal leant over his balcony, crowing: What, Mian, can't see a bit of blood? What'll you ever do in life with such a feeble heart and liver? That wasn't a child speaking, Vakilin swore. He was repeating grown-up talk, he was. That's the way they really feel about us!

Oh, go along with you, Nirmalaji! cried Vakil Sahib, exasperated.

But Vakilin consoled her son: Don't let that little butcher scare you, beta. When he was four years old his little noonoo had its tip chopped off—they do that, you know. And he howled and shrieked fit to bring down the ceiling. He thought the whole thing had been chopped off and he cried: Offer *dua*, offer *dua* for me, Auntie, that it grows again! That's your brave Afzal for you. Next time he does his bold talk, tell him I told you all about this.

And Vakilin had always had a bee in her bonnet about Afzal's mother. When they met in the common staircase, she greeted her affectionately as Sarvarji and Sarvar responded with equal warmth. A fragile, pretty woman, fading and soft, with graceful manners and polished speech, Sarvar seemed altogether too finely finished a specimen to be entirely real. Until, one day, Vakilin recalled, the mask had slipped when Limca, Manik's dog, had jumped on her in the landing and left mud on her kurta. Then had emerged a violently vituperating virago who had damned the dog and its masters in an astonishing tirade that had shocked and discomfited the entire building and left unforgettable reverberations in Vakilin's tenacious memory. The years had not erased some of the words, particularly the ones about barbarous and uncouth people's filthy curs that defiled the purity of one's namaz.

Then there was the crisis in the biology lab. Such neat, intricate diagrams my Manik used to draw. But he had to abandon biology because of that Afzal. Ruined his entire career and he did so badly with the physics–chemistry–maths combination. Might have been a doctor today. In school, Afzal teased Manik without mercy, laughing: Two ways of performing dissection, Mian. Jhatka and halaal. Manik blanched at the sight of the wincing frog, still a little conscious. And Afzal went on: One quick blow—that's jhatka. And a slow, measured sawing—that's halaal. Come on, let's give you a bit of training. Needs centuries of practice, Mian.

Manik had abandoned biology. Afzal had christened him Menaka.

Now Manik was in his final year with physics and Afzal had switched to history.

Recently there had been another spot of bother between the two of them. Manik was walking back from the university, Afzal cycling slowly alongside. The Elgin Bridge over the Ganga was jammed with traffic. Afzal carried a project file and was in a mood for banter.

What's that you've got? asked Manik.

Project file, informed Afzal.

What're you working on?

Afzal grinned. I thought of working on the fourth battle of Panipat and the victory of the new Ghaznavi from Afghanistan.

A time bomb began ticking in Manik's head. Your Pajama bin Laden? he mocked.

Afzal laughed. Good one. No, I'm actually working on Mughal mosque architecture. But how're you doing, Daktar Sahib? How's the physics coming along? Oh, cheer up, yaar. All is not lost just because frog-cutting scared you off. You can always practise alternative medicine—unani, ayurved, homeopathy or one of those abracadabrical voodoo things.

He had touched a raw nerve. Manik was touchy about his missed opportunities. Suddenly the time bomb detonated. He snatched away Afzal's project file, tore it in two and flung it into the river. The Ganga was swollen after the rains, flowing much too fast. Manik began to laugh like a madman, a strange light sparking in his eye.

What did you do that for? cried Afzal.

That was a jhatka, Mian, Manik mimicked him. One quick stroke.

The traffic had thinned. Manik sped down the bridge, an awesome inner fission in his head. Afzal stood propped against his bike, simmering, his eyes bloodshot.

Osman Bhai and Vakil Sahib were disturbed, tried to patch up the rents. You did wrong, Vakil Sahib scolded his son.

Such an old friend. Fifty years our families have been neighbours in this building. You didn't stop to think how he'd feel? Utterly insensitive you proved yourself, hazrat.

Did he ever stop to think how I felt? Centuries of halaal, sneered Manik to his father, lead to a few, quick jhatkas.

Where is that written? asked Vakil Sahib, wrathful.

In tomorrow's history books, retorted Manik.

Authored by whom?

Manik made no reply. He sat on the floor, patiently de-ticking Limca, his dog, plucking the ticks out with a pair of tweezers, dropping them into a bowl of blue kerosene oil.

What are you doing?

Manik's teeth flashed. Ethnic cleansing, he answered.

What?

Sure. I've exterminated whole colonies. Papa ticks, mama ticks, baby ticks, baba ticks. Ugh! No, seriously. Took me just half an hour. No tick has got a face. All die.

What a putrid thing!

I'm not enjoying this. I do it without hatred. I've got to do it. No running away from this situation. It's nature's way. Fight without emotion. Do what must be done. That's the Gita, no?

The boy looked dangerously volatile. Spoke too fast, too excitedly.

When you swallow antibiotics to destroy your viruses, aren't you practising extermination? When you spray your room with HIT to kill mosquitoes? When you fill the air with All-Out fumes? What're you doing? Turning your room into a gas chamber.

Vakil Sahib experienced a sinister dread at his son's wrong-headed rhetoric.

What sort of talk is this? he shouted, resorting to high-decibel tactics. Your tongue's grown too long for your head, hazrat! And you there! he turned to his wife. No more nonsense from you about this loafer's lost daktaree line. It was his own pussyfooting squeamishness that made him abandon biology!

He was a soft-hearted lad who couldn't bear to hurt a fly, protested Vakilin with asperity.

Vakil Sahib decided to use all the latent court-room potential packed in his vocal cords: THEN WHERE'S HIS TENDER HEART GONE NOW? AND HOW COME HIS THOUGHTS HAVE RUN AMUCK?

No reluctant witness could ever stand up to that stentorian voice. No wife or son could defy it. Nothing like a bit of good old-fashioned chauvinism, he used to think, in moments of domestic wrangling. It worked when nothing would.

The party for the Pakistani guests was planned with painstaking care.

The guests, when they came, were the soul of courtesy. Handsome, soft-spoken men; breathtakingly lovely, bejewelled women. Perfectly attired, murmurously gentle in their greetings. Their speech was music to Vakil Sahib's ear, their grace and elegance the wonder of Vakil Sahib's heart. Vibrations of a fuller, finer, unfragmented day filled the room. For when Vakil Sahib longed to hear the mellifluous glide of Urdu, he tuned in to Pakistan TV. Now, magically, here in his room, a hollow seemed filled, an absence reoccupied.

It took a few minutes to break the ice. Which Osman Bhai tried to do with characteristic buffoonery: If I were you, Vakil Sahib, I'd be wary of touching that box of Karachi halwa Jamal Bhai has brought for you. Handle it with care, I beg you. No knowing what may be hidden in it. We might all go up in smoke, ha, ha!

Vakil Sahib answered with a gallant Urdu couplet of his own composition:

T'would be heaven to be done to ashes, beloved,
If lost love returning be the fire which lit.

The guests were charmed. Smiles broke out. Murmurs of suave appreciation. It was smooth sailing after that.

What a beautiful fabric! exclaimed Vakilin.

Japanese crêpe, smiled the lovely lady.

In the course of the next hour Vakilin enviously gathered that the women used German hairwash and French perfume, that the bags they carried were Italian and the cosmetics which they liberally plastered on their faces were American. There was a small bottle of perfume for her too. Arré, you can't get such nice things here. They cost the earth, she said sorrowfully.

No, now you can get all this phoren stuff, Bhabhi Sahib, broke in Osman Bhai. That grocer of ours tried to sell me a foreign-brand bag of flour! I lost my temper and shouted: A vilayati company selling us aata now at three times the cost! *Lahaul vila Quvvat!* What bewakoofs run this country! When they aren't scoundrels, they're numbskulls, this sarkar of ours!

The guests ate and praised. Vakil Sahib's only anxiety was the rascal Nankoo's disappearance again. He had been sent to Nathu halwai's shop to fetch two kilos of kalakand and he had been away a whole hour.

Wah, Bhabhi sahib! applauded Osman Bhai. For a meal as delicious as this, I'm sure our friendly neighbours won't mind giving up all claims to Kashmir!

Oh, come on, Osman Bhai Sahib, what a slick-tongued tease you are, *kasam se*. Vakilin smiled broadly. We believe in looking after our guests. Why, in seventy-one, after the Bangladesh confusion when so many of your men were prisoners of war here, they were fed mutton every day ...

And once, an old Pathan came across the border from Pakistan to meet General Manekshaw much after seventy-one. Manik, who hadn't spoken all this while, suddenly found his voice: He came up to Sam Manekshaw and laid his turban on his feet and said, Huzoor, my three sons were all prisoners of war in India. So well looked after they were. Even provided Korans in jail. Allah bless and preserve you, sir.

Something had changed in the air. The smiles had become false, the expressions had set. And when Vakilin set little bowls of kheer on the table and Vakil Sahib said: A five-thousand-year-old dessert, popular even in the Indus Valley days, one of the young men said politely: That was in Larkana, no? In Pakistan?

And when Vakil Sahib said: Actually it ought to be an Aryan recipe—since it's a milk-based preparation, the same young man said smoothly: But the Aryans came from Iran, no?

Thinking back to that party later, Vakil Sahib squarely blamed the Mahabharata serial on TV that evening. As luck would have it, the episode screened was the disrobing of Draupadi. Draupadi, spitting brimstone and fire, reproaching, challenging, sneering, appealing, weeping tempestuously, twirled in a vortex of unreeling silk, her sari uncoiling round her spindling form, tugged by Dushasana's brawny arms. The Pandavas sat, shamefaced, the elders hung their heads, the Kauravas licked their chops and away, in the top right corner of the screen, stood smiling Krishna, holding up his index finger from which a cascade of silk ceaselessly spun out, to keep Draupadi's frame eternally draped. The guests were shaken, repelled.

All this in a holy book! their faces said. A woman's purdah shamelessly removed, with the consent of all those emasculated Hindu men!

Vakil Sahib felt he had some explaining to do. These tales aren't meant literally, he said. They're all symbolic. This one means: Lord Krishna shall veil the unveiled, confer purdah on the disrobed and honour on the dishonoured if one only appeals for His help.

But look, her long black hair, so brazenly exposed! Dragged publicly by that man! the lovely lady shuddered. And Vakilin was thinking to herself: As for disrobing, forgive me, I shouldn't be thinking such awful thoughts, but Mrs Sachdeva, my old friend who came over from out there, has those terrible memories of our women paraded naked in the streets of Lahore during those troubles.

The pressure of unspoken things weighed heavy in the air and the strain was felt by everyone. Someone tried to change the subject.

How do you get this just-right flavour in your kachowries? the younger lady asked.

I'll tell you how, Osman Bhai pre-empted Vakilin. The urad dal has to be soaked overnight and then ground rough. You grind together ginger, cardamoms, big and small, cinnamon, pepper, a pinch of red chilli. Also a good bit of aniseed. Fry the lot together until it's brown. Stuff the kachowries and do the final fry. Remember, the flour's got to be kneaded soft, very soft ...

Wah, Osman mian! exclaimed the Pakistani cousin. When did you learn all this?

Osman Bhai looked suddenly uncomfortable but Vakil Sahib gave vent to a loud guffaw.

In forty-seven, muhtarma, he answered. When the rest of the family was moving westwards from Aligarh, our Osman Bhai's father, Farzan Mian, all alone, was travelling eastwards with my father, Sailesh Chandra-ji. Great friends and roommates at Amritsar. Ah, you should have seen him then, my father used to laugh when they were both very old. Beardless, head tonsured and a thick tuft knotted at the end, even a sacred thread. For costume just a dhoti and a shoulder-cloth. That's how Farzan Mian accompanied my father through the rampage between Mathura and Kanpur. Disguised as his pious Brahmin cook! My father even taught him some recipes and you should have heard him hold forth on Hinduana cookery all through the train journey. If you don't believe me, ask Osman Bhai here. That's how our Osman Bhai knows all about karela kalonji and kathal masaledar. Farzan Mian owed his life to Hinduana food or Osman might never have been born.

Too late did Vakil Sahib realize that a gaffe had been committed, a forbidden secret divulged, something that Osman Bhai hadn't told anyone. In the stark silence that followed he was aware of Sarvar's electric-shaft glance at Osman Bhai and strove hard to rescue the evening by diverting attention to Nankoo's disappearance. Osman Bhai actively helped him, narrating Nankoo's traffic policeman effort. By the time the elephant entered the scene, the comic relief was tremendous, all the guests laughing louder than necessary, the hosts repeating every funny detail, squeezing maximum comedy from its resources. Then Vakil Sahib told his guests all about Nathu halwai, his old client. Charged with murder some years back, though to hear his sweet voice, syrupy golden in its unction, who'd believe it? But there it was. Vakil Sahib's impassioned argument had got him off and Nathu's gratitude had outlasted the passage of years.

He sends me a little something from his mithai shop. Every day without fail for fourteen years. I thought you'd enjoy kalakand and gulab jamun and a glass of milk badam to wash it down.

The guests protested that they couldn't, just couldn't manage a morsel more but Vakil Sahib was adamant. You can walk it off, Jamal Bhai, he insisted. Osman Bhai and I haven't missed our morning forty steps together for fifteen years now.

No, not a single morning.

Except when one of us was out of town.

And the time when I was operated for you-know-what.

Vakil Sahib and Osman Bhai exchanged meaningful glances and Vakil Sahib smirked. The guests looked on. Nankoo's timely return relieved Vakil Sahib's tension though Vakilin took one shrewd look at the kalakands and demanded: Call that two kilos, you wretch? She called her husband in and whispered her suspicions so long and with such intensity that the guests began wondering. Gulab jamun, melting soft in rich, perfumed syrup, saved the day and by the time the last spoonful had been swallowed and exclaimed over, Vakil Sahib had begun holding forth: Jehangir gave us kulfi, though the correct pronunciation is kufli, I believe, and Akbar, did you know, drank only Ganga water.

nineteen

In his shady, high-ceilinged room, Professor Mathur brooded on historical truth and media truth, provisional truth and perennial truth. And most of all on the independent truth of that dispensable little insect, the individual, who directly experienced history but left its pages unsigned, namelessly slipping away through the holes in history's honeycomb.

Apart from examinerships and his pension and the postal order from Britain, he also took on English tuitions. Teaching English was a hobby. He belonged to a generation for which range had been given primacy over specialist constriction. There were more takers for spoken and written English than one might expect, given the anti-colonial spleen in the air. And yet, he found the language slipping out of control, like an untameable colt or calf capering at liberty in the vast terrain of its adopted land.

The grocer, the vegetable hawker, the barber, all, all, have patiently corrected my English from time to time, Professor Mathur used to lament mock tragically. Give me a cake of Pears Soap, I say. And the grocer says: Cake? We have Britannia, plum and plain, but what is this you said, Mathur Sahib? Pears Soap, I repeat. He attends carefully, then utters an inspired cry: Oh, Peers! You mean Peers! Of course we have Peers! I ask for Oh-de-cologne and he gently admonishes: You-de-cologne, Mathur Sahib, you-de-cologne. I go to the Grand Prix Hair Cutting Saloon and refer to it as the Gran-Pree and

the barber says: Yes, this is the Grand Pricks Saloon, welcome.
Okay, I submit, I accept defeat, I stand corrected. By now
I've come to believe at times that I know no English. Where are
Afzal and Danish?

They having break fast, informed Munna.

The professor was mystified. Breakfast at six in the evening?

They breaking roza fast, clarified Munna gravely.

Ah! breathed the professor. But breakfast is always in the
morning.

Is there a boundation? asked Munna.

The professor sighed. First of all, there's no such word as
'boundation'. You boys are overly fond of this word.

Munna placed his essay on the table between himself and
the professor. The essay was entitled: *My Struggle with the
English Language* and Professor Mathur read it with an
expressionless countenance.

*In my Primary schooling when I started first the study
of English I was not knowing that in future I would
have to fight with English and in that combat my victory
would never come.*

*I started my book of English with 'A' for 'Apple', 'B'
for 'Book', 'C' for 'Cat'. Gradually the train of English
reached on a platform of short poems such as 'Baba,
Baba, Black Ship' and 'Twinkle, Twinkle little star', and
short stories like 'lion and Rat' and 'Rabbit and tortoise'.*

*Till my fifth standard I had to do very few things
in English—rembring some important meanings to
remembering question answer of the lessons which had
already been taught by teachers. When my study level
went upwards I had to increase the standard of
remembering. I used to remember like a parrot very
common essays—for instance 'Mahatma Gandhi', 'the
Cow', 'the postman', 'Diwali' et cetra, and 'An*

Application to Principal for Leave'. It happened till eightth standard and I was proud of my English. I was thinking as if I were an Oxford return who knows each and every aspect of English—and for my tipe of people there is a saying in English: a figure among ciphers.

Professor Mathur looked up from the exercise book, regarded Munna quizzically.

About the parrot, there's something I must read out to you, my lad, he said. He fetched the book from his revolving bookcase.

Ah, here we are. This is a character named Sam Weller saying to his employer, Mr Pickwick: 'vich I call addin' insult to injury, as the parrot said ven they not only took him from his native land, but made him talk the English langwidge arterwards.'

He mimicked Sam Weller's cockney to near perfection and Munna was puzzled. Isn't this Weller person an angrez? An angrez distorting angrezi?

Why not? There're illiterates everywhere, lad. And stupid literates too.

So what's wrong with my English? Munna looked peeved. These English can twist up their own language and still it remains literature but if I twist it up I'm failed! Why this boundation on me?

The professor had no answer so he resumed his reading of the essay.

Being an assistant in bank, my father used to press me to study English and maths more and more because he was considering me an engineer of twenty-first century. But still I was ill-worthy son of good father. The more he said me to study English the more I started to run far from English. I was thinking that English was very tough and I was seeking a way to get ride of it. English was a wire of 440 volts and untouchable for me. Whenever my father asked me anything of English I started equivocation and in some hard circumstances my father used his palms on my cheeks. What I should have done that time? Like a poor creature I started to weep or cursed English. My father used to preach me: See, if you want to become anything in your life, you must know English, otherwise you shall clean the utensils in road side hotels, understand. I used to listen but after some time all the sayings vanished from my mind. When I became a student of high school my syllabus and standard of teaching English both prolonged but I didn't. I was remain still in my old track. Now I write essays on 'The Wonder of Science' and application to the principal replaced by 'Letter to Friend'. I thought if there voices, genders, participles, gerunds, verbs, let them be there and why I should take any tension for tenses? Now I am in my first year I am still facing the giant of English but I have a hard-on intention this time. I will break the mountain and will clear my forepath and as poet Browning says in poem 'Prospiss'—the power of the night, the press of the storm, the post of the foe; where he stand, the Arch Fiend in a visible form, yet the strong man must go.

The essay ended with a triumphant flourish and Professor Mathur slowly turned back the sheets and surveyed the pages, now prettily patterned with red rings, inserted punctuation marks, crosses and corrected lines. Munna searched his teacher's face anxiously. But the professor said nothing, just kept his eyes upon the sheets with an abstracted air.

When he began to speak, it had nothing to do with Munna's essay. He began describing his last visit to Scotland where his younger son lived. He described well. In a combination language—Hindi, Urdu, English—he described the gently moulded hills, green and brown and blue-grey in patches, with the mist floating across their crests in a big, fleecy fume. The brilliant green meadows, lochs full of swans and intricate shadows, the water deep-green or silver. Cities of stone in many modulations of grey from chalk to slate to dove to charcoal. And the palest biscuit or faded camel-brown. Erected in large-hewn rectangular blocks, the same sort of stone the British used in their Indian constructions. And the perennial mist smoking about the tops of the ranges.

I like museums and graveyards, boy, and I usually carry a notebook. In England and Scotland I like studying and picking up Indian traces. I like studying the way histories interlock. Wait, let me show you some of the little things I've taken down.

He fetched a notebook, turned its ruled pages.

In a museum in Stirling castle I came across a model of the Lucknow Residency being recaptured by British soldiers under Colin Campbell. And a sepoy flag, captured by a Highlander in Delhi. In Edinburgh castle I saw the Silver Seringapatam medal of 1799. Struck to commemorate the defeat of Tipu Sultan— in gold, silver, gilt, bronze and tin. Awarded according to rank, the silver ones being for captains and subalterns. The medal showed a lion crushing a tiger beneath it under a waving flag. I remember feeling a strange hollowness in the pit of my stomach. In other war museums I came across other tattered flags, Indian flags, mounted and preserved—Holkar's, Scindhia's. Then, in England, in a Kentish city I came across memorial words on the walls of a cathedral. Let me just read some of them out to you. Here's one about soldiers who died 'whilst serving in Afghanistan, between the years 1838 and 1842, either from the fatigues of service or in action with the enemy ...' followed by the names of twelve sergeants, eleven corporals, three buglers and two hundred and sixty-four privates. There were other Indian battlefields mentioned on the walls of that cathedral—Sobraon, Aliwal, the Sutlej, Ferozeshuhur, Punniar, Cabul, Jalalabad. Hear this one: 'Sobraon, the Crowning Victory of the British arms in India. In sacred memory of James Burnett. In him the rigid discipline of the officer was so tempered by the gentleness of his disposition as to make military obedience a service of affection.' I read of the despatch of the 'enemy', then with disquiet I realized the enemy was my own people. But I loved the sonority of that language, its solemn roll and graceful ceremony. Ah, here's an account of the march to Chitral. Chitral was a small state occupying a mountain valley in what is now the far north of Pakistan close to the border with Afghanistan. The march to Chitral met some opposition from the forces of Jandul along the way, but the main obstacle was physical. A large part of the route, which crossed three large rivers and four mountain ranges, was unmapped and proper roads had to be made to take the enormous train of thirty thousand, six hundred and sixty-nine pack animals. The journey took one-and-a-half months. The East Kent Regiment, who called themselves the Buffs, with a company of the Seaforth Highlanders, were the only British troops to cross the ten-thousand-foot, snow-covered pass into Chitral. The garrison, which had already been relieved by an earlier force, was resupplied and the flag flown to impress any other possible enemies. Again that word, mark.

He turned some pages, looking for something more to interest his pupil. He found a poem, written by Sir Francis Hastings Doyle and titled 'The Private of the Buffs'.

This poem is written in honour of a young boy, who might indeed have been your age. His name was John Moyse. Professor Mathur observed Munna's intent face, his eyes fixed upon his own. He began reading:

Last night among his fellow roughs
He jested, quaffed and swore;
A drunken private of the Buffs
Who never look'd before.

Today beneath the foeman's frown
He stands in Elgin's place
Ambassador from Britain's crown
And type of all her face.

Poor, reckless, rude, low-born, untaught,
Bewilder'd and alone,
A heart, with English instinct fraught
He yet can call his own.

Ay! Tear his body limb from limb
Bring cord or axe or flame!
He only knows that not through him
Shall England come to shame.

Far Kentish hopfields round him seem'd
Like dreams to come and go
Bright leagues of cherry-blossom gleam'd
One sheet of living snow;

The smoke above his father's door
In grey soft eddyings hung
Must he then watch it rise no more
Doom'd by himself so young?

Yes, Honour calls!—With strength like steel
He puts the vision by;
Let dusky Indians whine and keel;
An English lad must die!

Neelum Saran Gour

And thus with eyes that would not shrink,
With knee to man unbent,
Unfaltering on its dreadful brink
To his red grave he went.

Vain, mightiest fleets of iron framed;
Vain, those all-shattering guns;
Unless proud England keep untamed
The strong heart of her sons!

So, let his name through Europe ring.
A man of mean estate
Who died, as firm as Sparta's kin
Because his soul was great.

The professor stopped reading, closed his notebook, sat searching the face of his pupil. Then he continued: When I first saw the Kohinoor displayed among the crown jewels of Britain, I felt an odd disturbance. Yes, they'd fought with exemplary courage ... they could grandly claim: India shall be a jewel in our crown. We fought hard too but some things we lost. The Kohinoor stood for all the things we lost. But maybe ...

He looked hard at the boy, sitting wide-eyed in front of him. Maybe there's something else we conquered in its place ...

He picked up the essay again. Bring this back on Thursday when you come, he said kindly to the stupefied lad.

Munna did not wait till Thursday. He was back the very next morning in a state of high excitement. He placed a sheet of paper on Professor Mathur's table.

I have written a poetry too! he announced, flushed with achievement.

The professor was taken aback. He remembered another pupil years back who had come with a poem he had named

'Arse Poetica'. He put on his glasses and scanned the notepaper which carried a stanza of verse. He handed it across to Munna. Read it out, he said.

Munna put on a special recitation voice:

> *Four hundred years see grew in sun and*
> *   sower.*

She, corrected the professor, despite himself. And shower, repeat after me—Sh. Sh. Shower.

Munna did not for once allow this correction to deflate him:

> *Four hundred years she grew in sun and*
> *   shower.*
> *Then India say a lovelier flower*
> *On earth was never seen.*
> *This speech to myself I take*
> *See ... She sall be mine and I sall make*
> *A language of my own!*

He looked up, victorious. Professor Mathur was at a loss for words. Moved.

What Private Mouse can do, I can do too, explained Munna.

Wah! applauded the professor. He decided to speak of the Kohinoor again. The original diamond was much bigger, boy. They've filed it down. A great pity. But this one we've conquered—this English language—has grown. It's growing and growing, my lad. On the lips of people like you and me. This jewel in our crown that we've worked hard to conquer. Its growth has known no limit.

No boundation, put in Munna, enthused.

No boundation, agreed the professor, relenting.

twenty

H ow much of real mathematics do you understand? sneered Neelesh. You fifty-per-cent-reserved-quota-walas have lowered the standards everywhere. You always have things coming easy. Easy admissions, easy jobs, easy promotions, easy success and never mind the quality of work you put in. At the cost of your betters!

When they were alone together in her one-room flat, with only Kartik for deaf-mute onlooker, Neelesh let loose his temper on Swati. Amazing, the things he got away with. She took it all. She knew that all his applications had recently been turned down. Six or seven job vacancies. And in twice that number he hadn't made it in the interviews. She knew he had exhausted all his attempts in the civil services exams and in the bank recruitments and in other public sector openings, that he was overage for so many other jobs and was now desperately trying to pick up a computer diploma. Coaching Kartik had been her idea. What was wrong with Neelesh teaching a bit of science and maths? she had argued. The other subjects she, Swati, could take care of. The idea had clicked with Kartik's mother. But English, no, no. English, Mrs Goswamy would personally monitor. No trusting these riff-raff tutors with a subject like English!

So Kartik now came every afternoon at three and stayed in Swati's apartment till six. Neelesh dropped in at five and frequently stayed back to share Swati's frugal dinner. He saved fifteen rupees a day that way and Swati was always welcoming.

Now she was planning to start a regular coaching institute, taking on more kids. A collaboration with Neelesh who, she discovered, was a bit of a wizard with figures.

But each time she voiced the idea, she timidly searched his face for signs of enthusiasm and was not encouraged.

He knew exactly what she meant by collaboration and what she covertly had in mind. He was surly, insulting, snide, jeering. But she seemed devoted to him. One day he asked her: Why do you look at me like a cow or a whipped dog when I say these things? Why don't you react? You lot are getting to be so vindictive now ...

She replied: I'm like this.

Centuries of endurance in her genes, he thought. But when one day she timorously suggested marriage, he pretended to be shocked. But you aren't even legally divorced, he exclaimed.

In my community it wasn't ever necessary, she said candidly. When one marriage didn't work, a woman just left with another man, if she found one.

Great, he thought. No legality or morality involved.

Now, of course, we've acquired some of your upper-caste vices. Like demanding dowries in marriages and even—yes, I know what I'm talking about—even the practice of untouchability. Some of us won't touch food cooked by an upper caste ...

She knew how to hit back but, over and above the immediate spirit of the debate, she doted on him with a humble, long-suffering ardour.

He pondered over her idea of a coaching institute. His mind strayed to her better chances of landing a job. For his part, he was even finding it difficult to scrape together the cash to buy his regular copy of *Employment News*.

But, of course, it was her faceless body he really came for. The only investment he made was the condom. Professional expense, he joked. Got to live by strict rules of Brahminical hygiene. No defilement allowed. At the clinic I work in they check me for HIV every month. I'm their prize provider. Some parties especially specify they want good-family Brahmin blood. That's me. If I wanted I could hike up my rates. I have to be careful whom I sleep with.

She heard him out without volunteering a word. In bed she served him, as slave served master. He lay back and she went over him, every inch of him, adoring, appeasing, with fervent lip and fragrant kiss and fulsome spittle and passion tears. She reached into crannies of him unexplored by touch until he cried aloud with the rapture of it and she had to put a hand over his mouth, twisted in the agonized contortions of pleasure, to stop him crying out louder. Until, unable to bear more, he seized and flung her on her back and mounted her and gave her such a frenzied, feudal banging, such a bashing and lashing and slamming and hammering that she wept in pain and the ardour of submission to an ancient master. That was what he kept going back for—that heady feeling of sovereignty. One day he would stop going back to her, he assured himself. One day he would drop her—just like that. She gauged his thought accurately, almost read his mind.

You try leaving me now, she quipped. I dare you to.

What'll you do? he challenged her.

I'll go straight to the thana and lodge an FIR. Abduction and rape of Dalit woman. Yes, I'm quite serious. You just can't get away from me now.

It dawned on him that she wasn't joking. She was that desperate about him, this he knew.

She studied his face fondly. It'll just be your word against mine. And by now you know who wins. She sounded triumphant.

Okay, you win, he conceded.

Still, when she suggested a Kalighat 'instant' wedding ceremony, he couldn't quite take to the idea. There was his large family back in Pratapgarh. Landowners whose land had shrunk, whose mango orchards had been sold off, and whose rambling old stone homestead had been partitioned into six smaller portions, two of which had a fresh coat of paint and were in good repair and the rest of which were crumbling. A proud old family of ancient stock, as they claimed, now fallen on evil days. They all thought he was working for the civil services examinations in the big city and supporting himself. They didn't know he was marketing his pedigreed Brahmin blood, he thought bitterly, his only saleable resource!

Now, marriage to this dumbly adoring girl here was another matter. Somehow he couldn't actually consider it. Still, when a caste Hindu married a Dalit there was a ten-thousand-rupee grant from the National Integration Office—Rashtriya Ekakikaran Anubhag—which stood just across the legislative assembly. That might pay for the computer diploma. There would be a loan facility to buy or build a house. And sooner or later, she would land herself a job with that fine-printed, laminated 'backward class' certificate of hers. When he screwed her, he would fling his sacred thread on the table where she kept that thrice photocopied and laminated testimonial. The irony of it had made him roar with jaded laughter. My salvation and yours! he had pointed at the sacred thread lying on the laminated certificate. My Gayatri Mantra is useless against that magic mantra printed on that sheet there, stating that Swati Maurya, daughter of Srichand Das Maurya, belongs to the OBC washermen's caste. So what the hell do

I do about it? Like those tantrik sages, I go on chanting and seek moksha through the dusky body of a low-caste woman. Old formula, he thought dourly. No, better check the condoms well each time. Best not to complicate the situation further.

But at Kalighat you can get married in a jiffy. A low-budget wedding and no one gets to know. If it's your family you're worried about. She had been to Calcutta and visited the Kalighat temple and one of her relatives had married there, she told him. It saves money, time, rituals and identity. No one will remember your face or mine. It's full of poor, red-and pink-sari-clad women and dressed-up young men. If there are no relatives present, it's that much cheaper. You can hire a priest for a hundred and one rupees to chant just the essential lines. It's called 'mantra money'. You hire a room for another hundred rupees and the ceremony's over in half an hour. Then, if you want a photo, you can go to one of the many studios and get yourselves clicked. So simple. And we'll be gone just a week. No one here will ever dream ...

He marvelled at her planning and her insistence. Why is that mantra so important to you?

She puzzled over it. Didn't really know the answer. Kalighat is a mahateertha, she said. The priest said each day is sacred there and each hour is auspicious. And each marriage there at the feet of the goddess is blessed.

Strange that she took her Hindu ritual so seriously. One would have thought they would discard some of it after it had excluded them for centuries. But no, every jot and tittle was important to them.

But we'll have to travel to Calcutta. I must tell you I can hardly afford the fare. And the expense of meals and lodging and transport ...

That's no problem, she quickly said. I've got something stashed away.

And I suppose if I refuse to go to the goddess and have the mantras chanted, you go to the thana and lodge an FIR? he joked cautiously.

She stroked his hair. Yes, she answered softly.

One night, walking down her lane, he had the distinct feeling he was being shadowed. He turned twice to make sure. The lane steamed with moonlight. A white dust of light descended between the terraces and motley parapets, blew down against old cornices and the stone latticework of overhanging balconies. A sort of radiation which heightened visibility instead of curbing it. He had the definite sensation of being watched but could spot nobody.

He told her of it the next day. She took it casually. She said it was the 'monster'. Her ex-husband. He didn't like the sound of it. She laughed, recklessly. It's me he wants to damage, not you, she said. You're perfectly safe.

When crank calls started coming for her on her landlord's telephone, he insisted on accompanying her downstairs. He heard her say: I'll send you an invitation card when it happens. Then she added in a sneering voice: So, why can't a woman have two husbands, one official and one all for herself? Then he heard her say: I'll say I wasn't ever married to you. It's the five families' word against mine and I don't care a hoot for them. He could see her go pale but she kept the bravado in her voice. He found himself admiring her pluck. She slammed the phone down and stood, trembling, her back to the wall.

The motherfuckers! she swore. They turn a blind eye when a swineherd or a barber or a washerman or a tanner puffs up the bellies of their daughters with his scum! Oh yes, they fold up the first marriage bloody fast and let the rutting females go their way with their favoured fuckers! But a Brahmin lover—*satyanash*! Then they'll stop at nothing, nothing!

He was jarred by her foul speech, her venom. Who's 'they'? he asked on the staircase.

'They' is the five families who stood witness at my wedding. What can they do to you?

Nothing at all. Break off all ties, I guess. Who cares!

She squared her shoulders and unlocked her room, switched on the light and picked up Kartik's punishment lines. His mother was taking her teaching seriously. She made him write out punishment lines. 'I will not waste my time.' Five hundred times. She imagined it was good for both discipline and handwriting. Kartik often left such assignments for Swati to complete.

Swati sat down and, face still aflame, tore through the lines, adapting her handwriting to Kartik's unformed one. I will not waste my time. I will not waste my time. I will not waste my time.

Neelesh watched her thoughtfully. It goes faster if you write it vertically. Pass it here—I'll do half.

An hour later, after he had left, Swati happened to glance at the incomplete lines in the open exercise book. Four hundred and fifty-five times, vertically down the pages, he had written: I will, I will, I will, I will ...

That night he had a brainwave. What if I make *her* appear in the civil services exams? And the banks and all the rest. She's just twenty-three. Unlimited attempts at the exam for her. No, for her there'll be an age-relaxation too. She isn't exactly dull and with a bit of coaching ... And I can avail of the ten thousand and the housing loan afterwards. Once she has a job we can try that Kalighat wedding thing. How easily solutions arrived if one was only a little flexible.

When they met the next evening he had organized his plans somewhat. She received him on the staircase, her face timorous, scared to hope, wondering if his oblique signal was a signal at all, wondering if she was imagining things, hardly able to contain her hope.

I've thought it over, he told her. I've decided to take up your offer—the coaching institute idea.

She looked disappointed. Said nothing.

Only, this'll be an institute with just one pupil. You.

What do you mean?

I'm going to coach you for the civil services exams—that's what. And all the other competitive openings in the list. You'll get selected where I couldn't.

Let's first go to Kalighat, she was insistent.

But, don't you see? he argued. If you marry me now, you might stop being a reserved quota candidate. We can't both be unemployed blokes—don't you see?

I know the rules, she said. I'll always be what I was born. She looked close to tears, accusing him in her heart for flourishing this trump card. So I get selected in the services and you get out of marrying me? she put it in all its stark heartlessness.

That's not it at all. First you get selected, which you easily will. Later, when you're confirmed in your job, we can marry. At Kalighat or anywhere else you wish. That fellow won't have any power over you once you're in a permanent government or public sector job. And my family shall overlook ... certain things. His voice tailed away.

She sat, studying her hands. Then she lifted her eyes to his face. Have it your own way, she said listlessly. I'll take any exam you want me to.

That's better.

The very next day he found study guides, manuals, syllabus booklets, model question papers piled up on her table.

I have had a private job offer, he told her. You'll let me pay for all this material when I draw my first salary, won't you?

An accounts job? she asked.

That. And one or two other things. It's at the office of a private press called Kal Bhairava Karyalaya. They print religious tracts for circulation to pilgrims at places of Hindu pilgrimage. It's funded by a religious trust. I've been called by someone called Kailash Brahmachari. The salary's negotiable and with the Goswamy woman's dole coming in, I can save my Brahmin blood for a while now.

It's saved for a while, she laughed joylessly. Meanwhile, my study material is ready but what's your tuition fee like?

He drew her to him, bolted the door. You know my charges, he whispered.

Later, as they lay in the half-light, she said with a tinge of bitterness in her low voice: Okay. Go ahead and coach away. Me, I'm just a worker. I'll study and get through any exam you say. You were always the teachers, you bloody Brahmins, and bloody scheming teachers too. I'm sure I'll make it on the strength of your coaching.

Don't forget the fifty per cent reserved quota, he laughingly reminded her.

twenty-one

Y ou may or may not have noticed that I have personally
    kept out of this narrative for some length of time. Now
that most of my characters, surviving or deceased, identifiable
or DNA fingerprinted, are known to you, I feel no necessity
to negotiate, explain or transmit supporting information.
The reason for my present intrusion is that in the course of
my researches into Master Hargopal Misra's life I met three
of his close friends, each as richly eccentric as Masterji himself.
And because what they had to say on the subject of their last
meeting with their deceased friend seemed promising in the
larger context of this account, I shall introduce them to you
at this point: Halim, the tabla repairer; Raghavram, the crazy
Vedantin; and Pawa, the area's half-wit. Masterji had sought
them out scarcely a week before the blast. He had been all
charged up with enthusiasm and full of deep contentment.
Bustling and businesslike.

Masterji couldn't rest for the excitement of it all. So much to
do. The harmonium to be tuned by old Malviya at Swar-Mandir.
His sherwani to be dry cleaned. Yes—he studied his face in
his cracked shaving mirror—a hair-cut might be called for. Or
should he allow a few straggly wisps to dangle artistically about
the ears? So. He surveyed his face gravely. He couldn't decide.
He would consult his good friends of the footpath, Halim
and Pawa and yes, even Raghavram.

Halim lived on a broad square of kerb where the Dayanand Marg crossed Hewett Road. At night he stretched a makeshift plastic awning over his stretch of pavement, pitching it like a sloping tent between the corrugated shutter of the bicycle shop behind and two iron pegs driven between the paving stones of the dry gutter. Halim's pots and pans and scanty household fitted neatly into an old tin trunk which the owner of the bicycle shop kindly allowed him to keep in a corner of the shop. Good nightwatchman, this mild old Muslim, he thought. He always greeted Halim with a polite *As-salaam wale qum* every morning, to which Halim courteously responded with the customary *Wale qum salaam*. Then, in his sweet, butter-silk speech, Halim would enquire after the other's mizaaj, his state of mind that morning, his begum's health, his little nawab's well-being, to which the bicycle shop-wala offered appropriate answers, trying his best to imitate Halim's courtly graces.

Halim's family had been repairing tablas and dholaks and kettledrums and mridangs since Mughal times, or so he said. He had a stone with which he rubbed the leather faces of the tablas to a fine polish. It had been in his family since the time of Shah Jehan, he said, holding it reverently in the palm of his calloused hand. Smooth to transparency, it sat on his palm like a wedge of ice, poised at melting point, liquefying slowly, too slowly for the eye to observe or the clock to measure. Drums had been the family specialty; kings, courtesans, street musicians his select clientele. Halim had tales to tell—of the time when Nadir Shah's battle drums rolled into Delhi and the time British drums escorted the captive Bahadur Shah Zafar to the fort. Now Halim sat, eighth or ninth or tenth scion of his lineage of drum-doctors, surrounded by confused snortings and trumpetings and revvings of engines, the squeal and growl of tyres, the blast volleys of mobikes, the thundering drums of traffic on a busy square. On one side of his patch was a massive Aptech hoarding, on the other an Infotech ad, across the street a fast-food joint.

Masterji cherished Halim for two reasons—his expertise with tablas and his enchanting memoirs, which Halim, slowly working the leather thongs in and out of the kathal-wood urns, prising them up or prodding them down or buffing away at the surface with the historic Shahjehani stone, meanderingly narrated. Stories of old Nadar's shop in Old Delhi in forty-seven when Halim lived there.

Nadar, a stalwart with a goatee, purveyor of hookah-tobacco, ice and firewood, had three brothers, Janab, Chhotiya Pahalwan and Naseer. Ah, what wrestlers! He could see them still in kurta and *tehmet* and on their feet curly-toed, decorative jooties. That Nadar! He could draw a bullock cart loaded with mountains of ice all alone. And he was long past sixty years old. And Chhotiya Pahalwan—wah! A back as broad as an army jeep. He could see him still, cleaning his teeth with charcoal at the street tap, swirling the water round his mouth and slosh-spewing it out at an angle, then beseating himself to a dekchiful of tea to which he added three pats of butter—to mute the heat, he said. And do you know, Masterji, what they said at Nadar's shop just before partition? You'll never believe this but rumour had it that Gama Pahalwan from Patiala had sworn he'd go over to Pakistan and train the army there to ascend Mount Everest before the Indians did.

Accha? Masterji, interested, picked at the crease of his pyjamas, tucked in his sherwani tails, and sat down on his haunches on the pavement, watching Halim work expertly on his tablas.

Yes, and there was this crazy mullah who started a rumour that the Turkish forces were being paradropped around the Jama Masjid, also that the Nizam, who had supernatural powers, had summoned a battalion of jinns to defend Hyderabad.

And talking of rumours, Masterji, hear this one. It struck terror in the hearts of the entire community—three veiled and burqa-ed women came in a curtained ekka, in strict purdah, you know. When the ekka reached the address given, no one came out. After a while the driver cautiously lifted the purdah, and kayamat! Not a soul in there! Just three shreds of paper with words in Urdu scrawled across. Prophecies of doom. One predicted famine, the other bloodshed, the third pestilence. At Nadar's shop we concluded it was the same jinns who had come over the Mitha-ka-Pul, draped in burqas. And it was construed that it was time for all men of the faith to leave for the new land. Most went away to Pakistan. But so many didn't, among them your humble servant. Me, I just left Delhi and came here.

But what of the Hindus? Did they not hear of these jinns? ventured Masterji.

Everyone heard of them. They thought their gods would be stronger than all the jinns. There was this Ramoo of Brahmin-gali, recalled Halim. His father's name, if I remember right, was Punno Khalifa. Now this Ramoo had drilled a few alley boys to holler *Har Har Mahadev* and *Om Namo Shivay* and *Jai Bansiwale Ki* and things like that. Each time the Khaksars in the Mandi called out *Nar-e-Takbir* and *Lar kar lenge Pakistan*, Ramoo's lot would counter with their own slogans. At a certain Madan Singh's house, Ramoo's gang had stored scores of staffs and lathis. This Madan Singh was a giant of a man, believe me. Lush moustache, solid bulk, brawny arms. They said he had broken the bones of both his arms once and when he had them set, the doctors replaced them with a ram's bones.

And, as for the Christians, Masterji, at Padritola there was a rumour that the Pope had instructed Mahatma Gandhi to ensure that not a single drop of Christian blood be shed. I remember one frightening night. There was a great banging and tumbling inside the church but nobody could pluck up the courage to go and look. This went on all night until finally they formed a group and, armed and fortified, they stole up to the great church door and peeped in. Behold, the sight they saw summoned the tears to their eyes! Halim fixed the leather thongs in a final knot, his face set in a frown of the deepest concentration.

What did they see? whispered Masterji in a stricken voice. His tender heart shrank from these gory recollections of a gruesome time, those massacres of innocents, those mortal wrongs.

Halim tested the resonance of the taut leather with a smart slap on the tabla's face, then spattered on it a jaunty tattoo with his fingertips. Ah, just right, he said in a strained voice.

What did they see? reminded Masterji.

What they saw wet their eyes, set them a-shake and a-shudder, Masterji, said Halim impassively, as though exercising enormous restraint of expression. Tears of big, big laughter. A donkey, half-blind, had managed to get into the church and somehow got locked in! All night it had banged about against the doors, trying to get out. That's what they saw, Masterji!

Halim ended his tale in the deadpan voice he used for his most mirthful narratives and Masterji's face relaxed in a sheepish smile. I have great news, Halim Bhai, he changed the subject. But first let me find Pawa and Raghavram and maybe we can all have a glass of tea at Billu's cart.

God willing, consented Halim.

So Masterji started up his moped and went in search of Pawa who haunted the next crossing, the one on the intersection of Ambedkar Marg and Madan Mohan Malviya Road. Pawa was the bazaar idiot. He loitered around the square and made a bit of money, massaging people's limbs. A grin split wide his goat face, watery brown eyes swimming joyfully in his head.

Pawa's mind had closed up circa 1980, so he still had long phone conversations with Indira Gandhi, prime minister of India. Indira, or 'woh', as Pawa significantly referred to her, often with a salacious shadow of a leer, rang him up often. She had two brothers, Pawa told his customers, Sanjay and Pakistan. Pawa planned to marry soon and he spoke of his sweetheart. A muscular Amazon with matted, dangling locks, who dressed in khakhi shorts and shirt and was dumb. She sold flowers and garlands outside the Alopi Temple and fiercely cycled past, gabbling shrilly at passers-by. She treated Pawa like dirt. But Indira Gandhi had assured Pawa time and again that she would personally arrange the match. So Pawa spoke of receiving a fridge, a radio, a tape-recorder and lots and lots of saris—all seventies' fabrics—he knew all the names—organza, American georgette, rubia, khatau ... Pawa could sing distorted lines out of seventies' film songs. He had the same sing-song tune for all of them. *These, these are the folk who took away my dupatta*, he sang simpering coyly. *Ask the halwai, ask the constable, they're the ones who stole my pink dupatta in the market square*. Then Pawa usually switched to another song, specially for Masterji's benefit: *What, what became of thy promise?*

He studied Masterji's palm and informed him that he would soon go on a long journey, maybe to Amreeka. Masterji was perplexed by what seemed most unlikely but then he remembered that God spoke through madmen and prophets. Pawa could not count money so people often wheedled him into massaging their arms and legs and paid him fifty paise or a rupee, telling him it was five rupees or ten rupees. Sometimes the man at the tea stall gave him a glassful of tea and a samosa for free. And once a week, Masterji treated him to a plateful of rajma and rice. Pawa ate it hungrily, then lifted the plate to his face and licked it clean.

They had given him electric shocks in Agra way back. He parted the hair at the back of his head and showed Masterji the scar. Even so, he had rigorous scruples. Don't give me any money before I massage you, he would caution the customer. When I get the money before the job I just walk away without massaging. Wait till I finish, then give.

Masterji waited till he finished and when the knuckles of the right hand and the left hand had been snap-snapped and the muscles of the wrist well squeezed and kneaded and soothed, Masterji gave him a rupee and asked him to perch behind him on the moped and together they went off in search of Raghavram.

Raghavram was, as usual, on the steps of the ghat, immersed in headlong discourse. When Masterji proposed tea, he proved resistant to persuasion. It was only when Masterji artfully picked up the thread of the discourse (whereupon the earlier hapless disputant slipped away in hasty relief) that Raghavram rose, his discursive deluge in full spate, and walked along with Masterji, the moped wheeling between them and Pawa shambling behind.

Say, Panditji, if there are two modes of Being, the sakar and the nirakar, and if Brahman is nirakar, the akash becomes shunya, why is it that the world likewise does not become shunya?

Raghavram was very dirty today and his face had the same swimming expression that Pawa's had. But whereas Pawa's countenance seemed permanently in a state of achieved beatitude, Raghavram's had the abstruse, intently involved look of the philosopher who is immersed in life-interrogating and soul-sustaining matters of faith and truth, making the humbler concerns of the flesh and social living redundant. He could neither read nor write and when his nephews discontinued his medication, his philosophic urgencies mounted in proportion to his schizophrenia.

Say, Panditji, what is the relation between manovigyan and Vedanta?

Raghavram had spent his childhood wandering the ghats, playing the square and four with tamarind seeds on the paving stones where the scholars and ascetics sometimes discoursed. He pondered over Masterji's patient explanations, shaking his head. Then another abstract query came swimming up.

Say, Panditji, if I were to take a pau of earth and divide it in half and that half in another half and so on infinitely, where would it go? Would its materiality be annulled? Say, Panditji, what are the causes of anger, of hatred?

Masterji fumbled with answers and Raghavram nodded and agreed. Ah, yes, it is moh which is the cause, Panditji. But why should moh be the cause? And Panditji, if I touch my brass pot I feel it is either cold or warm. Or both cold and warm. Or neither cold nor warm. Which means cold and warmth undermine one another and do not exist. So what is the cause behind these feelings?

Raghavram was about fifty. Very smelly and unkempt. His wrinkled dhoti fastened high above his knees like a loincloth, his face avid with a dazed, mystical idiocy.

Say, Panditji, my brother Jairam says that the idea that every Being has both jiva and matter is wrong. If Shankar Teli had jiva, why did he die? A person told me that in Brahmalok there is no pleasure. Is that true?

Masterji perceived that today Raghavram was in an advanced condition of contemplation. Raghavram did not know that philosophy was a subject taught in all the universities. He was surprised to learn that many editions of the Vedanta had been printed and he took long to get over the revelation. Raghavram had listened attentively to scholars at various ashrams. Now, in that wandering mind of his the questions reappeared, dismantled and reshuffled, the old discourses all scrambled up and tossed together.

They made it to Billu's tea stall. Halim joined them at the wooden bench and Masterji, after some coughing and clearing of the throat in preliminary bashfulness, broke the great news. The soirée, the NRI and foreigner guests, the printed invitation cards (silver on glazed cream paper), Mayank's sprawling sitting room, ragas Vasant, Pilu, Aheer-Bhairava and Jaijaiwanti that he intended singing. He went on to tell stories of the legendary maestro, Alauddin Khan, who worshipped Goddess Sharada and dedicated all his music to her. Then he remembered to tell them that the celebrated Raghunath Rai of Gwalior would be present, a man who had played so significant a part in his early commitment to music. He recounted how he had once bragged before his village mates that he had sung a raga at a big conference and had won the trophy, when, in fact, it had been won by Raghunath Rai. Then Raghunath Rai happened to visit their village as part of a wandering mythological dance-drama troupe in which he supplied the playback. And how he learnt of the little local upstart's tall claims of having won the maharaja of Gwalior's durbar trophy. And how, gracious that he was, he did not betray any of the lies. How he corroborated everything—the raga, the prize, everything.

He saved my nose. Ah, that's greatness! sighed Masterji.

That's fineness, observed Halim.

That's when I resolved to abandon trickery and start practising in earnest—six, seven hours a day—and here I am, Pandit Hargopal Misra, Maihar gharana. He did not actually say—the one without peer—but the suggestive slope of his sentence urged the idea necessarily into the auditor's mind.

The tea finished, they parted ways. Masterji collected the tablas in a large cotton bag, slung the bag carefully on his moped's handlebars, took leave of his footpath mates and rode away. When, returning home, Masterji unlocked the door of his tiny room, he found a polythene packet slipped in, lying on the floor. A couple of cassettes. One called *Titanic*, the other carrying the picture of a blonde, brazen, provocatively pouting beauty and the title *Ray of Light—Madonna*. Mayank naturally. He had kept his word, tracked down the music he was desperately looking for. Masterji dumped his tablas down on the chowki and fumbled about the shelf for the lead wire of his small two-in-one cassette player.

The music swept about the room, the same soundtrack he had heard in Mayank's sitting room. But disappointment filled him as the music unspooled out of the little instrument. There was no name to the tune; just a brief tingling rush of notes like quicksilver droplets colliding to form bigger droplets, giddying around a magic space—ga re sa dha dha, etc.—before being submerged by a massive all-capsizing swell of symphony.

Masterji stared at his two-in-one in dismay. Lost, his precious scrap of melody, lost in uproarious racket. He tried the other cassette. A moist, saturated voice with a delicate vibration humming in its drenched depths. He liked the voice but the background clamour put him off. The words of the verse circled around his room—*substitute for love, substitute for love* ... Halfway through the cassette, he switched it off, realizing he wouldn't find here what he was looking for.

twenty-two

S uleman's novel back from London! Sakina Bibi was consumed by curiosity. Oh yes, they've accepted it, he informed her curtly.

An Urdu novel—published in London! she gasped, hugely impressed.

Why ever not? Lots of Urdu publishers in London—massive reading audience in Britain.

Why've they returned it? she ventured timidly.

Editorial readjustments, he answered, unsmiling, and, lifting the parcel, held it against his side like a precious infant and went up the stairs and into his chamber.

It took Sakina Bibi a few intense inhalations and exhalations and a few vigorous heavings of her big bolster-bosom to grasp the essentials. A real, large-as-life published AUTHOR in her humble kothi! A real, authentic NOVEL written in her poor, crumbling dwelling! And if he became famous, maybe in a few years there would be a brass plaque on the front door and maybe there would be a permanent exhibition on in the room he inhabited. This is the chair in which the legendary Suleman Ali sat, this the table at which the immortal work *Ghair-e-Ibadat* was composed when the author was but twenty-five years old. This is the chowki on which his gracious landlady, inspiration and muse, Tehseen Sakina Begum placed his meals, his tea, double-roti and gosht-chappati. This his balcony, these his papers, files, fountain pens, dictionaries, glasses. And this, here on the opposite wall, is a portrait of Tehseen Sakina Begum, patroness of this mansion, once a humble hostelry, done circa AD 2000, oil on canvas, by the renowned painter Mehtab Mansoor Jung. Tradition has it that the same Tehseen Sakina Begum read and reacted to each chapter of *Ghair-e-Ibadat* and her influence upon the legendary Suleman Ali is a byword in the history of Urdu literature. That last bit jarred somewhat on Bibi's fluent fantasy. After that last time she hadn't had a chance to peep into his novel. He had sternly admonished her and he used to put away the notebooks in his tin box and padlock it.

She wondered what happened to the Rajput princess in the novel—and her Mughal bridegroom. She wondered if Akbar managed to placate the Rajput clans to accept the match. She wondered if the editors in London had preserved that lovely, heart-teasing sexy scene. She remembered how she had thrilled to the sweet, guilty titillation of that dainty-daring scene, how it had brought back the days when that impoverished Nawab Shaukat Ali Khan had squandered his last gold mohur on her, for the joy of ... by kayamat, what fools these men can be ... for the joy of placing his lips once, just once on her ... ah no, one does not speak of such things, those foolish, fainting ecstasies ... but that passage, ah! Why did it make poor Shaukat's face come swimming up from the depths of the river bed, resisting the flow that was time, come shivering together in a heart-jump instant of shocked and aching recall?

She would just have to read that passage again. Get Suleman out of the way. The notebooks he could lock up but maybe the big parcel containing the finished work he might just omit to secure.

Strange fellow, this silent Suleman. When he had first appeared, a bearded young man speaking a soft, chaste Urdu (except for a slight Punjabi grate somewhere) she had told him frankly: I don't normally take in young lodgers, Mian. But you're my very own Shakila's sister's brother-in-law's son, which also makes you my Zahid Mamu's chacha-jaan's half-brother's kin. So you're family and welcome. And if I was sure how old my Nusrat's daughters are now, I'd ... ah well, Allah willing, it may yet come to pass. All I need is a photograph and your walid sahib's address in Bhopal.

He hadn't cooperated. But then she had written to Nusrat, who sent a photograph of her eldest daughter, Rubina. But what a photograph! The girl in a shameless sari—eight inches of midriff exposed! Uff! What were times coming to! Muslim girls with eight inches of midriff exposed and bindis on their foreheads too. Sakina Bibi had written a severe reprimand to her cousin. Kindly understand, dear Nusrat, that this is a serious, devout, five-prayers-a-day young man. I'll trouble you for another photograph, a more decent one, in a more modest dress, please. The second photograph came, this time Rubina in a decorous salwar-kameez and her head appropriately draped in a wide brocade dupatta and her eyes cast down. But Suleman still wouldn't supply his walid sahib's Bhopal address. Playing hard-to-get. Even these unemployed ones who can't earn their dal-roti play hard-to-get. These hardened men, ah! she thought bitterly. But he was a romantic at heart, she convinced herself. His novel proved that beyond all doubt.

Getting him to take an interest in Rubina was going to be hard. The one thing he was interested in, other than his novel, was visiting crowded shrines. She had told him of all the local pirs, fakirs, poet–saints, healer souls. Sayyad Baba, Munnawwar Baba, Line Baba, whose green ceramic-tiled and twin-minareted shrine sat straddling the railway station yard. Hindu–Muslim shrines to which Hindus came and Muslims came and none went back uncomforted. He used to be annoyed though he said nothing but his face expressed his contempt. These linsey-wolsey combination faiths! his frown said. Mongrel mock-moralities!

No, Suleman Bhai, no, she remonstrated. Let not your young years scoff at these sacred ones ... why, it is said that even Mallika Victoria saw Haji Waris Ali Shah, the saint of Dewa Sharif, in a dream. And when the Mallika came to visit it, she was impressed by the saint's elemental simplicity and she said: *Wallah*! This is an independent sarkar! There's a ten-day fair at Dewa Sharif and it starts with a Hindu festival. When the karwa chauth moon is sighted, the urs begins.

This last detail seemed to annoy him intensely. Only, Mallika Victoria never did visit, he snapped. Not by any history book. So much for your *anaab-shanaab* stories!

She looked momentarily disconcerted but she could never be subdued for long. Her impatience to reread those teasing passages in his novel grew ever more importunate. Then she sprang Richard Sahib on him.

There's an interesting mazaar in the middle of Thornhill Park, Suleman Bhai. It's the grave of a British soldier killed during the mutiny. Only thirty years old, poor man. The gardeners of Thornhill Park put a rail around it and planted roses. Then childless Hindu women and barren Muslim women began coming with Friday sheets and incense and lo! All were blessed by Richard Sahib.

He looked venomous. Anglo-Hindus and Anglo-Muslims, these little Richard Babas!

She looked hurt, admonished him sadly: It does not bode well to jest about these mysteries, Suleman Bhai. Were you to visit the shrine of Richard Sahib on an evening, the sight that'll meet your eyes shall be enough to still all reckless mocking. Go, Suleman Bhai, go one day and experience it for yourself—the holiness, the hush, the hope ...

Good for your Richard Sahib he died in Hindustan, Suleman muttered balefully. Only in Hindustan would his grave receive a dozen silk sheets each Friday. In England it'd only be draped in moss.

How do you know, Suleman Bhai? she argued. Have you seen graves in England?

He bit his lip and fell silent, as was his way. Then speechlessly turned and sped up the creaking staircase. She was pleased to see him thus affected. He had seen his mistake, his young hot-headed arrogance of youthful disdain. He was ashamed—his face clearly betrayed his self-reproach.

Half an hour later she heard him leave the house, no doubt bound for Richard Sahib's grave in Thornhill Park to offer penitence. Ah, the novel now. She was held up for a moment by Pappoo's Mother, who unknotted a much-folded banknote from the pallu of her sari and flung it on the table, saying that it was a pity that certain people tried to parade as generous benefactors, only to defraud the poor and pass off fake money as real! Bibi patiently picked up the hundred-rupee note without looking too closely at it, meaning to examine it later, and put it in the drawer of her old Burma teak dresser. Then she sent Pappoo's Mother on an errand and hastened to Suleman's room.

He'd left the MS on the table, Allah's karam! She shuffled the pages, found favourite stretches, feasted her old, dreaming heart. The young Rajput nobleman brought his Mughal friend home to spend a few days at his fort in Chandelgarh. How the young Rajput's sister and the Mughal friend chance to see one another in the still waters of a lake. Then again through a filigreed screen. Then a third time. The girl, playing chaupar, looks up to see the young Mughal in a pavilion upstairs, watching her intently. Later, in one of the perennial Rajput–Mughal skirmishes, the young Rajput brother is slain. The Mughal friend deserts, brings his Rajput friend's sword and turban un-besmirched to his mourning mother and sister. That night he declares his passion, proposes flight to the girl. She proudly declines. So he goes back to Agra and seeks the Emperor's help. He has some uncomfortable explaining to do as to why he deserted. But Akbar realizes the diplomatic wisdom of replacing war with Chandelgarh with a matrimonial alliance. The marriage proposal is formally sent with pomp and pageantry. The girl's mother, the Maharani of Chandelgarh is promised honourable retirement in the young Mughal's villa.

Since none of the Rajput clans will support the alliance, Man Singh arranges for the ceremony to be held under his patronage. A nikaah first. Because without a nikaah no marriage can be. Bibi enjoyed the wedding scenes most. The songs, the meher, the Emperor's gift, placed in a golden, gem-crusted casket. The grand durbar hall garlanded with marigolds, lit with ten thousand oil lamps until the waters of the lotus pond shivered with shoals of buoyant sequins. Gongs clashed. Trumpets, conchs, then the gun salute. Maidens broke into song, rained flowers, rice. Ah, the lovely Braj verses, the Sufi songs, all the grace and lyricism of a Hindu–Muslim union of verse and melody, passion and poetry. So magical that it was obvious that the enchantment was beyond human achievement, a medieval romance in a poet's rhapsody, no more. Bibi thrilled to it, dabbed at the corner of her eye with her crumpled head cloth. Thank Allah, those publishers in London had not deleted those haunting passages although there were a lot of editorial queries and directions and suggestions in the margin in a scrawl she could not decipher. But it was certainly neither English nor Urdu. Must be some special editorial code. Two tick marks okaying the date of the nikaah. Against the gun salute again two tick marks. The Emperor's gift in its jewelled casket had a question mark against it. The hour of the baraat had been corrected and changed to four-thirty, but did they follow the English clocks in Akbar's time? she wondered. But no major alterations, thank God. She read on.

The ceremony over, the old Maharani, the bride's mother, in a dramatic volte-face, denies the young couple her blessing and jumps into the sacrificial fire. The heads of the clans spring to their feet, chanting. They fling sandalwood, oblations of ghee and the sacrificial herbs into the blazing fire in which the Maharani's body is slowly charred to raw flesh turning swiftly to ashes, shreds of smouldering silk, gold jewels burnt brighter, purer, more sterling for their trial by fire. It is the same havan-kund around which, after the nikaah was over, the young wedded couple stepped the seven-circled way. Bibi was saddened by this piece of tragedy. The young couple's love blighted forever! Why must such things be? Why must love most vulnerable, most trusting and tender, never survive the ravages of situation? Ah, Shaukat.

And here at last was the passage she specially sought. The one that made the breath heave in her bosom and a fine dew rise upon the lined forehead. The young bride loved her groom's bearded face against her soft, pale flesh, the way he laid it against her perfect, pearly, conch-shell breasts. She loved his halting, courtly speech which, despite its soft-spoken grace, held the possibility of an alluring, covert brutality which appealed to her bold Rajput heart. He was fascinated by her austerity, her shrinking exaltations, her piety. On karwa chauth day the young bride fasted, touched not even a drop of water all day long. Then, having beheld the moon through a sieve at nightfall, she touched his feet, as a Hindu wife must, fair idolatress that she was, and he lifted her up and set her on the couch, flushed with love and wine.

Sakina Bibi recalled how Suleman had consulted Professor Mathur about the karwa chauth fast. Professor Mathur had retorted: Wah! Imagine living in this land for centuries and not having the foggiest notion about its other cultures. There had been a spot of bother. Suleman had countered: And do you know anything about Islam? Professor Mathur had answered: I do—a little. But I don't represent the average. The average Hindu knows precious little of Islam, he had conceded. And the average Muslim or Christian knows just as little about Hinduism. The exchange had left Bibi troubled. She turned to the script again.

There were times when the young groom found his bride grown silent, staring out of the pleasure pavilion blankly at the sky. Her mother, her brothers ... At such times her groom burned with a stronger passion and had to force himself on her. Sakina Bibi experienced enormous excitement at this romantic rape scene. The way the young bride's soft white body is despoiled, kneaded, clawed, bitten. She read the passage over and over again. The violence of love—ah! The films she liked, those courtly Muslim socials—*Mere Mehboob*, *Mere Huzoor*, *Bahu Begum*—didn't have this explicitness. Everything, every delicate tribute, every chivalrous nuance, every rose-petal scented page of verse culminated in this, this! When the princess dug her teeth in her husband's gagging hand, it only sharpened his desire and left Bibi restless, ah, Shaukat, Shaukat, Shaukat. Lying in his mildewed grave in the Hazratbagh cemetery. Bibi's mind stirred in its romantic mist. Those delightful Muslim socials. Full of grace and shayari. Tragic nawabs, haunted poet–heroes, glittering damsels, qawwalis. Ah, *Mere Huzoor*! Raaj Kumar strumming his passionate agony into the taut strings of the jangling sitar. Drumming it into a musical chaos of such an inflamed pitch, such an agitated clamour of emoting, that he cut his fingers on the tortured strings and the blood dripped into the music like an extra burning splash of pain! And Jubilee Kumar in *Mere Mehboob*. Pale and anguished in his black sherwani. Singing his verses to the unknown beloved. Sakina Bibi's misted eyes gazed into the evening, scanning the creped surface of the air. Whipped clouds like clods of butter in a buttermilk sky. A georgette fog hung around the minarets like a tinselled head cloth. Just so, one length long, the other swung widthwise. Jubilee Kumar. Dead too, like Shaukat.

She had preserved a large coloured poster of *Mere Mehboob*. Put it in the gallery. A pink-faced Sadhana with a fringe across her smooth forehead, resting against Jubilee Kumar's dark sherwani breast. Jubilee Kumar's charged eyes smoky with passion. And stretching in a band across his wavy locks, the title of the film and the casting. Those wretched cricketer louts had pasted another poster over it, a smaller one in the centre, superimposed, showing a bosomy, modern starlet moueing suggestively into space. Plumb in the centre of her *Mere Mehboob* poster so that it now read 'Mere boob'. Bibi had uncomprehendingly let it stay.

That very evening Sakina wrote to Nusrat again and the following week Rubina arrived. Rubina was all of fourteen years and pretty as a picture. Along with a dozen smocked, laced, ruffled, piped, pleated, tasselled and tinselled salwar-kameezes she also brought her satchel containing her *Elementary Mathematics for Secondary Schools* by Ranganathan and Sen and her *English Prose Selections*, edited by M.C. Das. Shortly after her arrival, Sakina introduced her to Suleman, with disappointing results. For Suleman's look suggested that as far as he was concerned Rubina could be girl or fish or fowl or cloven-footed beast of the sands. But Sakina had her designs carefully chalked. A day later, while Suleman was out, she went sneaking up to his room, clutching Rubina by the hand and drawing her along, a finger on her lips and every tread tense with caution. She crept up to Suleman's divan, extracted his key from beneath his mattress, put the key to the padlock of his steel trunk, propped up the lid of the trunk and lifted the notebooks of Suleman's novel with an expression in which glee mingled with reverence. She placed them on the divan and, wetting her forefinger from time to time, turned the pages till she came to the delightful sensuous–erotic sequences. She beckoned to Rubina and mutely bade her to read. And as the girl's eyes devoured the letters on the page, a pink flush rose in her cheeks, a liquid shine in the eyes, fascination getting the better of embarrassment as she followed Bibi's pointer finger down the lines, right to left, then right to left and so down the pages until the loud groan of the kothi doors alerted them both and, swiftly replacing the notebooks in the trunk, key turned in lock and placed under mattress, they sped across the room and down the stairs. And not a moment too soon, for Suleman passed them on the stairs, gruffly returning their salaams, making Bibi whisper to Rubina: That one might as well be a-mourning for Hazrat Ali three hundred and sixty-five days of the year, all the woes of the world beseat themselves on his brow like the vultures in the graveyard neems, Ya-Allah!

Then Sakina undertook Rubina's training in the winsome wiles that made artful beguiling a refined code and subtle temptation an elegant skill.

Lift the hem of your salwar just six inches higher up the dainty calf when you fill the water pots at the courtyard tap. Let the silver anklet gleam round the snowy foot. Let slip the tinselled stole from the shoulder, thus. Don't urge it away, don't cast it off, no. Let it stray away from the fulsome little roundnesses, thus, and be you engrossed in lifting the buckets, bending over and keeping the hemline dry even as the level of the neckline falls as does water in a glass jar on a thirsty afternoon. If you chance to look up and behold his intent eye, bite the lip and lower the lash, thus, ah, well done!—and smile the blushful, bashful way.

Then as an afterthought Bibi added: And when you offer namaz do it with the door ajar. And when you read your angrezi book do it on the steps of the staircase. Let him see you know angrezi too.

And so it happened that Suleman, descending the staircase, came upon Rubina poring over her *English Prose Selections*. And chancing to sight a name in the large print of the page, was driven despite himself to ask: What's that you're reading?

It's a story called 'Kabuliwala', she answered demurely. It's about a man from Kabul.

He stood riveted to the spot. Then, impelled by an irresistible impulse, he suddenly sat down on the step beside her.

What was he like, this man from Kabul? he asked in a strange voice.

His name was Rehmat, she told him. He was the friend of a little girl named Mini. He brought her sackfuls of almonds, raisins, pistachios.

Really? intoned Suleman, interested.

Yes, they have heaps of fruits in Kabul. Khubani and kishmish and pista and plums and grapes and ...

Not in Kabul. Around Kandahar, and a long time ago. Melons and mulberries, peaches and pomegranates and figs, whispered Suleman almost as though he was speaking to himself. Now all the orchards have been cut down, the water channels broken. Now they have fields of poppies for opium. But all that was around Kandahar, not Kabul, you understand. Who's written this story?

Rabindranath Tagore, she turned a page, checked the title and told him.

He didn't know, said Suleman. In Kabul now you have men without arms and legs, only stumps.

She was taken aback. He seemed to be talking as one possessed. How do you know? she whispered back, tremulous.

He smiled a furtive smile all to himself. I'm descended from the Prophet's companion Quais and I have seen the Cloak of the Prophet too. That's how I know.

Suddenly he appeared to recover his wits and shook himself wrathfully. Tried to cover up his lapse, affect interest in the book she held.

So what does this Rehmat do?

He brings fruits for the little girl and they become great friends. Her mother doesn't like him. She thinks the world isn't a safe place. So many things to fear—drunks, thieves, dacoits, snakes, tigers, malaria, cockroaches—and she's mighty suspicious of Rehmat. But Mini doesn't listen to her and she thinks Rehmat is all right. He calls her Khokhi and jokes with her and asks her: When will you go to your sasural, Khokhi? And she asks him: What have you got in your bag, Kabuliwala? And he says: Elephants.

Suleman was anxious and adopted an unnatural jocularity. So when will *you* go to *your* sasural, Rubina? he asked.

She cast down her eyes coyly as she had been taught. When Allah decides, she murmured. Then she lifted her eyes and looked deeply into his and added: Or you do.

He caught the vibration, grew alarmed, saw that he must persist in diversion.

So does she actually go to her sasural? he asked, playful.

She dimpled mischievously. No, *he* does.

How?

He goes to jail for stabbing a man. He calls the jail his sasural. When he comes out of jail he visits her and it's really her wedding day and then he remembers his own daughter back in Kabul and he thinks: She must be big now and I must go back and get her married ...

Here, Sakina appeared at the head of the stairs and her massive bosom swelled with the pride and satisfaction of an achieved design.

Ah, there you are, you two! she greeted them. My Rubina reads angrezi so well. Have you heard her read? Read, beti, read, she urged and overcome by a fit of conniving discretion, withdrew. She returned to peep a moment later and was displeased to find Suleman vanished and Rubina alone, book in hand, staring into space. She bustled down the stairs, puffing.

What's that you're reading, my shehzadee? she asked, piqued. An upside-down book? It was increasingly clear to her that kismet had denied her the good fortune of overseeing a tender romance.

But what of Rubina? Once, only once later, she attempted to open conversation with Suleman on the stairs. Boldly, in the same jocular mode that he had used to cover his awkwardness, she asked coquettishly: What have you got in your bag, Kabuliwala?

He started, then remembering, said in an unnatural voice: Elephants. So upset did he seem by this exchange that she never tried speaking to him again.

But the sapling implanted by Sakina had indeed taken root. Not a night went when Rubina did not lie repeating the words of Suleman's novel, the language imploding in her mind, sending tiny shivers of excitement through her body, making her press her legs closer and draw them up as visions of the young Mughal and the Rajput princess, of herself and Suleman, filled her secret thoughts with ever new and bold inventions of sensual promise that led up to such strong–sweet climaxes that she often overslept, waking dizzy, shamed and scared and drawn still more surely into this overpowering new opiate of imaginings that had started in her fourteen-year-old life. Wonderment at the first brush of touch and fanciful visions of the final all-breaching invasion inebriated Rubina's pristine fantasy with a strength that conquered every instant of her waking and dreaming life.

twenty-three

On Sunday mornings Aditya read out the paper to Suruchi in bed. Security 'beefed' up in Ayodhya, he read. She burst out laughing. In the circumstances, that's a pretty unfortunate verb, she remarked.

I remember a newspaper howler that went one better. It said: Vigilance 'porked' up in Aligarh, you know, instead of 'perked' up.

It was the sort of kinky thing they liked laughing over.

Last second of October I was invited to inaugurate a function in a kids' school, she told him. I asked a little girl what the second of October signified. She replied: It's Gandhiji's Happy Birthday. So I asked another kid: Who was Gandhiji? He answered solemnly: Gandhiji was a man who kept three monkeys and made salt. I didn't know where to look and neither did the poor headmistress. I tried hard to condense my Gandhi info into a ten-minute speech but by now they were clearly confused by too many Gandhis. The Italian one or the Indian one? The one that's fond of animals or the bent one with the stick? That's right, I said, the one with the stick.

Now that her adopted son Vineet was away at boarding school, Aditya spent his weekends at her bungalow. He had to be discreet. Not that Suruchi cared. It was only for official reasons that some semblance of a charade was minimally necessary. Still, the whole thing was a perilous exercise, Aditya reclining back on an inclined pile of pillows, Suruchi in a position she could barely sustain for more than a minute.

It's not your heart I'm going to break but your spine, she whispered in his ear.

His face was pale. Thirty-five years of starvation, then this. She perfumed her nipples for him with Kanauj perfume. The scent of mogra or the fragrance of rain-drenched summer earth. He gobbled on them hungrily. Her strong hands supported his deformed back. Her lullaby-soft voice was confidently teasing: Remember, I've got a signed blank cheque. I can drive you to ruin.

You've done that already, he murmured.

He handed her the article he had come across in the 'Sunday Supplement'. She tried on his glasses and found she could see better with his glasses than with her own. Said so.

That's because we look at the world the same way, he said.

The relationship between them had developed suddenly but she scoffed at the idea of anything permanent.

That formula doesn't work any more, she had told him. The model's gone defunct. Love is like an email message sent to a wrong address. It bounces back and the machinery spells out: Sorry. Daemon Failure. Can't locate it.

Once he had asked her why she insisted on seeing him at all and she had replied: Oh, I don't know. You're a sort of business partner in a personal enterprise and sometimes you become my soul's neighbour ...

In the silence each was busy with their own thoughts. He had lately revived promising hopes of winning his case in the immediate future, recovering some of his capital. Renovating and refurnishing the house. Going in for that tricky spinal operation in Delhi, no matter what the risk. Then, magically mobile, getting into his car, the old Ambassador, one day, stepping on the accelerator, driving down to her bungalow with a formal proposal of marriage. Nothing less!

Surely she would brush aside the idea. But maybe, with his recovered capital ... He shook himself out of the reverie. Humbug! That case would drag on for decades, the battery of the Ambassador had discharged long ago, the chances of his ever driving again, nil.

But when Vineet came home for the holidays, what then? Had she sent Vineet off so as to have the house to herself? For the sake of this affair, trivial though she claimed it was?

Why did you send Vineet off to Darjeeling? he asked.

I thought he needed a change of air, she said. It was getting too much here—all his cyber politics. He used to be sitting at the internet all the time, visiting Pakistani sites and exchanging nasty abuse, visiting Israeli sites and doing anti-Palestinian talk. Hours and hours. He had so many Jewish friends and he was full of rage. I adopted him when he was just a year old and I'm sure I gave him a very peaceful childhood and I used to wonder where he picked up all that fury. Whose anger was this kid carrying? It became a problem.

How about counselling and gym and creative pursuits?

Nothing worked. He was simply possessed. I tried talking to him about what I call 'psychic pollution', you know, this garbage of negative emotions afloat in the air and all the hate out there in the World Wide Web. He always had a smarter answer. One day things peaked. I found him weeping uncontrollably, banging his head against the wall, hammering his fists on the table. He almost broke the computer. I had to give him a tranquillizer. It turned out that a disco in Tel Aviv had been bombed by Palestinian guerillas and twenty-five teenagers killed. His best chat friend used to frequent that disco. I kept telling him: Don't worry. He'll turn up at the chat site one of these days. But he didn't. Vineet waited a month-

and-a-half for Saul Navarro to come online but to no avail. He kept saying to me: He's dead. Those Palestinians have killed him and I'm going to kill all these bloody Palestinians and Arabs and Pakis even if I have to go to Israel to do it! It got so bad that he stopped going to school and used to stay up all night abusing at Pakistani sites until the First Term exams came and he dropped out. He just wouldn't go. That's when I decided something had to be done fast. And boarding school has completely cured him. Take a look at this letter.

She leaned across to the bookshelf and extracted an envelope.

Dear Mom (he read), *Couldn't tell on the phone because of Pandey snooping behind. It's not a big hurt. Just a cut lip. The doctor came and put two stitches. Now I'm eating only ice cream and drinking milk shake. Ragging's on. It was an accident really ...*

Suruchi took the letter back and continued: I was frantic with worry. He telephoned me from a phone booth and gave me the details. There's this new boy, Shakeel, who chummed up with Vineet from day one. The seniors used to provoke him with remarks like: Holiday? What's barawafaat, yaar? I guess that's the day after gyarahwafaat. During the month of Ramzan they brought tempting things up to the dorm and poor Shakeel, unable to resist, used to eat, then go and throw up in the bathroom. Vineet kind of took to the boy. Then this ragging began.

A dozen senior boys used to come to the dorm at midnight and wake Vineet and Shakeel up and demand: Fight, you two. Go for each other. And the poor fellows had to obey. Vineet told me that without a word being said they would pretend to deal out strong blows but they took care to keep the impact light. Then one of the seniors noticed and shouted: Hey, that's not fighting at all, you bastards. You're shamming. Fight harder. Let's see some blood! So the battle cry started: Let's see some blood!

Then an accidental blow from Vineet landed on Shakeel's face, gave him a black eye, and Shakeel hit back instinctively, tearing Vineet's lip and a loud cheer went up and Vineet's fist crashed against Shakeel's temple and Shakeel hurled himself at Vineet and battered his head against the wall and suddenly Shakeel froze and so did Vineet and one of the senior boys shouted: Oh, shit! And the others ran to fetch water to wash the stains off the wall before the warden came. But Shakeel and Vineet just stood there and didn't know what had come over them for a couple of minutes. Then all the seniors came rushing up with towels soaked in water and set about scrubbing the wall. It didn't clean up of course. And when the warden came the seniors said: They were fighting, sir, these two. The matter was reported to the headmaster and both Shakeel and Vineet have to give up their Saturday tuck for a month. But one thing's sure. Vineet's politics has changed drastically.

Aditya had listened to her intently. How tough it must be, being the single parent of an adolescent boy, he observed.

She swung her hair out of her eyes. Oh, not at all. When I speak to my son I find I'm using my father's voice and my mother's voice by turns. I guess our parents' voices become ours and travel down the generations like our genes. I don't feel single at all.

Aditya kept silent. She was silent too, her eyes fixed, unseeing, on the article she did not care to read. She could, of course, forego the promotion. But after such a long and bitter fight ... It was a triumph, a big jump for her. She had guiltily toyed with the idea of staying back, but her mind had scorned the thought. To give up a cherished promotion for the sake of a mere man! Aditya, she would say, my promotion list is out. I joined last week. Chairperson of the Moradabad Development Authority.

But each time she imagined his face. So for the present she said nothing. Not just yet. One of these days she would take him out for coffee, then break the news to him. Gently.

twenty-four

It had to be now or never. Perhaps if she got to speak to Marcia Gosse on the phone today, she would finally be able to expel her shadow from her head. Once that was achieved, the silverfish might be left to do their work on the questionable letters and cards. After that she would only preserve the letters Brian wrote to her in the initial days of their courtship, before Marcia Gosse appeared on the scene. Maybe she could photocopy them—to give their content a new lease of life. Once she could get herself to accept the unpleasant truth of Brian's prolonged defection, once she could retrieve her own badly mangled self-esteem, there was hope that she would come to regard the entire sordid business as another one of nature's old and dicey games.

But she couldn't keep going to a different PCO each time. She had already made such a fool of herself at all the nearby ones. And the PCOs at Ambedkar Road were too far away. She would work up a flaming leg pain if she tried walking down but maybe a rickshaw, well, that could always be done. Meanwhile she discovered that the PCOs she had been frequenting were manned by different chaps in the evenings. Change of duty at five. So, instead of trying in the mornings, she could always try after five in the evening. That's what made Lynette Shepherd change her hours at the park.

A flaxen floss of dust still hung about the trees. In the main road, sodium lights hennaed the air. A half-moon tilted against the Pragati Tower like a headlight blacked. Sitting on her bench, sipping her coffee, she fell unwittingly into her old habit of speaking aloud.

She took another sip. Her lips fell silent though her head did not. All of me, all my giving, all our years together, everything added up, was less than this wretched male instinct. And had I known earlier, when I was still young, nice-looking, when revenge was possible ... Too late now. There's just this faded mind holding hungrily on to an unfading heartburn and I'm unresigned to live with this betrayed feeling till the end of my days. Then her head set up a contrary chant: Be kind. Be kind to these small, human defects, these shabby little thefts. Be kind—it is the only thing that matters.

But then there was this funny physical problem—when she thought all that was over for good. An old woman of her age! In the dead of night, her cotton nightgown pulled up, her hands seeking the ley lines of forgotten pleasure, imagining the two of them—Marcia Gosse and Brian. Together. In that railway guest house. Was it misery that her heart sought as a final, extorted recompense? Until the visions became a revelling, a surging beat of the blood, a fractious arch of panic that was nothing less than a shrill spurt of secret and insidious pleasuring. Was she drunk on the new energy flow that grief released? Feeding on the moral power of being wronged? Converting pain to pleasure? She drained her cup, wiped it dry with a paper napkin, dropped it carefully into her basket and rose. She would try Jagat PCO first, the one this side of the main road.

She did not notice the plump little man in the maroon T-shirt who stared after her. Something about her slow, retreating form had awakened in his throat a sharp twist of sensation.

As though his brain had long ago decoded that essential movement, the way the spine held itself, the way the arms stirred and the heavy legs picked their way. It wasn't the external slump, the slowness, no. It was something else—prior and more essential.

It's Mrs Shepherd, isn't it?

She looked at him in suspicion. She clutched the plastic handle of her basket a little more tightly. Sized him up. Couldn't place him.

Sorry? she said.

But of course! the little man squealed. It's Lynette Shepherd! It is, of course, it is! he persisted, growing petulant.

Yes. But ... I'm sorry ... I mean surely we've met but my memory ... excuse me ...

Matthew Gardiner, he produced his name like a visiting card. Fifteen Lavender Terrace—remember me?

She opened her puffy eyes wide in surprise. Oh, MATT Gardiner! Why, to be sure! For a moment I thought ...

What?

Matt Gardiner! I can't get over it! She repeated the name, wagged her head from side to side in disbelief. Well, well, small world ... Forty years.

More.

Where've you been, Matt?

Now it was a social cake-and-coffee voice. She had recovered.

Oh, lots of stations. Jamalpore, Cawnpore, Alabad, Jubbulpore, so many others. After I retired I went off to Calcutta with Matilda who's poorly after her operation.

Matilda?

My wife.

I do remember. How strange, she mused. We—that's Brian and I—we've had stints in all those places. She smiled weakly.

I know. So what's a girl like you doing all alone in this park? he asked playfully, in a horrible travesty of the big bad wolf.

It irritated her. Actually I came to make a phone call.

From this park?

No, from Jagat PCO outside the gate. Thought I'd rest a bit here. It's so hot in my flat.

Ah. Under the greenwood tree? Ha ha! No, under the laburnum tree would be more like it. Jolly things, laburnums. You used to live in a house called Laburnum Lodge. Had a coupl'a trees drooling yellow flowers all over the thatch.

She nodded wearily, thought of her old house with its laburnum trees. Indian laburnum. Amaltas. Cassia fistula. Its fruit like pale gold grapes. Like a fall of jingling coins. Glass baubles on a Christmas tree.

What's become of that house? Your Laburnum Lodge?

It wasn't ours, she answered. We rented it for just thirty rupees a month from the Gandhis of Metcalfegunj— remember them? It was sold to a doctor. To some Gupta or Agarwal. Pulled down now. Big pathology lab in its place.

She wanted to get on with the phoning business. Wished he would take himself off. But he stuck by her side, walked her down to Jagat PCO, accompanied her in, would have dialled on her behalf like a secretary if she had allowed him.

What's this? A Calcutta number?

She cursed him. Nosey Parker. Why wouldn't he just clear out? Couldn't he see he wasn't wanted?

Who's this person? This Gosse? Old chum? he wanted to know.

Yes-s-s-s, she hissed in desperation.

The phone kept on ringing, ringing. She counted up to thirty tring-trings, pressed the repeat button. Thirty more. She gave up.

Hard luck, what, Lynette? he observed, jocular. You can always try later. Maybe tomorrow, Lynette?

She sighed, resigned herself.

Maybe yes, let's see ... She turned to go.

The next evening he was there on the bench before she reached. She clicked in annoyance. He told her a lot of boring things about plants. She gave her cup of coffee to him. He protested. Accepted half. Said: There's only one cup. She said: There's the lid of my flask. He said: Okay.

He slurped his coffee noisily. She looked at him in some distaste.

Ah, this is jolly coffee! he gushed. Remember that song, Lynette? *The night they invented champagne. It's plain as it can be, they thought of you and me* ... He sang a couple of bars in a tuneless tenor, then went on to tell her about the areca palms and araucaria palms: ... none of them were Christmas trees, mind you, Lynette, though in this climate it's the best we can do at Christmas ...

She interrupted him: In Alabad, Brian and I planted a tiny araucaria. I wanted a bigger one but it cost too much, even in those days. We planted it together. I asked Brian: How much time do you think it'll take to reach my height? Gate-high? Balcony-high? Ten years, who knows! We won't be here in Alabad then, said Brian to me. That's just what happened. We had to leave it behind when we moved to Mughalsarai.

I know, he said. I tended that tree for three years after you all left. It was taller than the gate then.

She turned to stare at him. You?

I was allotted the same house. You left. I arrived.

She digested that in silence. And my lilies and gladioli? she asked, a little shaky.

Those ones too, he said, lapsing into Anglo-Indian patois. So many of them. All over the blasted place. No system.

Yes. I used to scatter lily and gladioli bulbs everywhere. Here and there—just like that. Deliberately forgot where. When they sprouted, what an unexpected surprise!

Pretty bad bandobast, Lynette, to see 'em sprouting in my potato beds.

She was appalled. You went and planted potatoes in that lovely front garden?

He grinned, showing a wide ridge of toothless gum. Lots'a potatoes, he said, enjoying her shock.

They fell silent. Amazing how, by some quirk of fate, he had always found himself in cities she had just left. Both Brian and he in the same railway service. Even the same batch. He had even lived in bungalows that she had lived in. Come across bits and pieces that had belonged to her. Broken trinkets in old cupboards. Discarded pottery. Her children's scribbles on the walls. As young people at the school social where partners were chosen by lot, she had picked up a twist of paper with another boy's name. Dressed in frilled laburnum-yellow tissue she had been. He had prayed fervently: Christ, let it be me. Let Lynette Fischer pick my name. Then she unfolded the paper and it was Arthur Wallis's name, not his own. In college, he and Denzil Menezes had written letters to her. Denzil's letter reached her. His own was lost in the post. Then he had lost interest in her. Heard she had married a colleague of his, posted at Jubbulpore. He mentioned this to her in a gallant reminiscent mode and she said cynically: Too late to make passes at me, Matt.

Forgive me my passes and my trespasses, Lynette, he said, waggish. Now, about this Calcutta phone call of yours ... He interrupted his own reverie.

This time she let him dial. She stood, frowning by his side, as though she couldn't care less if the call got through or not. He hullo-ed, held the receiver out to her. Incredulous, she grabbed it, spoke. A child's voice at the other end. Boy or girl she couldn't tell.

May I speak to Marcia Gosse, please?

The child's voice grew uncertain. Hesitated.

Tell her it's Lynette Shepherd, Brian Shepherd's wife. Lynette's hands were shaking but her voice had achieved a studied calm.

I can't, said the child in a rush.

Why? Is she out?

Here Matt abruptly reached out and took the receiver from her and spoke into it: It's all right, Julia, this is Uncle Matthew. Tell Gran I'm here with Auntie Lynette and it's all going to be okay.

He placed the receiver firmly in its cradle and turned to face Lynette.

The reason she can't speak to you is that she's partially paralysed and in a wheelchair and slightly speech-impaired, he said carefully.

Lynette felt her legs go limp.

Shall we walk back to the park? proposed Matt, paying up.

They crossed the busy street and re-entered the park in a charged silence. In a second's illumination it came to Lynette that Matt Gardiner wasn't here by chance.

Who sent you, Matt? she asked bluntly.

She did, he answered. Or rather Matilda did. They're friends, you know. Marcia is in no state to decide or do anything.

So that's how you went to Laburnum Lodge and—

That's right. The Parkers next door directed me to your apartment. I found it locked but the chowkidar said you'd probably be here. It's taken some doing, tracking you down, Lynette.

She was conscious of rising animosity. Why are you here? she snapped.

I came to tell you her condition and ... He took something out of his pocket. And also to show you something. Here.

A photograph. He handed it across. Stupefied, she took it. She put on her glasses and stared at the scrawny figure sitting humped in a wheelchair. Who was this shrunken crone with the spindly hair? Surely not Marcia Gosse! She looked tiny, her soured eyes piercing in their sunken sockets. The flesh had melted off her face and all that remained of the old chiselled, sweet-contoured profile was a pinched beak of a nose overhanging puckered lips. It came to her as a shock that Marcia Gosse had it in her to grow old and paralysed when she had stayed in such a potent state of preservation in Lynette's mental world. The red-lipsticked, head-tilted presence in the earlier photograph was a grandmother, decayed and ill.

She's terribly upset by your phone calls, Lynette, informed Matt. She can think of nothing else. You're the biggest bogey in her mind. The last time you phoned, her blood pressure shot up so alarmingly they had to rush her to hospital. Lynette, my dear, won't you spare her this? She's in a bad way and she feels awfully threatened.

But I don't threaten, protested Lynette. I just wanted to ... to humanize the thought of her. Cast her out of my head. I've tried so hard. Months.

He shrugged. Pretty mutual, I reckon. Anyway, she's a nervous wreck.

Just what I am, thought Lynette.

You've got nothing to hide, Lynette, except your own misery. But she does have something to hide. Victor's known nothing all these years, you see, and it's too late to confess such things. Lynette, where're you?

She was trying to understand exactly why she had been trying to reach across to Marcia Gosse. After coming across those papers she had spent months describing and re-describing

Brian's ambiguous relationship to her own satisfaction, as though by giving it the just-right articulation she could overpower the situation and reduce it to its ultimate triviality. A fling or an involvement? A prolonged state of emotional confusion, one of those sort-of, almost-but-not-quite culpable neutralities acquittable by all standards except maybe by the shrinking secret heart. Then, finding those letters, she had known it had been much more than that.

She recalled herself to the present with a start to hear Matt pleading: So Lynette, I'm waiting for a promise that you won't trouble her again.

Trouble! All the rage reared in her heart. The painful reasonings fell away.

Are you ordering me about, Matthew Gardiner? Forgiveness can't be forced, men. Do you think I haven't tried? It's harder than you know. She may have lost her looks and her health but c'mon, look at me. I've lost a lifetime's faith and all my memories have gone wrong.

The violence of her grief and wrath, so carefully held in check, erupted in explosive vengeance.

I'm not taking orders from you or Matilda or her, Matt. Why should I? I've been under treatment for depression too. You can go tell her that. You can also tell her that I've preserved all the charming, gushy letters and cards she sent Brian thirty-five years back. I found them recently as I was searching Brian's files for some title deeds. And for your information, when Brian was oh-so-passionately-in-love with me, writing me love notes all the time, she was there with him, sharing his guest house, his bed. She wasn't even unattached at the time. Where was Victor then? Back home in Vizag, I guess. No, it isn't boring and trite. It may be happening all the time all over the world but it concerns human pain and dishonesty and ... and the helplessness and loneliness of discovery ...

Her voice had risen to an uncanny pitch, her old body was shaking violently. She rose, flung the thermos into the basket and hobbled away faster than she knew herself capable of, not looking back, unheeding his appeals.

Back home, she paced the terrace a long time, went indoors, came out, went in again and stood in front of the faded mirror on the chest of drawers and studied her face intently. She watched its lights go out, its outlines dim and stray, reassemble and set, only to dismantle and realign. Changing slopes appeared, crags and moraines unfolding an ancient, terrifying self, neither man nor woman nor beast. That night Lynette made a bonfire on her terrace. Dumped her packing case of old letters on the cement floor. She had travelled from place to place, lugging those cartons along. The first week of December each year she called the 'advent'. A private ritual of opening the cases and sunning the old papers. Beating out the silverfish, those fancy lace makers, smoothing out the ragged fretwork of their doing. Sometimes, unwittingly, she found herself reading a paragraph here, a page there. She read the words written thirty-five years back, the purple ink blotched, the words smudged upon the page. She read until the dangerous lunge in her chest alarmed her.

She stood and watched them as they turned into kerchiefs of flame. Saffron runnels erupted in flares, twitched in vermilion-edged sashes. Big fangs of indigo rose, slanted into kingfisher pennants. Small ragged fronds of paper lined with tattered frills of fire. More kerosene needed. The fire leapt to receive it, blazed dangerously, then steadied itself into a big, tapering banner, embedded in smaller wads of flame. Ridge upon ridge of livid incisors, illuminated escarpments highlighted in a big, steady, triumphant peak. She fed in the smaller bundles. Some sheets puffed, billowed, tumbled into hollows and collapsed. Some flinched, grew pocked, knobbly, mottled. Some twirled into wincing sulphur-green scrolls. Cards turned indigo, amethyst, opened up in dainty, unexpected florets of flame, exploding in roseate stalagmites. Those Hindus worshipped fire, thought Lynette. In the fullness of time, this is what it all came to, this all-reducing combustion. A fire sacrifice, a relinquishing of claim in the brief drama of igniting and extinguishing.

The fire sank to a low glower until in the heap of charcoal petals there glimmered its last crimson dregs. Lynette clutched the single letter she had kept back for reasons she understood and did not understand. Then, impulsively, she let it go and it fluttered onto the smouldering heap. She stood there, afraid, unmoored, until a great simple quietude closed over her. So much for pseudo memories. At least, she thought, there was in this some mutuality of redemption and not a cheap psychological victory.

twenty-five

F or a few weeks the professor had the plot for a radio play humming in his head. An investigation into the truths of history. He called it *The Roll Call*. He needed half-a-dozen male voices for it and one female voice. Sakina Bibi might be requested to supply the female voice but what of the half-dozen male voices? Munna was hopeless with an English script and Suleman was usually unobliging. He spent a week pondering the question. Lines of dialogue began reverberating in his head. Disembodied voices. His auditory imagination could construct their pitch and timbre. Some guttural-grating, others slick-unctioned in persuasion and innuendo, certain others teasing, challenging, impertinent, bantering. He used the voices to generate faces and body language. Until one afternoon, dozing at his desk, he heard right beneath his balcony, in the cobbled close, the very voice he had conjured in his head. Saying: Uff! This one is toh another! He probably thinks Amrish Puri and Om Puri are suburban colonies!

The professor pricked up his ears. Absolutely the right vinegar laugh.

Now, Allah and Jesus are responsible folk, yaar. They look after their own. But imagine going to Lord Krishna and saying: Sir, I have a stomach ache. Nah, he'll ask you with a smile: So, what is this stomach and what is this body? What is this ache? What are you?

A guffaw. Just the right bolt-rattling rasp.

Now, I must admit Sheikh Sahib's tabeez worked wonders for me. I light incense before it daily.

Have you converted? Like that poet woman—what's her name?

I converted long back. I converted to every religion in the world.

Silence.

You're not a Hindu any more?

That could only be described as a stage silence.

Of course I'm a Hindu. Half of me is Hindu. The other half's open.

Half-hearted! I know your type.

No, honest. I'm willing to walk nine steps out of ten towards anything. If Mahomet can't go to the mountain, the mountain's got to come to Mahomet. But our Hanuman, yaar, he can carry the whole mountain, ha, ha.

Professor Mathur's excitement was beyond expression. Here was his cast! If only he could get them to consent. But over the months they had come to regard Sakina Bibi and Suleman and himself as oddities. He had been the butt of numerous loutish pranks and he had no idea how to approach this lot.

He lifted the chik and appeared at the balcony. He cleared his throat, introduced a note of bemused indulgence into his voice.

Not playing cricket today, bete? he asked.

They looked up, suspicious.

Do you know, boys, when the Kargil war was on and your cricket game in full swing, Sakina Bibi and I used to be like Mirza and Mir in *Shatranj Ke Khilari*. Have you read it?

A collective shaking of heads.

But we've seen the film, one ventured. Who were those two fellows you just mentioned?

Mirza and Mir, repeated the professor, the two passionate chess players in Munshi Premchand's novel. They played chess while Awadh was lost to the British.

Oh ho. He means Saeed Jaffrey and Sanjeev Kumar! cried another, seeing the light.

The professor was humbled. His prospective cast grew discursive.

Ha! Think of it. Indians and Pakis playing on a British pitch. Same as the Raj, sahab. Divide and rule was the name of the game. Two teams and get them to fly at one another's throats. Not cricket, sirs. Going up to England for—wah wah—the Lords Test!

Get on with it, you clown.

What I'm saying, Prof, is this—British pitch *vagaira vagaira* is all okay. BUT—and there's the rub—BOTH India and Pakistan have beaten those Brits internationally, so far as the game is concerned. At their own game. That's cricket.

That's the way of history, grunted the professor.

Beaten in the game they taught us ...

Let me read something amusing to you. I promise you won't be bored. The professor fetched his favourite *Pickwick Papers* and found the page. Here's an account of a cricket match in the West Indies. This is a character who has this jerky way of speaking, describing the match.

'Capital game—well played—some strokes admirable,' said the stranger, as both sides crowded into the tent at the conclusion of the game.

'You have played it, sir?' inquired Mr Wardle, who had been much amused by his loquacity.

'Played it! Think I have—thousands of times—not here—West Indies—hot work—very.'

'It must be rather a warm pursuit in such a climate,' observed Mr Pickwick.

'Warm!—red hot—scorching—glowing. Played a match once—single wicket—friend the Colonel—Sir Thomas Blazo—who should get the greatest number of runs. Won the toss—first innings—seven o'clock a.m.—six natives to look out—went in; kept in—heat intense—natives all fainted—taken away—fresh half-dozen ordered—fainted also—Blazo bowling—supported by two natives—couldn't bowl me out—fainted too—cleared away the Colonel—wouldn't give in—faithful attendant—Quanko Samba—last man left—sun so hot, bat in blisters, ball scorched brown—five hundred and seventy runs—rather exhausted—Quanko mustered up last remaining strength—bowled me out—had a bath—and went out to dinner.'

'And what became of what's-his-name, sir?' inquired an old gentleman.

'Blazo?'

'No—the other gentleman.'

'Quanko Samba?'

'Yes sir.'

'Poor Quanko—never recovered it—bowled on, on my account—bowled off, on his own—died, sir.'

They were in splits and the professor was gratified. So there you are. That was colonial cricket for you. Brian Lara's the answer to Quanko Samba, my boys. Now let me read you an account of an imaginary cricket match played according to Marxian principles in Soviet Russia before its crack-up.

He could see he was making an impression, already turning from area crank to area guru in their eyes. He fetched the *Penguin Book of Modern Humour*, found the page.

Ah, here it is. Four hundred and eight. This is a delightful little piece called *Cricket in the Caucasus* by A.P. Herbert.

He read the piece through—all ten pages of it. Of a game of cricket played in a Soviet village. The umpire drunk, the local poet declaiming. But doubts disturbing the other players. Now that the village had been collectivized, everything was held in common. All were brothers and comrades. How could two teams of brothers play against one another? That went against the principles of comradeship and brotherliness. Yet, a decree from Moscow insisted that there must be two teams of eleven players, each under a captain. But two teams competing against one another was 'capitalist heresy' which sought to divide the workers. Someone suggested that all the players could play on the same side. It was further proposed that all runs should be shared in common. Then, since men are unequal in capacity, the strong men should throw the ball from a greater distance and the weak ones from a smaller distance. This would ensure equality. All this was doubtless good applied communist theory but the commissar insisted that the game had to be competitive so as to tone up the flagging spirit of initiative visible among comrades everywhere. Two teams hostilely striving for victory, runs belonging to individual players, the same distance for all. There were murmurs. Clearly this was capitalism raising its ugly head. Or the counter-revolution. And if the commissar grew too insistent he would just have to be killed. The commissar is killed. But then there's no one left to explain the rules of the game. But rules are made for the bourgeoisie ...

Professor Mathur had them all chuckling. So you see, my lads, colonialism's packed up, so has communism. You can't play the same game in all historic contexts. That's rank absurdity. What's all this humbug about the gentleman's game? No gentlemen left, lads, only salesmen. Or have I said that before?

He thought of reading out an account of a cricket match between the teams of Sebastian and Caliban but decided against it.

By the time they left, Professor Mathur had talked them all into agreeing to act in his play. Initially excited, they could not help exhibiting their disappointment that it was a mere radio play. It could at least have been a TV serial in fifty episodes, some regretted. Or a film. Maybe if it turned out well, we could stage it here in the haatha. Or in Sikandar Chowk Park, suggested Professor Mathur. They grudgingly conceded that. And the remuneration? Come on, Professor Sahib, you must be joking. Actors for free? We'll split up whatever the AIR gives me and maybe I'll add a bit to it, promised the professor. But later, later, when we stage it, maybe we can price the tickets at thirty, twenty and ten rupees depending on whether the chairs are Professor Sahib's plastic ones or Sakina's backless benches or ordinary bustee charpais or plain durrees on the ground. Rehearsals in Sikandar Chowk Park every afternoon?

What'll you give us to eat, Professor Sahib?

Tickets no problem, Professor Sahib. A few large, typed sheets photocopied and scissored. Posters from ACME Computers in the main alley—leave it to me, Professor Sahib. The fellow is a good pal.

Lighting? That'll be easy—Sahu Electronics will gladly do it.

Stop, cried the professor. You forget this is a radio play to start with ...

He had trouble containing the enthusiasm of his cast. So that when he finally sat down to write *The Roll Call* he was as infected as they were.

His hand didn't close upon a pen with the old assurance. In ten years even his handwriting had changed. Gone were those careful flourishes, dips and sweeps and curves. His fingers had to economize on energy and so the letters were slipshod, unconcerned with their postures on the page. Sometimes, as he wrote, he grew tired of it all, tempted to sweep the words off the board—defunct, tiresome pawns. But write he must, impelled to throw the dice, see which word appeared in this strange game in which all was chance and all was chosen.

It was coming to him in loose pieces, this radio play, with large gaps that refused to fill. As though the inspiration itself was built of transparent presences and large opacities, as history was. Or as fragments of a human narrative, shattered to bits, so that all that remained of the tale was shards of story, crumbled masonry, twisted pipes, things smashed and powdered to unidentifiable grit. Something that survived a mega blast, something excavated and put together with improbable adhesion. For example, the teacher's voice taking a roll call of the boys he had taught in the village school and later trained as soldiers for the Rohilla army in 1857, voice intershading music:

I returned to my village after a year. I returned alone, lice-infested, dragging my stump-foot, carrying a list in my head. I stood beneath the pipal on Wilfred Sahib's land and my last roll call burst from my overwrought heart.

Kedar Pundit.

Silence. The rustle of wind in dry leaves.

Kalandar Beg.

Silence. The glushing of the stream.

Mohsin Khan. (Zeeshan's voice rising in panic.)

Silence. A jackal baying far away.

Ikram Ali.

Complete silence now. (A hysterical note in Zeeshan's voice.)

Amrendra Singh.

Silence.

Shyam Bahadur.

Silence.

Ram Sajiwan.

Silence.

Then, suddenly, Zeeshan calls out God's name. Complete silence.

Finally, in despair, he calls out his own name.
Zeeshan Ali.
He answers: Hazir huzoor.
He tries again, tentative, waiting: Zeeshan Ali?
And answers, the voice a little farther off, blurred.
Tries yet again: Zeeshan Ali.
An echo, far away: Hazir.
Pauses. (Rustle of wind, waves breaking.)
Zeeshan Ali!
Silence.
He calls again: Zeeshan Ali?
Silence.
Now there is terror in his voice.
He calls out: Zeeshan Ali, son of Imtiazuddin!
Silence.
He calls: Imtiazuddin, son of Malik Mansoor.
Silence.
He calls: Malik Mansoor, son of Mirza Meraj.
Silence.
He stops calling.
Faint music starts, ebbs into complete stillness.

This was the ever-shifting roll call of history in which the names of the cast keep changing, presences turn into absences, narrators and narratives fade out but the provisional and perennial themes roll on. Professor Mathur had scripted the last bits in a rising rapture of engagement. He felt painfully involved with the concourse of human lives in the mass and each in its irreducible selfhood, he spoke for all the generations of the dead and silenced, he spoke for the future destined to slip into activated time and shade out of it. He was exalted, supercharged.

He summoned his cast and his self-professed muse, Sakina Bibi, and read out his play.

The cast were unimpressed. They had a number of objections.

What's all this about, this shouting out of names like a college classroom, Professor Sahib?

It's about the roll call of history, explained the professor. One day I shall go on calling out my name and I shall get no answer ...

Aha! I get it. Then you'll probably say: Hullo, I seem to be dead! But, Professor Sahib, if you're dead, how can you call out your name?

The professor was visibly crushed. He had no answer.

Also, Professor Sahib, this script clearly isn't working. No action, no emotion.

The action and emotion are all implicit, bristled the professor, defensive about his brainchild.

May the temerity be forgiven, ventured Sakina Bibi. Your play is most, most heart-squeezing but, Professor Sahib, surely a love interest might make it more humane ...

This play, explained Professor Mathur patiently, is about transparency between caste and communal groups. A real dialogue.

The transparency that followed, like a spurt of spontaneous combustion, took Professor Mathur by unpleasant surprise, the dialogue uncontainable by the poor playwright, by any playwright, except maybe that old rogue dramatist, history, he reflected later. One thing led to another.

See how they breed. In fifty years, in a hundred, what'll the census figures be? We'll be the minorities in our own country. Give them a chance—they're not going to spare you. It'll be fire and sword and jazia again. Why do you want to encourage foreign ways in your own country?

Foreign? It was we who came as conquerors and beat you to it. This mulk was ours, won by the strength of the arm and the blood of our hearts and the glory of our faith. And ours to be again, God willing. We're biding our time. Till then you might consider us resident aliens.

That's why you've got those universities on jihad? You're counting on this namby-pamby tolerance of ours, are you? But I say, how cheap is our tolerance and how half-hearted our will. It's dishonourable, this easy indulgence, this line of least resistance. I say, beware the fury of a wronged race, no matter how peaceful it is. We do not forget. We've never forgotten. Shame to those whose tolerance rests on the humiliation of earlier generations. We respect the enemy's potential for evil. We do not preach an emasculated forgiveness. I say, you and I are not equals in spiritual maturity. If you were in power, would you be capable of the same tolerance?

Please, please, pleaded Professor Mathur. Do you know how St. Augustine defined true religion? He wrote—and this is Latin—*Ama et fac quod vis*: Love and do what you want. That's what true Hinduism maintains.

Are you a Hindu, Professor Sahib?

Only on official forms, to be honest. But, on the whole, all things considered, I do think I'm one. There's one thing I'm sure of. And I speak only for myself—though I was happy to hear one of you voicing a similar attitude the other day—I am a Hindu because my being a Hindu allows me to be a Muslim or a Christian or a Buddhist or a Jew or whathaveyou whenever I wish. It's a bit like carrying a remote control with multiple channels. I have an Islamic channel, a Christian channel, a Buddhist, a Jewish ... there's this dish antenna in my head which freely catches vibes from any faith. Just that. And I won't change. Let me quote Frost to you: They shall not find me changed from him they knew, Only more sure of what I thought was true.

Frost, Augustine! Oh ho ho ho ho! They'll cut you down—give them a chance. *Kaat dalenge.*

Excuse me. The Hindus aren't all that mild and tolerant as they claim—everyone knows that. That's only a myth, a façade. They're barbarous. Look how they forcibly converted Christians in the North-East. Burnt Bibles in Rajkot. Now they're objecting to the use of wine in Mass.

Yes, and they doused men with kerosene and set them alight during the Bombay riots. And what of the Sikhs? 1984? Men trussed up with tyres, trucks driven over them. Babes hurled into bonfires. It's only the Buddhists who're truly peaceful.

Peaceful? I visited Anuradhapura in Sri Lanka. Used to be a sacred place. Became the site for one of the biggest massacres.

There's nothing we did that you hadn't done to us. No wonder we go saffron when you build universities of jihad. And who set the pendulum moving anyway?

Who's pushing the pendulum now?

Please ... let me speak ... one word. Why not let the pendulum come to a halt with time? An experiment with trust ...

Hah! I lay down my arms and you can then come and mow me down!

Why must we be hypnotized by history? Who was it who said history's a nightmare from which we never manage to wake up? Let's prod ourselves awake. Let's say: This is us, here, now. We're only accidentally connected to those people in the past, so why should we share their follies?

Point is, Prof, will all this liberal buck-buck affect them? Will they be equally liberal? Is tolerance and appeasement always to be our incubus? If they're in power, will they, can they feel the same way?

It's this *us-ness* and *them-ness* ... muttered the professor.

Yes, us-ness and them-ness. You want to wake up from history, Prof? Right. I know only one thing, Prof. If a Muslim mob attacked you, you'd run to your Hindu saviours bloody quick. Your us-ness would be your only protection. You wouldn't hold up your history book and read them a lecture. You'd discover exactly where you belonged.

A Hindu mob mightn't want to save me.

What price your liberality, then, Prof?

But if a Hindu mob attacked me for being a dirty liberal, would any Muslim liberals come to my rescue—that's the point? Would you come, Akhtar?

I'm not sure.

Would you want to?

Yes. This was said very low.

There. You see in me not a Hindu but me, me, Professor K.B. Mathur. And this was you, you, the private individual, not the rusty voice of history. This is the voice I want to hear oftener. The history-defying voice.

Oh, come on, Prof.

No, tell me first: Why's this voice so low? So guarded? Because you think you're bound to be shouted down. Because, for every history-defying voice, as you call it, there are a thousand history-avenging voices.

Sorry, I value my safety. And because I ... I'm frankly not convinced.

They left a while later, all of them uncomfortable, conscious of having lost their heads, said more than was socially necessary, all of them aware of having spoilt some old and easy camaraderie. No one more guiltily conscious of the damage done than Professor Mathur who found himself suddenly without his cast.

He stood alone at his balcony. Until Sakina Bibi spoke up behind him: Hope lies only in being careful and silent, Professor Sahib. You're stupid, may the offence be forgiven.

I am that, granted the professor. But what's wrong with stupidity, Bibi? Let's experiment with stupidity since cleverness hasn't worked.

Oh you! I know of one man who experimented with stupidity. Only he called it Truth.

Yes—and let me read out to you something he wrote right at the end, when he was bitter and defeated.

She shrugged. Read out of books! That's all this chronically silly man could ever do!

He spun the revolving bookcase round, selected a volume named *Walking Alone*, showed her the cover: See here, Bibi. Here he is, walking from village to village—at a time when independence was being celebrated in the Capital. Walking with a small band of volunteers, trying to persuade, persisting in his theories. And here's what he said at the AICC meet in Delhi—I've marked it out—it keeps coming back to me: How must the Hindu–Muslim question be tackled? I must own defeat on that point. I know that mine is today a voice in the wilderness and yet claim that mine is the only practicable solution.

All I know is, Professor Sahib, don't you try walking through a riot alone. If there's any real plain speaking, the sparks fly. Friendships end.

And yet, you're Muslim and I'm Hindu and we understand each other. Yes. And we're the real minorities—we, the unpartisan ones. We're always the real minority—in every country and every history. We, the common-sense-walas. Except that common sense changes its meaning—becomes the common man's sense, not ours.

twenty-six

Shirin often returned from work to find the washing brought in, clumsily folded and arranged upon the ironing board; the milk boiled—though each time there was an overspill of dried slime curdled on the gas ring and on the kitchen slab. Once she found the fridge defrosted and cleaned. She noticed these things without comment but on such days she sat longer with him, watching TV or just chopping vegetables or mending clothes at his bedside. The medicines seemed to be displaying their cumulative effect. Now she emerged from the bathroom in the mornings to find the mosquito net removed and put away, the bed sheets folded and her house plants in the balcony watered. His movements were slow but his speech, though still a trifle awkward, decidedly intelligible. At what stage Shirin herself stopped snapping and hissing at him, she could not exactly place but now, it seemed, they sat together a great deal in the balcony, studying the street below, even when the sun grew unpleasantly warm.

She marvelled at how the Sunday mornings appeared to meld together all things in a large comfortable daze. She seemed to be sitting in a tubful of sun, limbs half dissolved, gelled in a warm, golden drowse. The sunlight sedated the traffic sounds and made them float in its thick, slow sediment. One couldn't even stretch out one's legs without half expecting a resistance of hot sunny yolk against one's toes. Often she surprised herself in a large moment of peace that felt oddly unfamiliar. That the two of them could ever share such calm was something she had never expected.

When they began talking to one another again, she could not place either. But one morning he told her of a dream. How he found himself crossing a border in a moving train. His mother carried a big tiffin box. She said: Eat, son. Eat your fill. His mother had Shirin's face, though.

Hearing this, she was saddened. Dreaming of food? Bad omen. Food dreams, wedding dreams, all spell death and of course, you're not going to die just yet, Jus. I too had a train dream recently, she told him. I dreamt my aunt was taken ill in a train. I was running from coach to coach, desperately looking for a doctor. But my aunt didn't have your face, she laughed. Uff, this is all a lot of hooey! Superstitious nonsense. Yesterday, at your psychiatrist's I had a hilarious encounter. I'd gone to submit your report and pick up the fresh lot of de-addiction doses. There was a biggish crowd in the waiting room. I sat next to a middle-aged couple. The woman was all groggy, slumped in her chair; the man was the protective, alert, managing type. Well, I addressed my sympathy at the poor slumped-down one. Asked her how she was feeling. Her pert companion answered for her: Much better, thank you. I asked her if she slept well. And how was the appetite? Again he answered for her: Excellent, excellent. Their turn came just before mine, and, as I waited outside the doctor's chamber, what should I see? The alert one was the patient! He was the one stretched out on the couch! The slumped-down female was the normal partner! One of these days, Jus, you and I'll reverse roles and become like that pair. I had trouble keeping a straight face when they emerged from the chamber and walked past me to the medicine counter.

He smiled weakly.

They took to sitting out in the balcony in the cool, milky evenings too, watching the metallic stars appear, one by one in the sky, like new-washed coins. When he wasn't looking, she studied his grained face in altered tones of light. He looked old, exhausted by harrowing thoughts.

When she found all her shoes and sandals nicely polished and arranged on the rack, she decided to question him about something that was bothering her.

Jus, she ventured carefully. As I came up the stairs last week I found the kabari carrying down some empty bottles. Your old brand. Then, the other day I spotted Raju, the paan-wala, carrying a suspicious-looking pack up to our front door. I hid on the landing two floors down and when he came down the stairs I asked him what he had brought for you and he said: Nothing, nothing, just magazines. Of course I didn't believe him. I've also regularly missed money in the cash box ...

She didn't complete her sentence, sat with her eyes riveted on him. He hung his head.

Look at me, Jus. Answer me. Am I right?

Still he said nothing.

You've been boozing again, Jus. Doing it while I'm at work. And all this while I've been trying to get you de-addicted. Oh Jus, you've failed. We've both failed.

Then she saw that his chin was trembling and his face crumpled up in tears. He wiped them away with his sleeve and when he couldn't stop, he hid his face in his hands, slumped forward in his chair. And she found that at some point she had knelt on the rug in front of him. Speaking, speaking urgently. At some point she had put her arms protectively around him, held him fast, resolved to stand sentinel over his enfeebled body and brain. Remembering in one large, shamed memory the times when she had belaboured him with jibes.

You've walked a hundred miles up and down this room, Jus, she sobbed. But you've reached me at last.

twenty-seven

M asterji had visited Mohan, his barber, for a hair trim and had allowed Mohan to talk him into getting his unruly locks dyed a sharp blacker-than-black that made his moustache look sadly out of tune. There was no option but to get the moustache dyed raven. Which made his eyebrows look off-colour. But when Mohan offered to dye them as well, Masterji put up a spirited resistance. A peep into the barber's mirror filled him with self-disgust but now there was no undoing the damage. He drew comfort from the sleek fall of his dry-cleaned and well-ironed sherwani with its matching boat-cap. He had also invested in a pair of svelte leather sandals. With all these corporeal preparations he had not neglected his performing capacities. He had gargled with warm saline water four times a day during the preceding week, abstained from pickles, hot tea and chilled water and put in an extra couple of hours' riyaz in the small hours of the morning. He had observed silence much of the day, speaking in eloquent sign language, giving his vocal cords the requisite hours of rest so as to be in good voice on his special evening.

Mayank had asked him to come at eight. When Masterji approached Mayank's parents' villa at a quarter to eight, the sight of it filled him with awe. The entire building was illuminated with trinkets of blue and white bulbs, the ashok trees in the garden wreathed with lights, a row of cars drawn up in the street, a traffic policeman monitoring the parking. Inside, a red carpet leading from the porch into the lobby. Alpana in rice paste and brightly coloured sawdust in intricate patterns on the floor of the drawing room with little clay lamps burning around it. Mango leaf and marigold festoons looped on the lintels, sandalwood incense in the air. A couple of photographers strolling around.

Masterji was gratified. All this for him! He walked in, self-conscious as a bridegroom, bestowing genial smiles on those assembled. Mayank met him at the front door and ushered him in. He was conducted to a small platform draped in snowy sheets, surrounded by clumps of potted plants, and introduced to the young percussionist.

Masterji arranged the folds of his sherwani and sat down cross-legged on the low platform. On one side of him he laid his precious Stradivarius in its case, on the other his flute. He conferred with the percussionist. He joined his hands, smiled affably and bowed his head in a graceful namaskar.

Not right away, Masterji, whispered Mayank. Wait a bit. Wait till the ceremony is over.

What ceremony? asked Masterji, perplexed.

In answer, Mayank offered him a card in a dainty envelope. True enough—silver embossed letters on matt-finished cream-coloured paper. It invited his gracious presence on the auspicious occasion of the engagement of Meena, daughter of Mrs and Mr M.V. Kaushal, to Rajesh, son of Mrs and Mr C.L. Pradhan of Pennsylvania, USA, on the 21st of March, 2000, at 8 p.m. at their residence, 109, Rana Pratap Street. Drinks and dinner to be followed by music. Classical vocal and instrumental recital by the celebrated maestro, Pandit Hargopal Misra, Maihar gharana.

The scene began to clear somewhat before Masterji's bewildered vision. Only now did he take in the jewelled, well-coiffed and made-up ladies, the well-groomed, Scotch-twiddling men, the waiters going round with trays of snacks and bottles, the lively chatter and swishing silks, the heady clash of a dozen perfumes. On the central sofa sat a young man and a young lady, surrounded by a crowd of dressy guests. On a table before them a jewellery box and several large, gift-wrapped parcels. Masterji cast his eye round the room. Sure, an NRI crowd—one could tell them at a glance from their designer Indian apparel matched with a decidedly foreign tautness of skin. Some Japanese faces too.

It's my sister's engagement, Masterji, whispered Mayank. The boy is a surgeon in America. His family's settled there. His father works in an American–Jap engineering concern. So we've got some American and Japanese guests too.

By now the context had become perfectly clear to Masterji. No soirée in his honour, this. He was here as the party entertainer. While the drinks went round, while dinner was served. And later the foreign and NRI guests would sit around, enjoying this Indian ambience. Of course there would be dinner for him as well. Singing for his supper, that's what he was doing. Like one of those pathetic singers in five-star hotel restaurants. Except that they were paid. He was here for free. All this he refrained from sharing with Mayank out of a sensitive regard for his pupil's feelings.

So when the engagement ring had been put on the girl's finger and when the gold mohurs had been presented to the groom's parents, and the sari and jewellery and the cosmetics and the coconut and vermilion from the groom's side offered to the bride-to-be, and clothes for the entire family given by the bride's parents to the groom's, when the cheering and the clapping and the jokes and the group photographs had ceased, then and only then did Masterji begin singing.

His labours had not been wasted. He was in good voice and if at times his throat grew a bit silted, it was from emotion rather than any vocal malfunctioning. His voice climbed the smooth shingles of the raga, mellifluously lingering over the lush labials, rattling the pebbly consonants in gurgling trills. He held one hand clapped to his ear like a mobile phone. He sang, then played the flute for a stretch, then presented another couple of ragas on the violin. The guests applauded, took out little cameras and clicked away at him, asked him eager questions about his gharana, about evening and morning ragas, about the history of the ragas he had sung and played. And by the time dinner was served, Masterji had begun enjoying the attention enormously. An American girl seemed very impressed and kept jotting down everything he said in a little pocket notebook.

Then, while everyone crowded around the buffet tables, a little old Japanese lady came up to him. She had a flat, lantern-jawed face, heavy eyelids and scanty tufts of hair falling into her eyes.

You teach me? she asked.

Mayank was right behind her, beaming. She wants to know if you'll take her on as a pupil, Masterji.

Masterji was dumbfounded. But she doesn't stay in India, does she?

She's here for a year. Visiting Buddhist places of worship and spending some time at monasteries. Her old mother's terminally ill with cancer of the liver. She wishes the end to come at Benaras.

Die in Benaras? A Japanese woman?

The Japanese lady explained: My mother she very very fear ... of the death. She ... like the death in Benaras. In Benaras ... bodies burn and the weemen wash the cloth near to it ... at the ghat ... and the children, they play the game ...

She means, in Benaras death is so much a part of living. It isn't anything unnegotiable or alien. So there's less to fear.

Masterji's heart was touched by the Japanese conception of death in Benaras, however romantic. Of course, he murmured.

But his fees are high, put in Mayank quickly. Thirty dollars an hour.

Okay, said the Japanese lady. No problem.

Masterji stared at Mayank, speechless, conscience-stricken. Over the little lady's head Mayank winked. Then, just as abruptly, Masterji's face underwent a remarkable transformation as an elderly man walked up and joined their group.

Hargopal Misraji? he asked courteously.

Masterji started. Where had he heard that voice? But of course it was! It couldn't be anyone else.

Raghunath Raiji! He put out his hands, grasped the other's hands, then, on an impulse, bent low and touched his feet. The Japanese lady was charmed. An elderly man touching an older man's feet! Where else but in India?

Raghunath Rai raised him, led him to a chair. Mayank had slunk along, looking oddly embarrassed.

The most natural question: How are you here, gurudev?

I have moved to the city for good. Enough travelling for a lifetime. I'm seventy-five now. And Mayank's parents have kindly rented me an apartment. The rent's exorbitant, of course, but I've started a Sangeet Academy, a private music school and Mayank is my first pupil. We adjust his fees in the rent.

Masterji could only turn and look straight into Mayank's eyes. Mayank shrank from his gaze. Then Masterji recovered his poise and said smoothly: An excellent choice, beta. Time you grew in the art. I could hardly recommend a better ustad. Raghunath Raiji once visited my village and did me a very great honour.

Raghunath Rai clapped an arm on his shoulder in affectionate comradeship and laughed. That's a secret between us, Hargopal.

Masterji nodded, gratified.

So now, Masterji, you have a Japanese pupil instead of my poor self, said Mayank, trying hard to be jocular. And she'll pay you thirty dollars an hour. Maybe by the end of the evening you'll rope in a few more. Think of it, Masterji!

It isn't the money, beta, said Masterji softly. It's something else. It's a different sort of giving and receiving. Not a cash exchange.

He was himself surprised at the fluency he had suddenly acquired.

By now Mayank, shamefaced, sped away to fetch dessert for them. Masterji turned to Raghunath Rai and asked the question uppermost in his mind.

Gurudev, why didn't Mayank's parents ask you to perform tonight? Why me?

Raghunath Rai laughed. They did. I refused. Besides, they knew I'd never consent to play for free as you would.

Mayank returned with two plates of halwa and the American girl who had carefully attended to all of Masterji's comments.

This is Karen, introduced Mayank. She's from Chicago and she's doing her PhD in Western Musicology. She plays the violin. She's here to collect some data on Indian classical music from the University of Khairagarh. Karen, Hargopal Misraji will be delighted to take you on.

Masterji looked at the American girl. A strange feeling of déjà vu swept over him.

Will you play something for me now? he asked her bashfully.

Sure, she agreed.

He offered her the Stradivarius. They retired to a corner of the dining hall.

She played. Very softly. The playful music spinning out like glinting copper twine. Wisps of notes floated and perched. Masterji took the violin from her, tried playing the same tune. But it was like sawing at an iceberg, filing off small, sharp chips of ice. He played a snatch of an Indian raga and suddenly the violin came alive and honey slipped down the strings, dripped off them in a placid pool around them. She laughed in a strange sort of rejoicing.

What did you say your name was? he asked her.

Karen, she answered. Karen Schumacher.

Shoemaker?

Yeah. My grandpop must've been one in Germany before he migrated.

Masterji was struck by the classlessness of it all. He tried repeating her name.

Karan? he ventured.

She corrected him: Care—En.

He tried again: Kay—Yer—

Now say N.

He obligingly said: Yun.

Now say: Karen.

He said: Kiran! Lovely name. It means a ... a thread of light. From the sun.

Oh yeah? she laughed.

Suddenly he understood the déjà vu feeling. That cassette Mayank had left. Ray of light!

Of course! he cried. You're like her. Ray of light. Ma-something. Ma-damma?

Madonna? she exclaimed, incredulous.

Yes, yes. You look just like her. Ma-Dohna.

She was in splits.

I'll pay you thirty dollars an hour, you teach me too? she asked when she stopped laughing.

Masterji was by now too ashamed. He said nothing. She took his silence for acceptance.

At a small distance he saw Mayank hold his hand up in a thumbs-up sign and felt suddenly outraged. That boy knows well that I have nothing more to teach, that I have reached the end of my knowledge. So he pretends he's studying for his IIT exam. And now that I know, he's sending me these unsuspecting foreign students who will pay me heavily and never be able to see through me during the short time they are with me.

Done, said the American girl. What shall I call you, sir?

Masterji, jolted back to the immediate present, said: Oh, anything you like. Guruji—that's what my pupils call me.

Okay, Gooroojee, she said. Where do you take your classes?

Look, said Masterji in desperation. I teach in the local Government Academy of Music. Why don't you come up one day and get enrolled. You can choose your teacher out of many able people.

But Mayank said you were the best, she protested. And I haven't time to enrol for the entire year. I have to pack it all in the space of three or four months. After that I'll carry on my PhD from Chicago and maybe come again next year. Maybe ... we could manage a fellowship or something for you and you could come down to Chicago.

The thought scared Masterji. Very sorry, he stammered. I can't go anywhere.

But why? she persisted.

Because of Kurkuri and Champa. And also Langoorie and Tipoo and ... and Mahashaya.

Family? she asked.

Not exactly. Kurkuri and Champa and Langoorie and Tipoo are dogs.

So can't you leave them with friends? Or hire an animal crèche or something?

You don't understand, he pleaded. They're strays. Nobody will agree to keep them. They dirty up the place. They depend on me for meals. They sleep in my room when it rains.

And that other one, the one with the long name? Maha-something.

Mahashaya—that's an old lame bull who lives in my lane.

Her grey eyes warmed his face. She shook her head in disbelief, shrugged.

Then may I take lessons from you privately—at your place, Gooroojee?

Please, appealed Masterji. There's a better teacher present in this very room. See that gentleman there—the one who was with us a while ago. That's the celebrated Raghunath Rai. Why don't you ask him? He'll give you your money's worth. Me, I'm not up to teaching a PhD student, you know.

She turned to look at Raghunath Rai, a thoughtful frown on her smooth forehead. Then she said: Okay, I'll ask him. But, Gooroojee, may I come up once and see your strays, the dogs, the bull ... ?

Of course, you're welcome, said Masterji, inwardly quaking at the thought of her stepping down his garbage-littered, slushy lane.

But how will you find your way there? It's in one of the smaller lanes behind Moti Mahal Cinema—not easy to find.

Mayank will drive me down if I ask him, she suggested.

Masterji shook his head. A car can't reach my house. My lane is very narrow.

Then maybe you can come and pick me up tomorrow. We can go on foot, Gooroojee, she said.

An idea took shape in Masterji's disconcerted brain. It was already past one in the night. He was afraid to ride home carrying the precious Stradivarius, naïve enough to suppose a night stalker might covet it. Suppose he left it behind with Mayank? Came back to collect it in the morning and picked this girl up as well? He voiced his plan. She agreed.

He would have to tidy up early in the morning. Buy some mithai and namkeen to serve. Tell the corner chaiwala to supply hot tea in his more presentable cups.

That's a beautiful violin you have there, her voice cut into his thoughts.

Yes, he said, lifting it proudly, caressing its dark wood. It's an antique piece. See here.

She peeped into its hollow belly, read: *Antonio Stradivarius Cremonenfis, Faciebat Anno 17.*

Wow! She whistled softly. That thing's worth a fortune.

So I have been told, he said modestly. I bought it very cheap from an old Anglo-Indian.

For how much?

A thousand Indian rupees. And a promise.

He looked stricken. Gulped as he remembered.

Shall I tell you something? Tonight, for the first time in years I forgot my promise. I was so puffed up with vanity ... I just forgot.

What?

I promised the man who sold me this violin that I'd only play hymns to Jesus Christ on it. Tonight I went and played Malkauns and Darbari Kanra on it.

His disturbed face touched her heart.

So what if you did? she said. All beautiful music is a hymn, isn't it?

He looked up, startled.

And in any case, you can go ahead and play a hymn now— just to keep your promise. Why don't you do it right away, while they're busy with dinner?

He hesitated.

Go on, she urged. We've got just a little time left.

He lifted the violin, tilted it against his left shoulder, leant slightly over it, drew a subtle pass at its strings with the bow. The violin inhaled gently under his touch:

> Ga re sa dha dha
> Pa sa sa ga re
> Ga re sa sa dha dha
> Pa sa ni re sa.

By the third line she began singing softly under her breath:

> *E'en though it be a cross*
> *Tha-at raises me ...*

And when the violin lifted its rarified voice into the higher reaches of the air, she followed it in a voice perfect and pure.

> *Still all my song shall be*
> *Nearer my God to Thee*
> *Nearer my God to Thee*
> *Nearer to Thee ...*

His jaw dropped. He stopped playing.

You know this one?

Of course. It's so well known.

The one in *Titanic*? he asked, excited.

That's right, she said.

What're the words? Tell me quickly please. I've been waiting for them for years. Asking everyone I met ...

It goes like this—have you a paper and pen?

I'm sorry I can't write English. You say them out in English—I write them down in Hindi.

Okay. It starts—*Nearer my God to Thee*—you understand what that means, of course?

Yes. Yes, said Masterji, taking down the words in the Devnagri script.

It's supposed to be the voice of the soul approaching death without fear ...

Masterji put an 'ee' accent on the Devnagri letter for 'thee', his heart beating wildly. He knew now why he had been brought to this place this evening and he knew what his payment was.

twenty-eight

Neelesh hardly recalled the sequence of events. It happened so abruptly. One moment Swati was tugging at the door and he heard the low squeak of wood on the cement floor. She lifted her hand to switch off the light in the corridor as she always did when he left after midnight. A mistake. Because her attacker, cautioned of their approach, had probably readied himself, taking advantage of the darkness. He had obviously been watching out for her. He pounced, laid hold of her, grabbed her in an iron clamp with one hand, brought up his other hand and jerked something all over her. She struggled, swung her head but it caught her on the right side of her face. Neelesh heard her agonized scream, saw the figure break into a run. Gave chase, shouting, but couldn't pursue far because of Swati's tortured shrieks.

Windows opened in the surrounding houses. Lights came on. He lifted Swati, trembling all over, the blood pouring down the front of her nightdress dripping down his shirt. He looked at her in horror. What had been Swati's face was a mass of bleeding meat, a shapeless sponge of raw, sizzling flesh. Acid! The word flashed in his head. He tried to staunch the blood. Couldn't. He hoisted her up, horrified, began to run, hailed a rickshaw, piled on. His right shoulder was drenched in blood.

The Parvati Nursing Home on Sapru Marg would not admit her. Nor would Markandeya Hospital, half a kilometre ahead. He tried Rehman Clinic, then Bethany's. Sorry, the men behind the reception counter inevitably murmured. Medical–legal. Criminal case. But the patient's condition is critical! he shouted at them. She needs instant medical attention! Please go to the Medical College or the Civil Hospital, he was told. Go to their emergency unit. Only government hospitals can register such cases.

Two hours later she was admitted to the Civil Hospital, semi-conscious for loss of blood. She would need a bottle of A-Positive blood, he was informed. The irony of it struck him even at the height of his horror. I'm an A-Positive, he told the attending physician.

What relation are you of hers? asked the man behind the blood-bank counter.

A brother, he said. The receptionist took that without comment.

Your name?

Neelesh Trivedi.

But the patient's name is Swati Maurya.

He had no answer.

The man behind the counter wrote on in silence. Neelesh went back to the women's general ward where she lay. They called him out to the pathology section to cross-check a sample of his blood and were satisfied. Good blood—matched hers perfectly.

The wound had been dressed. She had been injected with Pathedines, put on a glucose drip. She would need plastic surgery at a later stage—if she could afford it. If she couldn't, be thankful her eyes have been saved, poor thing, though her face is permanently disfigured.

Back at the ward, he sat, staring at her in enormous fright. Half her nose was gone, they had told him. Corroded by nitric acid. A cheek eaten away, a jawbone exposed. Now, where her face should have been there were only gauze bandages, cotton padding, criss-crossing tapes. He watched his blood slide, drop by drop, down the tube and slip into her swollen vein.

Morning brought a sub-inspector from the Bailey Road Police Station, accompanied by a couple of constables. The hospital had sent in its report. The interrogation in the duty room to which Neelesh was summoned unnerved and infuriated him. The original question:

What relation is the patient of yours?

A friend.

You told the receptionist you were a brother.

I am a sort-of brother.

The sub-inspector leered, wrote in his notepad.

How did this happen?

We were coming out of her house, she is a tenant on the top floor and the landlord lives downstairs. We opened the front door—it's at the foot of the main staircase. A man pounced on her and splashed something ...

What time was it?

Around twelve-thirty in the night.

What were you doing in her house at twelve-thirty, sister-fucker?

Neelesh kept silent, his blood boiling.

Has she no family?

They don't get along.

The inspector uttered an obscenity. Were you in the habit of visiting her regularly? Her neighbours often saw you leaving her house at night.

Yes, I'm coaching her for the civil services exam.

At twelve-thirty in the night?

He said nothing.

Why was the patient dressed only in a cotton nightie? the sub-inspector asked with a lewd grin. The hospital staff have stated that she had nothing on underneath.

His gorge rose but he controlled his rage.

Is she your kept?

Silence.

Or are you hers?

How many others like you does she receive? How much does she make from this calling?

Neelesh looked away, tried concentrating on a diabetes-control poster on the wall.

What do you do for a living?

I'm not employed. I coach the patient.

How does she pay you? In cash or in kind?

Neelesh felt a sharp pain condense on the side of his head.

What does she do for a living?

She's an occasional teacher. Does tuitions. She is preparing for the civil services exams, I told you.

The sub-inspector eyed him shrewdly.

You are a Trivedi, she is a Maurya.

Yes.

The sub-inspector wrote that.

Did anyone see the face of the man who hurled the acid?

It happened too fast. I've never seen him before.

Do you suspect anyone?

Neelesh hesitated, then said: It might have been her ex-husband. Or someone hired by him.

Her husband is an OBC too?

I suppose so. He shrugged.

What makes you suspect him?

She used to receive threatening phone calls from him. He used to damage her two-wheeler ...

Again the sub-inspector made a note.

We'll have to question the patient. Record her statement.

But the patient is in no position to speak.

We'll manage. And we might have to detain you till the matter is cleared.

But why? You surely don't mean I had anything to do with this. You can't involve everyone who brings a seriously injured patient to hospital!

The sub-inspector declared maliciously: Your part in it can't be overlooked.

But the patient has nobody with her. Her people have broken off with her. If I'm arrested—his voice had developed a desperate edge.

Keep quiet. We're not apprehending you yet …

The sub-inspector's voice trailed off significantly and Neelesh grasped what was meant. He had to arrange for cash, buy them off.

Please, he implored. Give this patient forty-eight hours. I ask only for forty-eight hours.

He would have to get in touch with his family in Pratapgarh. Fine mess to be in. Mix-up with a Dalit girl and now a police case.

Suit yourself. We'll record the patient's statement now.

From the doorway of the ward Neelesh watched them.

Did you recognize your assailant? Lift your right hand if your answer is yes.

She lifted her right hand feebly.

Was it your legally wedded spouse?

Again she lifted her right hand.

You are absolutely certain of this?

A final time she lifted her hand.

When did you last cohabit with your husband?

She made no sign.

Did your husband know Trivedi here? She waved her hand sideways, signifying no.

Did he know about your relations with Trivedi?

She lay, unmoving.

Did you have relations with Trivedi that night?

She lifted her hand extra firmly in an emphatic yes. You had to admire her defiant spirit.

The sub-inspector turned and threw Neelesh a salacious leer.

That's all for now, he said as he rose to go. Forty-eight hours, remember. We might have to interrogate the patient again. As for you, we'll have to call you to the thana for further questioning ...

Then the three policemen clumped down the corridor and Neelesh heard the jeep start and grind its way down the gravel driveway. He came and stood beside Swati's bed in a cold sweat. She extended her free hand to his. Limply he took it in his own. How to break the news to his people in Pratapgarh? How much cash could they arrange? And what if they failed or refused to muster up that much? The untimely rains had spoiled the year's harvest. His elder brother had also lost his case at the district court level and had appealed to the high court, engaged costly lawyers. And when they learnt of Swati, what then? There was only one option.

He took out the slip of paper with the phone number and studied it in undecided silence. Put it back.

Some time during the day he went back to Swati's apartment to fetch some cash that she kept locked up in a tin trunk. He had some chhole-bhature off a cart in front of the hospital and washed it down with sweet, milky tea. Bought some medicines for her, cleared some bills.

The night was bad for her. He kept awake, watching the glucose drip. Next morning he walked out, drank tea off the same cart, bought a newspaper. And was stunned to find, on

the third page, in bold type: ACID THROWN ON DALIT
WOMAN'S FACE. He read it through in mounting agitation.
The press reporter had given a strange slant to the story,
completely omitting the fact that it was the woman's husband,
another Dalit, who was the prime suspect. He bought another
paper and read in its local page: DALIT HUSBAND CHASTISES
ERRANT WIFE. This story recounted how a morally
outraged husband sought to punish his adulterous wife for
illicit relations with a caste Hindu abductor by disfiguring her
face. The two newspaper reports left him tremendously
disturbed. The situation was rapidly gaining in complexity,
incorporating a deliberately partisan tone. Impulsively, he
made his way to the hospital's phone booth, took the slip of
paper out of his wallet, and dialled ...

I've thought it over, he said. I accept your offer. I'll try to
join ... yes, the State Bank Head Office Renovation tender ...
but how about my security arrangements? And there's a little
complication with the Bailey Road police that has to be sorted
out.

He hung up, much relieved, though a bit apprehensive at
what he had taken on. He went back to the ward, told Swati
he would be back in an hour, and took an auto-rickshaw to
Patel Nagar where Kailash Brahmachari had his offices.

twenty-nine

When the badmash did not return even after an hour, Vakil Sahib decided to go in search of him. For a long time he had suspected that Nankoo frequented Nathu Halwai's on the sly, used his master's name and carried away packets of choice mithais which he devoured on the way. He had no proof except that the haramzada kept working up terrific bellyaches every day and had to be dosed on Pudin Hara and Hajmola Churan by Vakilin. So Vakil Sahib picked up his carved Nainital swagger stick and strode down the road, crossed it and, skirting Sikandar Chowk Park, entered the bazaar behind. He would first check with Nathu before launching into punitive action.

He spotted Nathu, placid and pot-bellied, sitting bare-chested behind his massive oil cauldron, frying gulab jamuns. A large bowl of syrup stood alongside the fire and Nathu brought out a ladleful of little golden balls and dropped them to fatten in the bubbling syrup. With his other hand he used his blue-checked shoulder cloth to mop his beaded forehead, occasionally swatting flies with it as well.

He greeted Vakil Sahib cordially. And did you like the dil bahars I sent last Thursday? he inquired courteously.

Vakil Sahib's suspicions were confirmed.

I received no dil bahars, Nathu.

Did not receive them? And what of the palang-torh burfi I sent three days back?

No burfi came for me.

But your boy, that Nankoo, took half a kilo of each! said Nathu in perplexity. In fact he was here a while ago. Said his master appreciated the palang-torh burfi exceedingly and could I send round another half-kilo?

Aha! exploded Vakil Sahib. The bed-breaker burfi has found its way down his swinish gullet, the son-of-a-sow! But pretty soon he'll get to know what a back-breaker burfi is.

He brandished the Nainital swagger stick. Which way did the saala go?

That way across the road and in at the park gate, pointed Nathu.

Ho! quoth Vakil Sahib. A kilo of back-breaker burfi to bring bahar to the dil! I'll give him such a one his dil shall stay a-bloom for days hereafter and his buttocks as well!

He strode energetically into the park.

It did not take him long to find Nankoo. Having feasted on the spoils of the morning, Nankoo had experienced, of a sudden, that old acidic bite in the pit of the stomach and the horrid bilious tide travel up his throat. He now sat hunched up on a bench, retching, hugging his knees, struggling manfully with the stabs of hot pain that pierced his belly and drove sharp heated needles into the basement of his chest.

Vakil Sahib stole up from behind, laid an iron grip on the rascal's ear, pulled him to his feet and shook his fist in his face.

Got you, beta! he greeted him with vicious joy. What was it today? Palang-torh, was it? And have you tasted the bottom-breaking burfi? Shall I serve your lordship a dishful?

He twisted the fast-reddening ear. Nankoo clutched his belly with a groan, released an acid burp in Vakil Sahib's face, so noxious that Vakil Sahib almost let go. Nankoo moaned softly and began vomiting on the grass.

Oh ho ho ho ho! Gorged yourself sick, have you, beta! roared Vakil Sahib. I see you need medical relief. First aid and third degree, eh? An injection at Dr Narain's clinic right away.

If there was one thing Nankoo was petrified of, it was an injection. Four years in the city had not quelled his rustic dread of the syringe. Vakil Sahib used this crowning threat as the capital sentence in his stormy tirade.

Anyone might think your employer starves you, skin-and-bones! Do we not give your royal belly its fulsome feed, wretch? To look at you, to look at your skinny self, one might imagine you were an illustration for malnutrition in *Saptahik Hindustan*. Come, come, come, come. Come, saala haramzada, we'll cure your belly disorders in a jiffy! Just one tiny injection of Aqua Pura at Dr Narain's clinic across the park and you'll shit out the stuff that's troubling your gut!

He hauled Nankoo to his feet and, thumping one hand on his forearm, tightened his grip on it like a vice.

No, Babuji, not an injection! Please, not an injection! moaned the rascal.

Why ever not, beta? Why ever not, say? Your belly is aflame. Just one little Aqua Pura and we'll have you cured. I discussed your problem with daktar sahib. My boy, Nankoo, has the belly-bonfire, I told him—we're worried. Nothing works. Not the mint drops, not the asafoetida powder, not the ginger essence nor yet the ajwain pinch. Daktar sahib said, he said, bring him to my clinic, just you bring him to my clinic, my clinic across the park, and one little Aqua Pura, one little Aqua Pura is all that'll cure him. So come, come, come, come!

And Vakil Sahib dragged the protesting wretch across the park towards the north gate, where the bazaar began and Dr Narain's tiny clinic stood.

Not an injection, Babuji. I fall at your feet, Babuji. Hé bhagwan, spare me, hé bhagwan! lamented the rascal, appealing, expostulating, protesting innocence, as his employer towed him behind him.

* * *

The late afternoon felt numb. The sky slate-grey and the sound of traffic like a low, distant battle. Trumpet alarms, drumbeats, thudding hoofs. Piercingly shrill beeps and low rumbles. The scrape of tyres on asphalt. A large, elemental glacier of sound that Shirin felt was as hard to cross as the congested street. Or as hard to get over as a fatal preference for the tragic. Did I see myself in a radiant halo, compensating for something? Do I just enjoy risk, recklessness? Too bad I burn my fingers each time. And here's this chronic attachment raising its demanding head again. Quickly, quickly, now, let me disengage my heart. Carefully, so not a speck remains. As quickly get across this current of feeling as across this difficult, congested street.

It'll soon be the twenty-second of March, Jus, she had said the other day. To which he had said meekly: Will you do something for me? Will you choose a film to watch on the twenty-second? Will you go and eat in Kowloon? Will you buy something nice for yourself with this? He took an envelope out of his kurta pocket and gave it to her.

Three hundred bucks! Where did you get this money, Jus?

He wouldn't say. Then suddenly she knew. How many empty booze bottles have you sold to the kabari, Jus, to raise this cash? Her voice was strained but there was a catch in her throat as she looked at him with stricken eyes.

Okay, she had agreed reluctantly. I'll go to the Regency Theatre and see what's running. It'll be funny. I'll try to sit in one of the corner seats in the balcony—where we used to sit—and pretend you're there with me. Like the old days. Do you know, Jus, other people vow they'll go on pilgrimage or donate something to a temple or gurdwara. Me, my only promise to myself is that one day you'll be fine and you and I will see a film together at the Regency. And ... and dine at Kowloon.

Please go, he had said. You'll have to go alone this year. Next year, maybe, on the twenty-second of March, if I'm well ...

Maybe, she thought, unable to fend off the sadness. She had planned a surprise of her own for him—a half-bottle of rum that she had left in the kitchen as an anniversary gift, a mute token of acceptance.

She bought a balcony ticket. They were screening *Sooryastha*—The Sunset—again. An old favourite, if somewhat underdone. She didn't care. All she cared for was the familiar charged darkness, the two corner seats in the balcony, the throbbing soundtrack and, sunk deep in the plush pushback of the seat, her bounding pulse, remembering him and her years ago. She couldn't attend to the film, the feeling got so strong. Halfway through the film, she decided to abandon it and the restaurant idea as well. Get dinner packed at Ringo's, things he could manage to eat, easy-on-the-liver things. Drop in at a video parlour and see if a cassette or CD of *Sooryastha* was available. If not, anything else they had. Also pick up his medicines from the chemist's.

Blindly, she picked her way, stumbling down the pre-dawn darkness of the movie hall, almost tripping over the carpeted steps, to the side exit where the metallic flare of daylight caught her in a dazzling instant of arrested clarity. Why hadn't she thought of it before? (Quickly, quickly, let me disengage ...) No helping it. She had fallen, head over heels, into the old, treacherous feeling, all of it, unadulterated, love taken neat without a drop of soda or lime or water to muffle its potent blow, she ruefully reflected, as she surrendered to its heady onslaught, crossed the street, meaning to take a short cut through Sikandar Chowk Park.

* * *

The boys were playing cricket in the haatha but even to a casual onlooker it was a limp game at best. Their hearts were not in it. Professor Mathur leaned over the trellised balcony and addressed the boys.

I've redone my play, so you can come up and give me your comments.

There's no bijli, Professor Sahib. Why don't you come down instead?

Good idea. Why don't we rehearse in the park in the evenings?

They didn't look enthused at all. He was conscious of a note of humble persuasion in his voice.

He collected his altered draft, picked up his black umbrella and went down the stairs. They were stacking away their bats in Sakina Bibi's murky little lobby. There was in the air a decidedly oppressive feel.

Hullo, he said, affecting a cheerfulness he was far from feeling. What's wrong, Munna? You're very quiet.

My mood is off, answered Munna.

Where's your mood off to? asked Professor Mathur, trying the hearty, jovial approach. It failed.

What's up, Afzal? What's bothering you?

I'll tell you, Afzal said dourly. We've wasted so many phone calls in this *Kaun Banega Punjipati* farce and none of us is ever called.

Naturally, reasoned the professor. That's the real gamble. Out of lakhs of phone calls, the computer chooses a hundred. Then, out of those hundred, only ten are chosen. And out of those ten, only two or three get to play in each episode. It's a chancy game, boys.

But why, I'd like to know, are we never the selected ones? demanded Vinod, as though he were interrogating a fickle Providence.

Cheer up. One of these days you'll be the chosen ones, reassured the professor. A gamble can work for you and against you. Ever heard of Horrific Housie, boys?

They hadn't. As they set off for the park, he told them about it. A weird sort of game. Prisoners of war allotted numbers. The numbers that are called out are shot. The remaining fellows run. Worse than Russian Roulette, no? Now, why can't I add this to my script to add punch?

* * *

Suruchi slowed down her Matiz and manoeuvred it to a halt near the east gate of Sikandar Chowk Park.

Shall we walk? she suggested.

He agreed.

Aditya, she said after they had walked a few paces. Slowly because of his handicap. I've just been promoted and transferred to Moradabad. I joined last week.

He turned to stare, disbelieving. For a moment she resented this imaginary right over her that he appeared to claim. When he stayed silent, she was irked. She wished he would speak.

But he wouldn't speak a word.

I'm shifting to Moradabad in a fortnight. I got this promotion after a long and bitter legal battle, Aditya. It's a backdated promotion. My seniority is now calculated retrospectively ... with effect from 1997. Huge arrears too. A terrible blow to all the people who superseded me illegally.

He still couldn't say a word. There was an odd sensation in his head. Live wires zigzagging across his brain. The discomfort hardened into a cold blade wedged painfully in a cleft at the side of his head. He thought that crevasse of pain would gape wider, deeper, overwhelm everything in a massive fission. He daren't tell her all the fanciful nonsense he had cherished in his head. That they had been brought together by some design, to be with one another in some crucial experience. It was always to be so. They had been dealt a strange hand. Not love but some overwhelming option to it. Not life but its alter.

Aren't you going to congratulate me, Aditya? she provoked him.

Something seemed to strain, give way under pressure. He couldn't trust himself to speak.

Come on, she said, what's it to be? Espresso, cappuccino, moccacino or frappe?

***

Vani Kabir left her scooter in the parking lot just inside the park and made her way to one of the benches. Clear my head first. That's most important at this point. Clear my head. She would just have to tell Parul the truth. Early that morning Parul had telephoned her. It's all fixed up, she informed her. Her voice sounded uplifted in certainty. I've arranged a lawyer for this defamation suit. Name of Tandon. Lives on Lytton Street. Fourth house down first by-lane. The papers are all ready but he'd like to meet you as well. So can you manage an hour this afternoon? Around four-thirty, say?

Vani had nothing to say, no protest. She could, of course, have put Parul off with: Sorry, I can't make it today, I've got an appointment. Or: Sorry, I'm not too well today. But how long would that have worked? She couldn't keep Parul waiting indefinitely, giving her flimsy excuses for avoiding the meeting with the lawyer.

So she had fortified herself to speak out. Tell Parul the unpleasant truth. The heart-storming, devastating truth that would make Parul's marriage come crashing down and her all-too-vulnerable sanity as well. She told herself that deep down Parul knew the truth all the time—even at her most defensive. But to rob her of her carefully structured defences, her social front, seemed a particularly cruel act of betrayal.

There seemed no way out. She would have to rehearse the words in her head. Choosing them with great care, preserving a cool balance between brutal fact and ameliorating doubt.

It was nearing four in the afternoon and the appointment with the lawyer just half an hour off. Parul had promised to meet her at Tandon's gate. The right words still hadn't taken shape. It was now or never, please God, let me find the right words to tell her what I know or grant me the grace of silence, please God, she fretted to herself as she seated herself on the poolside bench.

***

Under the laburnums, on the far side of the lotus pond, sat Lynette in a mood of rare contentment. And Matthew in a fit of abnormal vexation. While she sat, heart slowed, blood turned to honey, thoughts rinsed in gold, he grew fractious, fidgety, until she longed to give him a rap on the knuckles as one would a restless child. Such a lovely afternoon, squiggles of tune in the branches. Dreaming of Lansdowne. 1955. The wind in the pines, the ground brown with pine needles, the stringy locks of trees, uncombed and draggled. Now sleep came unbidden in lavish downpours. She even dozed off on the bench. Deeper and deeper variations of sleep until all that stayed constant was a tenuous memory of self.

I feel like fulfilling an old dream of mine, Matt, she said. I must stretch out on this grass—it's so tempting. Will you wake me up in half an hour? I know your train's at seven.

What on earth, Lyn! he exclaimed. You can't do that.

Do what?

Sleep on the grass. An old lady. What'll people here think?

Deliberately she put aside her basket, rose and lay down on the grass. She closed her eyes and spoke slowly: What'll people think of me? What'll I think of me? Ah, it's good to let it all go, Matt. So good to be rid of oneself.

She opened her eyes a second and thought of saying: And you can tell her to relax. I'll never ring her up again. Tell her I've destroyed all her letters.

But there was an obstruction somewhere. Correct moves and good intentions weren't enough. Forgiveness involved a complete overhaul of self and she knew she would have to wait for that to happen. She didn't insist on keeping to standards of conscience she couldn't humanly maintain and she felt released, suddenly, of her own demands on herself. The sort of freedom she had known when she let the last letter slip out of her hand into the flames.

* * *

Masterji felt most self-conscious at the prospect of a beautiful, blonde American girl riding pillion behind him. He hoped none of his acquaintances at the Academy spotted him—he would never hear the end of it. He slung his violin on his back so that it might form a barricading wall protecting his diffident bachelorhood from her fragrant person, gave his moped a kick-start, and with a courteous nod asked her to climb on. She did.

What is your name, Gooroojee? her tuneful voice spoke up behind his right ear.

Actually my name—the one my parents gave me—is Hargopal. Misra is my surname. Hargopal is one of Lord Krishna's names, he added. For he carried the impression that all American tourists had links with ISKCON.

Do you know, Gooroojee, I've named you Francis, she said playfully.

He was bewildered.

We have a saint who created a brotherhood called the Grey Friars. He wanted to make all the world one vast Friary, in which men might live in peace and brotherhood. For Francis, the first Friar was Jesus Christ.

Isamasih? he asked, surprised. A new thought. Isamasih as Big Brother!

I thought of you and your stray dogs and your lame bull and I suddenly remembered St. Francis's words. Lemme see—how did they go? Oh yeah, Friar Christ, Friar Francis, Friar Wolf and Sister Swallow, Brother Fire, full of power and strength, Sister Water, so limpid, pure and useful, Brother Sun and Sister Moon ...

Masterji's moped wobbled in sheer pleasure.

Where is this saint's temple? he asked.

In a place called Assisi. In Italy. But the order exists all over the world. He lived in the Middle Ages and of course the Church persecuted his followers—doesn't that always happen, Gooroojee?

Men can't live in peace, that's true, Masterji observed sagely. But how marvellous to think that such peace has been imagined. Sun, moon, fire, water, wolf, swallow, all one family and Isamasih too! And that hymn, Kiranji, what did each line mean?

It means that every moment we're drawing closer and closer to the time we're to meet God. Even when one's got to pass through torment, it's all welcome, because one's moving nearer and nearer, nearer and nearer ...

In a burst of sudden elation Masterji hummed, ga re sa dha dha, and tried to fit the words he had learnt: *Nyahrah mai Gawd too Theee, Nyarah too theee* ...

She laughed aloud. The wind blew her blonde hair into her eyes.

Kiranji, he said in deep emotion, you've revealed the words of this hymn to me. I meant it when I said you've been a ray of light.

Madonna? She laughed still harder as the moped turned a bend and entered the shady short cut through Sikandar Chowk Park.

***

Sleeping with her was fine but marriage? Actually, Neelesh thought guiltily, now he didn't much feel like sleeping with her either. He only did it once in a while as a polite gesture of continued regard. And he knew she realized it too and grieved over it in secret.

He had brought her that evening to meet Kartik in the park. Kartik's mother had been appalled at the fact that his tutor had been involved in a criminal assault—even if she had only been the victim, even if the police had mysteriously dropped the case—and had vociferously discontinued the evening classes. Kartik had been forbidden to meet them but one evening, shortly after Swati was relieved from hospital, he had rung up and said he wished to meet Swati Auntie and have Himalaya Kheer—which is what they called ice-cream—with her.

This was Swati's first evening out. She had her dupatta drawn across her face for even Neelesh couldn't help flinching when his eyes fell on the burnt plateau of her mangled face.

She tried to preserve her optimism. Was full of plans.

Now that I'm Dalit and sort-of disabled both, she quipped, do you think I can avail of two reserved quota positions? Don't you think I've almost made it to the civil services? And once I'm through I'll save up and get the best plastic surgeon. See me then—you won't know me.

He had always admired her grit and never more than now. Still, she didn't seem a woman any more. He was full of complex angers. At his fate under this dispensation that denied him employment which would enable him to get her the plastic surgeon she needed. At her villainous husband who got away scot-free. At himself for no longer desiring her. At his abject submission to Kailash Brahmachari's machinations. At what he must do soon.

When he stayed silent for longer than ten minutes, she grew anxious, nagged: What are you thinking all the time? Why are you so quiet?

To which he always replied: I'm like this now.

The fact of the matter was that he longed to get away. From her. From the city. From the situation. From himself. Break out or break up. His heart smarted with many unforgiving rancours.

He helped her sit on the grass with Kartik, asked which ice-cream they would like.

Toota-foota! smiled Swati, looking so hideous that he had to look away. Toota-foota was their name for Tuti-fruity.

Right, he said, toota-foota it's going to be. And went off to the nearest ice-cream parlour across the street.

thirty

Remember me? Siddhantha? Yes, I'm still around, overseeing the placement of these episodes. If I have let myself fade out midway like one of Professor Mathur's radio play characters, it was only to stop myself obtruding unnecessarily into the scripts of others. Now that what was going to happen has happened, I cannot escape the imperative of searching that last fatal instant of their lives. I know it is presumption to suppose that death can ever come within the compass of living imagination, much less offer its reality up to language. But my characters might have experienced a compression and acceleration of time and thought in one pang of atomized knowledge in which all the resources of their selves flared and merged in super-fast reception of the event.

One—little—Aqua—Pura—what—was—that—hai—bhagwan—please—please—I—must—I—o—mother—waiting—Jus—I've—got—to—reach—Jus—it's—me—cappuccino—or—espresso—oh—help—Suruchi—must—tell—sleeping—on—this—grass—mercy—this—poor—child—home—must—get—violin—out—of—this—must—home—I—must—I—I—

It is equally possible that they knew nothing at all. Their stories just ended there but this other story doesn't. By now you know that Suleman went missing, that his novel was seized by the police and also the roll of film with his photograph.

You know that the Swatantra Bharat Party called a strike and that a rampaging mob stormed Sakina Bibi's kothi and discovered the hundred-rupee note from Pakistan, then, not finding Suleman, the mob fell on Rubina. The little Rubina whose imagination was aflame with fantasies of flower-perfumed tender-turbulent wedding nights, was dragged into the courtyard, naked, and she learnt, in shrieking agony that all her visions were wrong.

I covered the incident and got my newspaper office burnt down.

It goes on, you see. I was fond of saying that history has taught us how to make the old mistakes in new ways. Now I'd like to add to that and say history is one hell of a flexi-holograph in which some rules get recast, some rhythms recur or reverse but the obdurate old truths reincarnate in new forms and all the old human stories get rewritten in new ways.